The Secrets We Keep

Sicilian Mafia Wars
Book 3

Meaghan Pierce

Pierced Soul Publishing

For my ex. Turns out listening to you drone on and on about your work in data security finally came in handy.

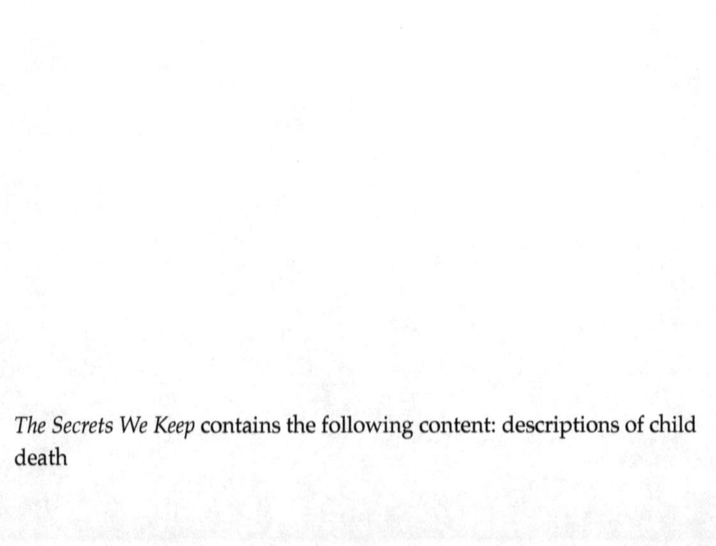

The Secrets We Keep contains the following content: descriptions of child death

Chapter One

The wind whipped her hair around her face as the ferry churned from Italy's mainland to the island of Sicily. She tucked it behind her ears to keep it out of her eyes but stopped herself short from pulling it into a ponytail. It hid the scar carved down the side of her neck.

People stared when they saw it, puckered and white. If they weren't staring, they were asking questions. She wanted to avoid both. Being the center of anyone's attention was something she tried to avoid.

A family joined her at the railing to watch the boat cut through the sea. A little boy who couldn't have been more than seven or eight climbed onto the bottom rung, head tilted out over the water while his father gripped the back of his shirt.

He had a missing front tooth when he smiled, and instantly she thought of her nephew. Pietro was only six when he died. He'd just lost his first tooth and was teaching himself to whistle through the gap. He was convinced he could learn to whistle an entire song if he tried hard enough.

Then it wasn't his smiling face she saw. It was his lifeless one, staring at nothing out of wide eyes, mouth open in a silent scream. She squeezed her eyes shut against the image, forcing it to the recesses of her mind.

Wading through her memories was like a sick game. The bad always came with the good, no matter how many times she practiced recalling only happy times, only smiling faces, only laughter. In the end, it was always overtaken by the way it had all ended. She was always left cold and alone with nothing but the horrible memories of that night.

She'd never be free from them.

The coast began to take shape, colorful houses backed by towering cliffs of green, and she gripped the bars of the ferry's railing. It had been too long since she'd stepped foot on Sicilian soil. She missed it. The people, the food, the sounds, the smells. Her life just outside of Berlin had been fine—comfortable and quiet. But nothing would ever compare to home.

The ferry blew the horn to announce their arrival, and the little boy next to her squealed with joy, jumping down from his perch and scurrying back inside. The boat slowed to prepare to dock, and with one last look at the shore, she descended to the lower level and climbed behind the wheel of her car.

It was new, but not flashy. She needed something plain that wouldn't draw attention, and the simple black sedan fit the bill. All she had left in the world was what she'd managed to cram into the trunk and the backseat. Before leaving Berlin, she'd sold all her furniture, given her cat to the neighbors who promised to send pictures, and packed up what was left.

It wasn't much, but she hadn't left the island with much, either. Only the clothes on her back and a healthy dose of terror and pain.

The ferry docked with a jolt, and eventually the cars in

front of her pulled forward. Carefully navigating the narrow strip of land serving as Messina's harbor, she wound her way inland, rolling the windows down to take advantage of the unusually warm temperature.

The sun heated her skin when she dangled her arm out the window, and she drove on impulse toward the restaurant she remembered from her childhood. Her mother was from Messina, and her family owned two popular restaurants boasting the island's best cannoli.

When she was a girl, they'd drive up from Catania to see her grandparents, who would happily let her eat as many cannoli as she could stomach, no matter how much her mother protested. Then she'd run around with her cousins until it was dark and her mother dragged her home again.

When she pulled up to the curb outside the bigger of the two restaurants, her eyes brimmed with tears at the sight of it. She only had happy memories here. It wasn't tainted. And it looked exactly how she remembered it.

Bright coral stucco with white shutters and a happy teal door. In the summer, the door would be left open for the breeze off the water, cooling the dining room and the sweltering kitchen beyond. In the winter, the bell over it jingled when you opened it to announce your arrival, and someone would always call out a greeting.

Tapping her fingers on the steering wheel, she debated getting out of the car. It would be easy to jog across the street and step inside to the rich scent of pasta sauce and basil and cannoli shells frying. They probably wouldn't even recognize her. She'd changed so much in the last three years. She was wholly different now—inside and out.

While she was debating with herself, the front door opened and a woman stepped out. Her throat constricted, and it was impossible to draw a full breath. *Zia* Aria. The woman's black hair was bundled on top of her head and secured with what was probably a pencil. She brought a cigarette to her lips and lit it, cupping her hand around the lighter and then blowing out a puff of smoke once the cigarette caught.

Zia Aria had been a smoker for as long as she could remember, with a wonderfully deep, raspy voice because of it. Aria leaned back against the side of the building, settling one arm over her stomach and propping her elbow on her wrist.

Someone walked by, and Aria smiled at them. The sight of it was like a knife to the gut, sharp and painful. *Zia* Aria looked so much like her mother it was excruciating. She couldn't do it.

Pulling away from the restaurant, she shook her head. It wasn't worth the risk. She didn't want anyone to know she was back. It's not like she was planning to stay, and even if they didn't recognize her, she didn't trust herself not to say anything.

The business she was here to handle so she could make things right was too important to jeopardize. She'd come all this way, spent all this time preparing. She couldn't ruin it in her first fifteen minutes.

Angling the car south, she followed the route she knew by heart to Catania, her fingers tightening on the steering wheel with every mile. She had to come back to do this part. It was her only option.

She drove aimlessly through the city, crisscrossing familiar streets, turning, circling, looping back on herself. Her breaths came faster, but she couldn't release the pressure in her chest quickly enough. It was suffocating, being this close to home and yet so far away.

All she had to do was turn right, and she'd be there. In front of her childhood home. Her knuckles were white on the wheel as she sat at the stop sign, but she couldn't force herself to turn. It was too soon, too dangerous. She didn't want to be seen in that old neighborhood anyway.

Someone honked behind her, leaning out their window to swear, and she jolted, pulling through the intersection and driving instead toward the apartment she'd found online. It was more expensive than the place she'd rented in Berlin, but it was within walking distance of her new job, and she'd saved up enough money to afford all the deposits.

Plus it was secure. And she needed the security right now. Needed to know at least something stood between her and the outside. Parking in a guest spot, she smiled at the woman who held the door open for her into the lobby and waited for the receptionist to acknowledge her presence.

"Can I help you?" the man finally asked.

"I emailed yesterday asking to see some apartments. Anna Marino."

The man typed something on his computer and then looked up at her with a smile. "A furnished two-bedroom with a short-term lease, right?"

She smiled in return. "That's right."

"We have two units available." He grabbed a large ring of keys from the drawer at his elbow and pushed back from the desk. "One faces the cathedral, and the other faces the water. Did you have a preference?"

"The water." She'd missed the sea, the sound and scent of it, holed up for so many years in Berlin.

They took an elevator to the top floor, and he led her down a short hallway and into a bright, open apartment. The furniture was modern and looked brand new. The apartment was beautifully styled and clean, but it was the view that drew her forward.

The city stretched out to the marina where boats came and went and the glistening blue of the Ionian Sea lay beyond.

She sighed, a little piece of her settling at the sight. It was perfect.

"Rates are very reasonable for an apartment this size in this location with the terms you're asking for. We could drop them if you wanted to sign a longer lease."

"No. Three months is all I need." It was the shortest they offered. She hoped to be done with her task well before the lease was up.

"I understand," he replied, leading her away from the kitchen with stainless steel appliances and a big round dining table and down the hall to the bedrooms. "If you change your mind within thirty days and decide to stay longer, we can usually accommodate that."

The main bedroom was larger than it looked on the website, with a wide terrace and an imposing king-size bed. The bathroom had a large shower, a separate soaking tub, and a double vanity. She hardly needed that much space just for herself, but she wanted to keep up appearances.

The second bedroom was smaller, with only a queen-size bed and a bathroom across the hall with a simple shower stall. She frowned, wondering if it would be easy to move the bedroom furniture out of the way and bring in her own.

"Is something wrong?"

She indicated the bed with a wave of her hand. "I was hoping to use this space as an office instead of a second bedroom."

"Oh. We can swap out the furniture for you. That's not a problem. A standard office setup would include a desk, a chair, and some bookcases. Did you need anything else?"

She shook her head, following him back out to the living room. "No. That would be perfect. Thank you."

"So," he said, turning a slow circle and offering her another smile. "Any questions I can answer for you?"

Her eyes drifted to the windows, catching on a yacht

leaving the marina. She was reminded of warm summer days, the wind in her hair, the sun on her body while she stretched out on the polished deck and sipped limoncello.

Then it was leering grins and the smell of gunpowder and blood. This plan had to work. She couldn't torture herself with all these memories without getting what she came for.

She turned back to the man and shook her head. "Where do I sign?"

Chapter Two

Luca watched his brother check his watch for the third time in as many minutes, the scowl on his face deepening. Nero Gallo was almost fifteen minutes late to their meeting, and Matteo was not happy about it.

"He's fucking with you," Luca said. "Don't let him get in your head."

Matteo took a deep drink of his latte and set it back on the table. Luca didn't like meeting on Gallo's turf any more than Matteo did. Even if it was the only way to make this sit-down happen. But Gallo being late didn't bother Luca nearly as much as it did his brother. Matteo hated the disrespect of not being on time.

Gallo wouldn't be dumb enough to ambush them. Not in the restaurant of this upscale hotel. He cared about his image too much to take so public a hit, but that didn't mean he wouldn't try some shit if given the opportunity. Which is exactly why Matteo had stationed not one but two cars of men at the front and back entrances.

Signaling the waitress for another cappuccino, Luca sat back and waited. Gallo would show eventually. He was too interested in figuring out what they might know and what exactly this meeting was about to miss it. His tardiness was a power play, and Matteo needed to chill.

"Gallo's going to do exactly what you think he will when you make your proposal," Luca assured him.

Matteo slowly dragged his eyes away from his phone and met Luca's gaze. "I know. He's going to play right into my hands at every turn because he underestimates me."

The waitress arrived with Luca's cappuccino at the same time he spotted Gallo and his two sons standing in the vaulted archway between the hotel's lobby and restaurant.

"Heads up," Luca said when Gallo spotted them and made his way over.

Matteo fixed his face with a bland expression, adjusted his cufflinks, and waited.

Gallo claimed the middle seat across from them, his sons sitting on either side. Dante, the younger of the two and the one currently engaged to the daughter of the Don running the Syracuse territory, sat on his father's left and fixed Luca with a sneer.

Luca fought hard not to roll his eyes. As if Dante Gallo could intimidate anyone. The kid was a notorious fuckup. Luca might feel sorry for Tessa Antonetti being stuck with the guy for life if not for who her father was. The two of them probably deserved each other.

"Well?" Gallo said in the haughty voice that had always grated on Luca's nerves. "You didn't drag me out here for a meeting to stare at me in silence, I hope."

Matteo's grin was razor sharp. "I have a proposal for you, Nero."

Gallo flicked a glance at his oldest son, Stefano, and clasped his hands in his lap. "I can't imagine why I'd want to do business with the Bianchis, especially not one who abandoned his own family for nearly a decade. But go on."

Luca saw Matteo's jaw tighten before relaxing again. "We're both interested in the same thing."

Gallo snorted. "I highly doubt that."

"We both want money and power."

At Matteo's nod, Luca laid a file folder in the middle of the table. Gallo's gaze danced from Matteo's face to the folder and back again.

"I already have money and power. I doubt you can give me more when you have so little yourself."

"That's where you're wrong," Matteo replied. "I may have spent the last seven years away from Sicily, but I wasn't wasting it. I've built quite a fortune, made some deep connections all across Europe."

"Good for you," Gallo said, eyeing the folder but feigning disinterest. Albeit not well. "I still don't see what this has to do with me."

"You saved Gallo Industries from your father's mismanagement. Used your connections in the Italian government to make it one of the largest transportation companies in the country."

"The largest," Stefano corrected.

Matteo inclined his head. "The largest. Certainly in value. It's worth quite a bit of money." He paused for dramatic effect, and Luca bit back a grin. "It could be worth a lot more if you expanded further into Europe and Asia."

"And I suppose you're the one who can help me do that?" Gallo wondered.

"With my connections and an infusion of capital, yes. I can."

Gallo tapped his fingers on the edge of the table, eyes glued to the folder. If the man was faking this level of curiosity, he was the best actor Luca had ever seen. But Nero Gallo was a greedy son of a bitch. His desire for money and the power it afforded him would win out over old grudges almost every time.

Luca suspected that's precisely why Nero had been helping Aroldo Varda wage war against them for the last few months. Another mark in the column against him. And a useless effort since Varda was now dead and the Agrigento territory was under their control.

"And if I accepted?" Gallo wondered. "What are you offering?"

This part of Matteo's plan to take over Sicily's throne and rule all five territories was the most ambitious yet. It had been easy to subdue the Romanos by taking out the family's biggest players and installing a puppet. Then moving on to Varda and eviscerating his loyal ranks.

Over half the island was now under Bianchi control. But where the Romanos and Varda had been hurting for cash, Gallo had plenty of it. Not to mention connections that went to some of the highest levels of government.

Taking him out without bringing the law down on their heads would be a study in strategy. Starting with this offer Gallo was sure to refuse.

"All the details are there," Matteo replied, indicating the still untouched folder.

Gallo shared a look with both his sons, but ultimately, his curiosity and greed won out, and he pulled the folder closer and flipped it open. Luca watched his eyes scan the page, mouth ticking up at the corner when they widened. He was no doubt as surprised as the rest of them with how much Matteo was offering to invest. Especially because Luca knew his brother was good for it.

"Your newly acquired Romano strip clubs must be doing well if you have that much liquid capital to invest."

"Not yet. But they will be. Giuseppe did a fine job of

running them into the ground before I got my hands on them."

"Before you stole them out from under the Romanos' bloody bodies, you mean?" Dante said, a frown deepening under his father's searing look.

"What's the catch?" Gallo asked, leaning back in his chair. "You want to inject all this cash into my company for what?"

Luca sat forward, reaching across the table to pick up the top sheet and flip it over, revealing Matteo's terms. He skimmed his finger down the page and pointed. He enjoyed watching the color rise up Gallo's neck and stain his cheeks a blotchy red. Gallo's head snapped up, eyes narrowing on Matteo's face.

"You want a 50 percent stake in my own fucking company? The company I dragged out of the gutter with my blood, sweat, and tears? You can't seriously expect me to make you an equal partner."

Matteo shrugged. "A small price to pay when we could easily quadruple the value of Gallo Industries together."

"And what if I don't need your help to expand into Europe and Asia? I'll take your plans and your ideas and make my own connections. Then I won't need you at all."

"If you could, you would have already," Luca replied. "You need us and this deal if you want to branch out into global markets."

"Don't tell me what I need, boy," Gallo snapped, and Luca gritted his teeth against the insult. "No one would want to make a deal with terms like that. And I don't need your money."

Slapping the folder closed, he shoved it across the table, face still beet red.

"Suit yourself," Matteo said, scooping the folder off the table and dropping it in his lap. "I'm sure your competition will be much more agreeable to my offer."

"Don't threaten me, you little shit," Gallo growled. "You may be Don of the Palermo territory, and you might have earned yourself some money through happenstance, but I'm not Romano or Varda. I'm not hurting for cash, and my empire isn't falling down around my ears. My men are well paid and loyal."

Matteo cocked his head. "Are you sure about that? Everyone has a weakness, Nero. Even you." Matteo lazily sipped his latte. "Are you sure Antonetti won't back out of your hastily thrown together marriage deal? No one likes to be second place."

"What the fuck are you talking about?"

"I know you were in talks with my father to have Dante marry Carina. Hoping to get your hands on her widow's inheritance, no doubt. Or maybe you thought she had some kind of stake in the Romano strip clubs. Funny how you didn't mind a Bianchi alliance a mere six months ago."

"That's different." Gallo waved a hand between them, but Luca could tell Matteo had thrown him off with that bit of info. "That deal would have been between me and your father, with much better terms than the shit you're offering me. You know nothing of what makes a good business deal."

"Oh, I think we know enough." Matteo shared a look with Luca.

"We know when you bet on the loser, you have to seek more powerful allies. Isn't that right, Nero?" Luca said, enjoying the way the man squirmed in his seat. "Running guns to Varda while he was at war with us hardly did you any favors."

Matteo held up the folder, drawing Gallo's attention again. "This deal is less than what you deserve from me after that blatant show of disrespect. But I'm willing to overlook your...indiscretion in favor of a mutually beneficial agreement."

"A controlling stake in our company is hardly mutually beneficial," Stefano said. "I'm not interested in sharing the power to make every single decision with you for the rest of my life."

"You could always buy us out in the future."

Stefano snorted. "Right. Like my father sai—"

"I don't need you to speak for me," Gallo barked. "Last I checked, I'm still the head of this family, the Don of this territory, the CEO of this company. *My* company," he added.

"Of course, Father. I only meant—"

"Shut up, Stefano."

Stefano's eyes sparked anger, but he held his tongue. There was a fracture forming there. Maybe one they could exploit.

"I don't know what game you two think you're playing," Gallo said, looking between them. "Do you think I'm stupid?"

"I don't recall making such an accusation." Matteo looked at Luca. "Do you?"

"I don't. No," Luca replied, sipping his cappuccino. "Are you stupid, Nero?"

Gallo's lip curled back over his teeth. "I'm smart enough to know when assholes dumber than me are jerking me around. You cannot take me down by force. I will not crumble like Romano and Varda before me. So I'm not going to fall for this pitiful fucking act you two have got going."

"It's not an act," Luca assured him. "You can take this deal, accept our generous infusion of cash, and lean on my brother's many connections throughout Europe—"

"And in the States," Matteo interjected.

"And in the States. And you can do so in exchange for a 50 percent stake in Gallo Industries. Or we can get what we want somewhere else. Take it or leave it."

Gallo rose from his chair and waited for his sons to do the

same. Buttoning the top button on his suit jacket, he stared down his nose at them.

"I think I'll leave it. And good luck bolstering my competition. You think I don't have safeguards in place to make sure no one can rise above me? I grease my palms very well."

"It's your choice, Nero." Matteo sighed and waved a hand, as if bored with the entire interaction. "Far be it from me to come all this way to try and bring a little peace to this island."

"From where I'm standing, you're the one who stirred up all the trouble to begin with. Be careful, Bianchi. You know what happens when you fly too close to the sun."

Chapter Three

Sunlight slanted over the bed in bright slashes, and she groaned, rolling away from the window and shoving a pillow over her face. She made a mental note to buy some fucking curtains.

She was just drifting back to sleep when banging on the front door echoed down the hallway. Heart leaping into her throat, she bolted up in bed and checked the time. Barely nine in the morning. Who would be knocking on her door at this hour? Had they found her already? No. No. She'd been careful. So careful.

The banging stopped, the silence more deafening than the noise, and then quickly resumed, making her jump. Tumbling out of bed, she hopped into a pair of leggings, nearly crashing into the bedside table, and tugged a tank top over her head.

"Who is it?" she called as she darted down the hallway and into the kitchen.

"Maintenance with a furniture delivery."

She peered through the peephole, her heart rate slowly returning to normal when she saw the men standing in the hallway, the building's logo emblazoned on their white button-down shirts and furniture loaded on carts behind them.

Running her fingers through her hair to smooth the worst of the tangles, she swept the door open and smiled. "I didn't realize you'd be coming by so early."

"Sorry if we woke you," the tall guy said, looking her up and down, his eyes lingering on her bare feet in a way that made her wish she'd put on socks. "We're supposed to swap out the furniture in the second bedroom for office stuff."

"Yes. That's great. Thanks."

She led them down the hallway to the second bedroom, closing the door to her room and concealing the rumpled sheets of the bed. No need for any of them to get any ideas about her bed or her feet.

"Want anything anywhere in particular?" the tall guy asked.

"Just the desk facing the windows in the middle of the room. The bookcases along that wall."

They nodded, and she retreated to the kitchen to stay out of their way. Her stomach growled, but she didn't have any food in the apartment. Normally she soothed morning hunger pains with a strong shot of espresso, but she didn't have any of that either. She should make a list.

Opening drawers in the kitchen until she found a tidy junk drawer with a small pad of paper and a pen, some rubber bands, and other various supplies, she added a countertop espresso maker and jotted down some of her favorite pantry staples.

Cooking was the one thing that had kept her grounded during her time in Berlin. Her family's recipes existed only in her head now. She'd recently started writing them down, keeping them in a notebook her mother would have loved. Anything to feel like she had a little piece of them with her again.

Glancing up at the view and the sun glinting off the water, she added blackout curtains to her list, underlining it twice. She didn't know why the morning had to announce itself so early. In a perfect world, the sun wouldn't rise until ten.

She didn't start her new job for a few days, so she still had some time to unpack and settle in. The first thing she wanted to do was wander the neighborhood and acclimate herself. She hadn't spent much time in this part of Catania before leaving the island. It would be best to get her bearings.

The hum of voices from the bedroom grew louder, and she looked up to see the men coming down the hallway with the mattress and box spring loaded onto the cart. They waved her away when she moved to open the door for them. After another two trips, the incessant banging of a hammer and squeal of a drill, and lots of swearing, the second bedroom was now an office, and the apartment was silent again.

Crossing to the living room, she bent to inspect the boxes she'd brought in last night and stacked behind the couch. Plucking the one she needed from the stack, she carried it down the hall. She set it on the edge of the desk and split the tape with her fingernail. Moving the unassuming t-shirts she'd laid on top out of the way, she lifted out the stacks of notebooks and set them on the desk.

Dropping into the chair, she reached for the one on top and flipped it open to the first page. Details about that night were hard to recall at first. Everything about her memory was fuzzy and unclear, like watching TV through static.

She'd read somewhere that writing it all down could help bring things into sharper focus. So she'd walked down to a local shop, bought a spiral-bound notebook and a pen, and carried it home.

Sitting cross-legged on the worn chair in the corner of the room she was renting, she'd begun writing down whatever came to her in a rapid stream of consciousness. Snippets of memories, flashes of what happened, things that popped into her head both before and after that night.

It was all so emotional at first while she grasped for what she wanted to remember and grappled with the pain of the loss. Over time, it became more clinical, detached, analytical. It was the only way she could look at it and not fall apart.

Then it became strategic. A plan to put her life back together. A roadmap to help her pick up all her broken pieces and reassemble them into something recognizable. Making the plan had kept her going when the grief and the pain were too much. Sometimes, it was the only thing that got her out of bed in the morning.

If moving to Sicily was the second part of the plan, getting a job at Gallo Industries was the first. And she'd been able to do that with a series of interviews online. She'd put her university degree and her remote work for a prestigious German engineering company to good use. She spoke four languages, was at the top of her class, and had several certifications. A perfect candidate.

She'd used all that and her willingness to relocate to negotiate an excellent salary and benefits package. But it wasn't the money she was after. It was the access. Nero Gallo had something she wanted, and she needed this job to get close enough to take it.

Working there was a risk, but one she needed to take. She didn't anticipate running into anyone who might recognize her in the IT department. None of them had ever bothered to notice her before.

And as an extra precaution, she'd dyed her hair and gotten colored contacts. Plus, her documents were excellent fakes that didn't come cheap. It was going to be fine. She'd have what she came for in three months or less. Hopefully less.

Sliding the notebooks onto the shelf in chronological

order, she carried the clothes into her bedroom and changed into a pair of jeans and a t-shirt. Before starting work, she'd have to go shopping for some office-appropriate outfits. Working from her tiny kitchen table in her little apartment outside of Berlin for the last two and a half years had spoiled her, but in the end, it would all be worth it.

Grabbing her list off the kitchen counter, she slid the strap of her purse over her head and stepped into the hallway, making sure the door was secure behind her. The elevator doors opened on an empty car, and she blew out a relieved breath. There were only three other apartments on this floor, and if she could manage it, she hoped to avoid meeting any neighbors.

The wind had a biting edge this close to the water; it would be too cold for short sleeves once November hit with a vengeance. The sun had slipped behind thick clouds, casting the sidewalk in shadows, and she turned right toward Gallo Industries. Today was as good a day as any to gauge how far she'd have to walk to get to work.

Following the crowd of people making their way to Catania's business district, she ran a nervous hand through her hair the closer she drew to the ornate building. A revolving door led people into and out of the lobby, and she saw white marble floors through the glass walls.

Gallo Industries speared up out of the concrete and jutted into the sky, taller than the buildings on either side. Each floor was a different department, with IT on the second floor, the executives on the top, and things like accounting and HR sandwiched in between.

It was an easy walk, only a few blocks, and she could make it in about fifteen minutes, maybe twenty if she was wearing heels. She hadn't worn heels in a long time. They weren't very good for running.

Someone bumped her from behind, forcing her to turn

with the flow of foot traffic, and she spotted them. Walking three abreast down the sidewalk with bodyguards in front and back, forcing people to move out of their way. Nero Gallo and his sons.

Why were they coming in the front? Shouldn't they be coming in through the parking garage? That's why she wanted to live close enough to walk. She didn't want to risk running into them or anyone else who might know her in the confines of an underground concrete tomb.

She melted into the crowd, scooting behind a tall potted bush, and watched them move quickly through the people who scurried out of their way. Nero looked angry, Stefano looked attentive, and Dante looked annoyed. They hadn't changed much at all.

Stefano jogged ahead of his father and held the door open, scowling at his younger brother when Dante darted in ahead of him. She counted to twenty before moving back onto the sidewalk, the knot in her belly loosening. They hadn't seen her. But if they came in this way often, she'd have to rethink her plan.

Darting quickly past the front of the office building, she crossed the street and continued up the block. The scent of bacon and coffee hit her nose, and her stomach grumbled. She stopped short on the sidewalk, apologizing under her breath when someone ran into her back and slipped into the hotel.

She could use a good espresso. Germans didn't understand coffee. Not the way Italians did. She'd had her first good cup of it in three years once she crossed the border from Austria and stopped for the night in Verona. The flavor was like heaven in her mouth. Full and rich and deep.

Her mouth watered at the thought. She'd make a quick stop for breakfast, then she'd get back to shopping and exploring.

Chapter Four

"Why are you pouting?" Luca asked, slipping his phone into the inside pocket of his suit jacket. "He gave us exactly the response we were expecting."

"I do not pout," Matteo replied with the same tone their father would have used when insulted.

"Sulking, brooding. Whatever this"—Luca circled his finger in front of his brother's face—"is. Did you want Gallo to come around or something?"

"Of course not. I wanted him to rise to the bait about Varda."

"Why?" Luca frowned. "We already know he was gifting weapons to Varda in exchange for protection should we ever come after him. And since Dom got caught during their last exchange, Gallo likely knows we know. "

"Because I still don't know who his main supplier is. He bought the weapons he gave Varda from a guy in Belgium, according to my contact in Frankfurt, but it's not where he gets the bulk of his product. Even if I destroy Gallo Industries, he can pivot quickly to weapons trafficking and amass another fortune in no time."

"Can he?"

"Yes. Always someone in the Middle East looking for guns."

Luca's brows shot up. "Experience in funding terrorism, brother?"

"I have experience in a lot of things," Matteo replied. "My point is, I don't just want to sabotage his shipments. I want to know where the fuck Gallo might be getting his weapons from."

"So you can cut him off at the knees."

"And then shove him face first into the grave."

Matteo's phone rang, and he got up from the table to answer it. Luca rolled his eyes. His brother's trust issues were a big fucking problem. He imagined they'd experience far fewer bumps in Matteo's plan if he didn't play all his cards so close to the vest.

It wasn't like Luca, Dom, and Carina were the ones who'd run out on this family for nearly a decade. Carina had done what she could to keep the family going with her marriage to Giuseppe Romano, and she had the scars to prove it. Dom had more than stepped up, dealing with their father until his death while simultaneously handling the enforcement and security at the casinos, leading the men.

The very casinos that would have gone belly up if Luca hadn't taken over their day-to-day operations a few years ago. His father had done his best to squander whatever money he'd gotten from his secret deal with Giuseppe for Carina's hand, blowing it on booze and women and ignoring the businesses that had always put food on their table.

Luca suspected it was Lorenzo's way of dealing with the death of his wife. She'd wasted away from the cancer until she was an empty shell. His father's downward spiral was the only sign Luca had that Lorenzo might have been even remotely upset at his wife's passing. And all of it got worse when Matteo stormed out two weeks after the funeral. Two years after that, Carina was married.

Things had been bad in the Palermo territory for a while. Until Luca and Dom took over and did their best to right the ship and get profits back up. They'd put in the hard work and the grueling hours and endured the late-night fights with their father to get the territory and the casinos back on their feet.

Matteo sweeping back in with his grand plans to conquer Sicily after their father put a bullet in his brain was all well and good. It was no less than what they deserved. But they were all tiring of his cloak-and-dagger bullshit.

As much as they all wanted to unseat Gallo so they could then go after Antonetti and be a force—the only force—to be reckoned with on this island, it was impossible to trust the brother who'd been gone for so long. Especially when Matteo refused to share more than one or two steps ahead in his plan or name any of his mysterious contacts or divulge exactly how he'd managed to make so much money in such a short amount of time.

Matteo wanted their blind faith, but sometimes it was impossible to tell if their goals aligned, and patience was thinning.

Movement out of the corner of his eye caught his attention. He looked up, expecting to see Matteo making his way back over from his phone call, but it was a woman instead. Thick ash-blond hair hung to her waist. She had it pulled forward over her shoulders, but there was no hiding her perfect hourglass figure.

Her eyes were an intense shade of blue somewhere between turquoise and sapphire, and she had a kissable top-heavy mouth. She accepted the menu from the waiter, and the smile she gave the guy made every thought of Matteo's assistant and the way Luca had been trying to get into her pants for months slide right out of his head.

There was something so familiar about her, but he couldn't quite place it. He'd never been with a blonde before. At least not one who looked like that.

He tried not to stare, but every time his eyes left her, they found a way to wander back in her direction again. Noticing the way she drew her bottom lip between her teeth while she read the menu, the delicate pink polish on her fingernails, her long, elegant fingers twirling a strand of hair.

He had to know her name. He couldn't leave here without it or her number.

The waiter returned to take her order, and he watched her mouth move, mesmerized. What the hell was it about her? She was like a song lyric he couldn't quite place, insistently nudging at the back of his mind without taking hold.

"Excuse me," she called when the waiter moved away to put in her order. "Can you tell me where the bathroom is?"

The realization slammed into him, punching his heart into his throat. Her voice. He'd know it anywhere, even after all this time. His stomach clenched as he watched her sling her bag over her shoulder and skirt around her table toward the direction the waiter indicated. It couldn't be her. He had to be mistaken.

He watched until she disappeared around the corner, trying to convince himself he had it wrong. It couldn't have been her voice. It was impossible. She was a brunette with hazel eyes. He'd watched them…

Shoving away from the table, he stalked toward the bathrooms but stopped short of pushing into the ladies' room. She'd have to come back out eventually. He reclined against the wall opposite the door and waited, hands tucked into his pockets to keep himself from fidgeting. Or punching a hole in the wall.

This was a mistake. She couldn't be here right now. Whoever this woman was, she'd walk out that door and see him and have no reaction. Because it wasn't her.

The door opened, and he jerked his head up, but an older woman stepped out. He forced himself to return her polite smile, then went back to staring intently at the door, barely able to breathe for the tightness in his chest.

He saw the swing of her blond hair before the door fully opened. When her eyes locked on his across the narrow hallway, they instantly went wide, her mouth falling open. Her fingers gripped the strap of her purse against her chest, and he thought he saw them tremble.

How? Why? It wasn't… He couldn't…

He pushed away from the wall, and she stumbled back into the bathroom. But she wouldn't get away from him so easily this time.

His hand shot out to grip her throat, and he shoved her into the wall so hard she squeaked. Her eyes were shining with unshed tears, but they never left his.

"What the fuck are you doing here?" he growled. "You're supposed to be dead."

"Luca."

That one word from her lips nearly brought him to his knees, so he tightened his grip on her throat instead. "I watched them bury you. I stood at the back of the cemetery, and I watched them lower your body into the fucking ground."

She reached up to wrap her fingers around his wrist, squeezing until he loosened his hold. "It's a long story."

"I'll fucking bet."

He stepped closer, inhaling her sweet honeysuckle scent. She might not look like he remembered, but she smelled exactly like he remembered, sounded like he remembered, felt like he remembered. He let go of her throat and pressed his body against hers, trapping her against the wall with his hands on either side of her head.

She didn't move when he dropped his face to the crook of her neck and breathed her in, but she tilted her head for him like she used to do to give his lips better access to her body. He jerked back at the sight of the long white scar running the length of her throat from the bottom of her jaw to the curve of her shoulder, where it disappeared under her shirt.

Gripping her chin roughly in his hand, he jerked her head to the side to study it. Too jagged to be a knife wound. It looked more like she'd scraped it across broken glass. But the last time they'd been together, he'd seen every inch of her naked body, and not a single centimeter had been marred by scars.

He released her but didn't move away. "Tell me, Sienna. What the fuck is going on?"

She flinched when he said her name, her hands moving up to sweep her hair over her shoulder, hiding her scar from view. "There's too much to tell. I-I can't here."

She squeezed her eyes shut and then opened them again. At this distance, he could clearly see the unnatural blue of her eyes, the hazel peeking through what must be colored contacts. Her hair was dark at the roots, her natural brown. Hair he'd run his fingers through countless times, eyes he'd stared into, wishing they could have more than stolen moments with each other.

He'd spent so many hours trying to figure out how to make it happen. How to make his father agree to let him marry Nero Gallo's niece. He'd almost done it. Almost gotten close to softening his father up enough to ask. Then he'd woken up one day to a headline in the paper. **Prominent Members of Gallo Family Slain. Police Have No Leads.**

Her entire family was wiped out at her twenty-second birthday party. Just two days after he'd seen her, held her, made love to her for the last time.

"What are you doing here, Luca?" she asked, her voice thick with the tears swimming in her eyes, jerking him out of his memories. "Why are you in Catania?"

His laugh was bitter, cold, and for the first time, she shrank away from him. "I live on this island. How are you back from the fucking dead?"

"I can explain, but I…" She drew her bottom lip between her teeth and released it, and he couldn't stop himself from reaching up to rub his thumb over her mouth.

"But you don't want to."

"No! I do." He heard the click of her throat when she swallowed. "But not here. Not in public. I'm renting a place not far from here. We can go back there, and I'll tell… I'll tell you everything."

He left one hand braced against the wall by her head and reached into his jacket pocket with the other. Keeping his eyes locked on her face, he dialed and pressed the phone to his ear.

"Hey," he said when his brother picked up. "Something came up, and I have a thing I need to handle. I'll meet you back in Palermo later."

Luca hung up on his brother's grumbling protests and slipped his phone back into his pocket. His eyes dipped down to her lips when they parted, and he was hit with the memory of how she tasted and the little sounds she made when he kissed her.

Before he dipped his head to make his memory a reality, he shoved away from the wall, turned his body so she could walk past him, and gestured toward the door.

"Lead the way."

Chapter Five

Every step was torture as she led him away from the hotel and back to her apartment. Never in a million years did she imagine she'd run into Luca when she returned to Sicily. He lived on the other side of the island.

The year they'd spent together had been stolen moments when they could both get away from their families. Trysts in hotels and the backseat of cars—and that last time in a field of wildflowers.

But it had been the happiest year of her life. She'd wondered, in the years since disappearing, if she remembered it that way because of everything that came after or because she loved him as much as she thought she did.

Seeing him, even with anger flashing in his eyes and a gruff growl in his voice, she knew it wasn't in her imagination. She'd loved him then, and she loved him still. The thought didn't soothe her. She'd already lost him once. This felt like losing him all over again.

He was silent on the walk, matching her pace but staring straight ahead. When the foot traffic thinned as they neared her apartment, he put distance between them. It shouldn't bother her. She'd grieved him, let him go a long time ago. She'd never expected to see him again.

But the anger radiating off him was palpable, his jaw tight, hands clenched into fists. It was probably better this way. For him to be angry, to hate her. If she got lost in him again, she'd never get what she came for.

This would be over soon. She'd explain as best she could without giving away too much. She didn't want him to stop her. And he'd want nothing to do with her. He'd retreat to Palermo, and they could avoid each other until it was done. Once it was, she wouldn't be anyone's problem anymore.

A mother and a young toddler were waiting for the elevator when they stepped into the lobby of her building, and they rode up in more silence, punctured by the occasional happy babble of the baby's gibberish.

When the door opened on her floor with a ding, she led him down the hallway and into her apartment. His eyebrows winged up when he stepped inside, and he appraised the space with shrewd eyes. Setting her bag and keys on the counter, she turned to face him, wrapping her arms around her torso.

"Would you like to sit?"

His gaze flicked past her to the couch, then back to her face. "How long have you been back?"

"Three days. Give or take a few hours."

He seemed surprised by that, but he made no move to come any further into the apartment. "I want all of it, Sienna." He shoved his hands into his pockets. "Every detail."

It had been such a long time since anyone had used her real name. It sounded so good in his deep voice, even when it dripped with anger. Moving to the fridge, she pulled out a bottle of water she'd ordered with her takeout the night before and took a deep drink. She set a second one on the edge of the counter for him, but he didn't take it.

She'd never told another living soul this story before. Only documented it in the pages of her notebooks. She hardly knew where to begin or what to expect from him once he knew.

"I assume you read about what happened to my family."

"The papers said someone broke in during a birthday party and started shooting. Your birthday party." His voice was thick with emotion, but his expression was unreadable.

"That was true." She took a deep breath. "We were eating dinner. One minute everything was fine, and the next minute it was chaos. Someone rang the doorbell, and my brother got up to answer it. There was a gunshot, and then…"

She forced the tremble from her voice, taking another drink to ease the tightness in her throat. "There were so many of them. Papa, my brothers, they barely had time to draw weapons before they were cut down. We tried to get to the kids, get them out the back. But more men came in through the kitchen."

Her hands started shaking, and she set the bottle on the counter before she dropped it. "The kids were screaming, crying, running. Rina made it to the door with the twins, but the next time I looked up, she was on the floor. Blood," she whispered, voice hoarse. "There was so much blood."

Unable to look at him, she kept her eyes fixed on the shiny silver surface of the refrigerator and the reflection of the marina. "I tried to grab Pietro. Marcello's youngest. And then pain exploded in my shoulder. More pain in my side." Sienna cupped her hand over the ugly scar on her stomach.

"Someone came to stand over me, so I held my breath and played dead. He fired, but he didn't hit me. It was Pietro. H-he shrieked when he died."

Her heart squeezed painfully in her chest, Pietro's face swimming into her vision. She still heard the sound of him dying in her nightmares. A noise she'd never be able to wash out, no matter how many times she punished herself for not doing more to save him.

"I lay there listening to pleading, crying, boots stomping around, and more gunshots. Then car doors slamming and squealing tires. I don't know how long it was, I think I might have passed out, but then I smelled smoke. When I opened my eyes, the room was filled with it. I could barely see faces. Except for Pietro's..."

"How did you get out?"

She jumped at the sound of his voice. Her eyes darted in his direction, where he stood perfectly still by the door, watching her intently. "I had to crawl"—she swallowed a sob and waited a beat—"over their bodies. I was afraid whoever attacked us might be watching the house to make sure no one got out. But I figured if they were, I'd be dead either way, and I didn't want to burn alive."

When he took a step forward, the urge to go to him was overwhelming. The desire to feel his arms around her, to hear him whisper comforting words in her ear, was something she thought she'd exorcised a long time ago.

"Rina was in the way of the door. Her and the twins. I couldn't move them to get out, and the fire had already consumed the front of the house. So I broke a window and half climbed, half fell out of it. I cut myself on a piece of glass."

She wrapped her fingers around her throat, tracing the long, thin scar.

"Where did you go?" His voice was soft, strained, and he took another step forward.

"My father had a safe house no one knew about. A bunker, really. I laid low there for a bit. Patched myself up and tried to figure out what to do next."

"Why didn't you come to me? Why didn't you let me help

you? I would have helped you, Sienna," Luca said, a note of desperation in his voice.

"I didn't know who I could trust."

"You suspected me?" His tone was an accusation.

"No." She shook her head. "Not you. Never you, Luca. But your father? Romano? Their alliance was new then. I didn't know how strong it was. The men wore masks; they didn't speak. I had no idea who they were or why they were killing us. I needed to get out."

She had an idea, though, and plenty of time to think about it while she recovered.

"Where did you go?" he asked after a long pause. "How did you manage it?"

"My father always kept money at his safe houses. Once I dug the bullets out of my body and sewed myself up, I waited three days to make sure I didn't have an infection. Then I took every bit of money I could find, more than I was expecting, a few supplies, and I went north."

"I went to your funeral." His voice was quiet. "There were so many bodies. They buried each family together. I guess since you were unmarried, they decided to bury you with your parents. I stood in the back so no one noticed me. I watched…" His breath hitched, and her heart squeezed in her chest. "I watched them lower your casket into the ground. If it wasn't you in there, who was it?"

She'd wondered the same thing when she read stories of her funeral. Probably a maid, but she had no way of confirming. "I don't know," she breathed. "I'm so sorry, Luca."

"You're dead. I *grieved* for you. And you didn't even trust me enough to let me help you."

She bit into the soft flesh of her cheek to hold back the tears, wrapping her arms tight around her. Every second of every one of the three days she spent in her father's bunker recuperating enough to run, she'd thought about going to him.

She dreamed about tumbling into his arms and hearing him whisper that everything would be okay, that he would fix it, make it right. That nothing bad would ever happen to her again.

Of course he had no part in what happened to her family. She'd never even entertained the thought. But trust was scarce in those days, and as much as she loved him, no one knew about their relationship.

She had no reason to think his father wouldn't sell her back to the person who had tried to kill her in the first place. Lorenzo Bianchi was a heartless son of a bitch.

She jolted at the thought and took a quick step forward. "Your father can't know I'm alive. If he tells—"

"My father's dead." He jingled a set of keys in his pocket. "He killed himself about six months ago."

"Oh. I didn't realize. I'm sorry."

"Don't be. We both know what an asshole he was. If he wasn't, I might have been there to protect you."

She moved closer, stopping short when he looked sharply away from her. "Or you would be dead along with everyone else. It was comforting to know you were still out there. It helped to picture you happy."

"There wasn't happiness without you, Sienna." He gave a mirthless laugh and scrubbed a hand over his face. "How could you possibly think there was?"

"I figured you'd move on eventually," she said softly. "Get married."

That thought sent a stabbing pain through her. It was harder to picture it, harder to want that for him when he was standing so close. She couldn't remember if she'd seen a ring on his finger at the hotel. She'd been too preoccupied with his hand around her throat and the feel of his body against hers.

"Have that big family we always talked about."

He surged forward without warning, gripping the back of her neck and hauling her onto her toes. She crashed into the hard plane of his chest seconds before his mouth covered hers. His kiss was hot and demanding, and she melted into it.

Linking her arms around his neck, she pressed tighter against him, groaning softly when his free hand circled her waist and pulled her in until there was no space between them. He slid his tongue along her bottom lip and then nipped it with his teeth, making her shiver.

His hand circled around from the back of her neck to squeeze her throat, gently this time, and he used his thumb under her chin to tilt her head up so he could deepen the kiss. She slid her tongue against his, teasing him until he rewarded her with a groan.

When she slid her hands into his hair, grazing her fingernails along his scalp, he rocked his hips into hers, and she sighed. This was the one thing they'd never needed to work at. Far beyond words, she knew the heart of him.

She'd spent a year mapping him, committing him to memory. The shape of his body, the things he liked, the sounds he made if she touched him exactly the right way.

He trailed a line of kisses along her jaw to her earlobe, tracing the shell of her ear with the tip of his tongue. Goosebumps erupted across her skin, and she moaned softly, tightening her fingers in his hair.

"Luca," she breathed, wanting more from him, needing more.

Luca froze at the sound of his name on her lips, then backed away so quickly she stumbled forward a step. His eyes slowly traveled her body from head to toe, his breath coming in shallow pants. He stared at her for a long moment and then turned on his heel and left, the door slamming behind him.

Somehow, the absence of him in this moment, that rejection she'd been so keen on avoiding, hurt worse than all those years without him.

Slumping against the counter, she dropped her head in her hands.

This was for the best. Luca would only be a distraction in this. If he knew why she was really here, he'd probably try to stop her. And she couldn't let that happen. Not even for the possibility of being with him again.

Chapter Six

Luca sat at the far end of the large conference table in Matteo's newly acquired office building, staring out the window as Matteo and Carina argued. He preferred meeting at home, gathered around the couches in his father's old study or the dining room table while they ate. Meeting in this glass-enclosed room felt cold and sterile.

Or maybe it was the fact that his world had imploded a few days ago. Seeing Sienna, hearing her voice, tasting her, knowing she was alive when he'd thought her dead for so long, mourned her. It had broken open something inside him, something he'd buried a long time ago.

What he'd read in the papers was nothing compared to her telling of it. And he knew there was more she wasn't saying. She was too easy to read. She always had been.

He should have asked more questions, pried more answers out of her. About why she was back, what she was planning to do, if she knew who'd done this to her. He should have been cold, clinical, removed.

But from the moment the first tear fell, all he wanted to do was scoop her into his arms and comfort her. To touch her, hold her, soothe her. He wanted to know the bastards' names so he could tear them limb from fucking limb.

Fingers snapped in front of his face, and he jolted, looking up to see everyone around the table staring at him.

"Enjoying your daydream?" Matteo wondered.

"Sorry, what was your question?" Luca shifted in his seat, ignoring Carina's searching stare.

"How are the new drink menus performing at the strip club?"

Sitting forward in his chair, Luca dug the correct folder out of the stack in front of him and flipped it open. "Very well, actually. The higher profit margin helps, but sales are better and steadier than this time last year."

He passed the report and waited for Matteo to glance over it. "Perfect. Let's roll this out to the other clubs and keep an eye on the numbers. Eventually, I want to open some clubs and casinos in Varda's territory. Mark it as ours."

"Am I not doing that already by wasting away in Agrigento?" Dom asked.

"Missing home, brother?" Carina teased.

"Let's just say I preferred my compound with a view of the Mediterranean."

"It was too far and still in our territory. Agrigento was Varda's seat of power, and I wanted to keep it that way."

"I remember the reasons." Dom waved a hand over the table. "That doesn't mean I like them. Emilia, at least, has enjoyed gutting Varda's hideously ugly house and redecorating."

"Happy to hear she's making herself at home," Matteo grumbled.

"Don't start," Carina chided before Dom could snarl a retort. "I think it's nice someone finally revealed Dom's softer side." Dom's lip curled back over his teeth, and Carina chuckled. "Such as it is. Soon enough it'll be you or Luca."

Matteo grimaced. "Please, you'll make me lose my lunch. And Luca is too busy making eyes at my off-limits assistant to think of getting himself saddled with a woman."

"I'll have to remember to tell Alexei he's been saddled with me," Carina replied, one eyebrow arched over unamused brown eyes.

Pursing his lips, Matteo turned to Dom. "Strongholds are bearing up along the Antonetti and Gallo borders?"

Luca let his mind drift again to Sienna and Catania. From the first moment he saw her four years ago, he wanted her. She'd been out celebrating her twenty-first birthday, grinding on some guy in a club, her ass pressed against his crotch, his hands on her hips.

He'd never felt lust punch through him like that, an immediate, desperate need for one person. Stalking across the dance floor, he stared the guy down until he dropped his hands and wandered off. He'd slid in behind her, taking the other guy's place and whispering everything he wanted to do to her against her skin.

Then he'd shown her. First in the bathroom of the club with her skirt hiked up around her waist, then in the backseat of his SUV barely shielded by the tinted windows, then at the hotel room he rented because he couldn't get enough of her, couldn't fathom not spending the night with her.

It hadn't taken them long to realize they were on opposite ends of the island. Him a Bianchi, her a Gallo. Their families didn't strictly hate each other, but they wouldn't have approved of them being together. There was no money in it.

She was the youngest daughter of the second Gallo son; he was the third son of the Bianchi Don who couldn't seem to get his shit together. But that didn't make him want her any less. They spent as much time together as they could, sneaking off to meet somewhere in the middle or contriving to run into each other at clubs and falling into a hotel room bed.

He'd seen her for the last time two days before her birthday, before the day that changed everything. He'd taken her on a picnic in a field of wildflowers. She had a thing about wildflowers, always stopping to collect them from cracks in the sidewalk or on the side of the road.

They ate, they laughed, and he teased her for spending her summer learning another language just for fun, as if three wasn't enough already. Then he'd rolled her onto her back, fitted himself between her thighs, and…

"Luca!"

Dom's shout jerked him out of his thoughts, and he rammed his elbow into the edge of the glass table. "Fuck. What?"

"What the hell is wrong with you lately?" Matteo demanded. "You've been acting weird for days."

"Just…" He rubbed his forehead. "Haven't been sleeping well. I'm fine."

"Well, take the rest of the week. Christ, take the weekend too, to sort your shit out or get laid or something because I need your head in the game next week. We're taking our first hit at Gallo, and I don't want it to go sideways because you're too busy thinking about pussy."

"Don't worry about me. I'll be ready. Besides, Dom is the one who gets to have all the fun."

Matteo raised a brow. "I can't spare you for an active op. But I do need you sharp so you can keep an eye on everything when it goes down. So go get your dick wet or whatever you need to do to stop moping around my house."

"I'm not moping around the house."

"Uh huh," Matteo replied, unconvinced. "Let's plan to meet again after the first strike. Dom, you can call in. I know you hate to leave Emilia alone. Now that you're a family man and all."

Dom slapped Matteo on the shoulder, squeezing until Matteo winced. "One day, brother"—Dom laced the single word with venom—"you'll have to get married to make little Matteos to carry on your master plans and rule over the empire. Unless you expect Luca or me to do it for you like we've done everything else."

Matteo shoved Dom's hand away and took a menacing step forward.

"Boys," Carina said, stepping between them and laying a hand on either chest. "Give it a fucking rest. Dom, tell Emilia I said hello, and I'd love to have lunch sometime soon. Matteo, maybe *you're* the one who needs to get laid."

Luca snorted as he slid his chair away from the table. "That's what I've been saying."

Pushing out of the conference room, he made his way to the elevator, going the long way around to avoid Matteo's assistant Maeve and the flirtatious smiles she kept sending him. A week ago, he'd have jumped at the chance to finally get her naked. Now the only woman he could think about was Sienna.

Pressing the button to take him down, he sagged against the wall. He really hadn't been sleeping well. That was the truth. But the last thing he needed right now was for Matteo, or any of them, to know about Sienna. He had no idea what any of them would do if they found out about her, and he wouldn't jeopardize her safety.

The doors slid silently open, and he stepped into the car, pressing the button for the lobby.

"Luca, wait up!" He shot his arm out to keep the doors

from closing but didn't make eye contact with Carina when she got on behind him.

"Are you still working out of the casino?"

"Habit," Luca replied, leaning back against the wall of the elevator as it descended. "Matteo keeps trying to get me into the other corner office."

"It would be easier, I guess. Then again, you'd have to spend all day with him." She made a face. "Could be torture."

Luca chuckled, then sobered. "Say what you really want to say, Carina."

"Are you sure you're okay?"

"Yes," he lied. "I'm fine."

"I don't believe you."

Voices echoed through the lobby's atrium when they got off, Carina's heels clicking across the floor as she kept pace with his long strides. Out of all his siblings, he was closest with his sister. Not that it meant much, since their father enjoyed keeping his children at odds.

But they'd spent a lot of time together after their mother died. Carina was only eighteen and newly back from boarding school. Then Matteo left not long after, and Dom was off in his own grief and anger. Still, they were hardly in each other's confidence, and Carina didn't know about Sienna.

"Luca." She laid a hand on his arm to keep him from climbing into his SUV. "Please. Tell me what's going on."

His eyes wandered from her face to a spot over her shoulder where the sunlight refracted off a street sign, sending a bright white beam of light arching over the sidewalk.

Out of all of them, Carina might be the only one who understood. Lorenzo had intentionally kept her and his enforcer, Alexei, apart for years. But this thing with Sienna seemed wholly different. And it wasn't the fact that she was a

Gallo that stood in his way on this, not really. Matteo wouldn't be thrilled, but Luca could deal with that if he had to.

What really bothered him was knowing she hadn't trusted him. His father might not have agreed right away, but Luca would have gotten him to come around eventually. And until he did, he could have hidden her, kept her safe, tended her wounds and loved her.

But she'd taken that from him. And it didn't matter that she was back. She wasn't here for him. She'd made that clear when she asked what he was doing in Catania. He'd do well to remember that.

She was more than likely here for revenge. Why else come back to the island after all this time? She deserved it. There was no question about that. And he wanted her to have it. Hell, he wanted to be the one to give it to her. Burn the world down and hand her the ashes on a silver fucking platter. Better yet, stand at her back and give her the match. Whoever had done this to her would pay a thousand times over.

But what then? Would she leave him all over again? Go back to whatever life she'd built for herself far away from here while she recovered and plotted and planned? He wasn't prepared to lose her a second time. Which is why he needed to stay away from her. Far away.

Leave her to her business so he could do his. She was three hours away, and a few days ago, she was dead. It couldn't be that hard.

"I've just had a lot going on, *sorellina*. You worry too much," he teased, but he could tell she wasn't convinced.

"When you're ready to tell me the truth, I'll be here." She turned to leave, then stopped herself, pivoting to face him again. "You should come out to Marsala for dinner sometime. We can catch up properly."

"Have you finally stopped firing cooks?"

Carina rolled her eyes. "I'll have you know Alexei is responsible for firing the last one."

"Yeah, because she kept bringing her son around, and her son let his eyeballs wander too much. You're lucky Alexei didn't carve them out of his skull."

She propped her hands on her hips, but her lips twitched into a small smile. Carina and Alexei were perfect for each other. They both enjoyed drawing blood entirely too much.

"In any case, the new one is very good, and I think she might stick." She tucked her tongue in her cheek. "No wayward sons to speak of. Or daughters," she added, a note of jealousy in her voice.

Luca shook his head. "I might be able to find the time this weekend. I'll text you. But really, Carina. You have nothing to worry about."

She reached up to pat his cheek, giving him a patronizing pout. "If you say so, brother. Whatever's bothering you, I know you'll sort it out. I've never known anyone quite as good as you at solving a problem. I'm serious about dinner. I expect to hear from you."

Luca watched his sister's driver open the back door of the black town car and wait for her to get settled before driving away. There was no problem to solve. He had no reason to drive back to Catania any time soon. He knew the truth now. Or enough of it to satisfy him. He'd leave Sienna to her problems, and he'd focus on his own.

His hands would be busy enough rebuilding Gallo Industries once they assumed control of it. No need to complicate matters further. Maybe he really did need to go out and get laid.

Glancing up at the building towering over him, he thought of Maeve on the top floor. He should text her, ask her out for a drink, and finally give her the ride they'd both been dancing around for weeks. Scratch the itch, get it out of his system, and get his head back in the game.

Staring at the phone in his hand, he slipped it into his pocket with a sigh, climbed behind the wheel, and headed for the casino.

Chapter Seven

Sienna swiped her badge on the keypad at security and watched her face and alias flash across the screen. The guard looked from the screen to her face and back again and pressed a button to let her through to the bank of elevators. Gallo Industries was guarded like a fortress.

She'd been surprised to see how tight security was on her first day, with everyone needing to be approved by armed guards before they could access the elevators. You couldn't even get to the executive floors without the right access card or an escort. An important thing for her to know and something she'd have to factor into her plans.

Bypassing the elevators and the line of people waiting for them, she took the stairs to the second floor. The elegantly decorated reception area was empty when she stepped out of the stairwell, and the receptionist greeted her with a smile.

"How's your first week going so far?" Angelina wondered. "Settling in okay?"

"It's good. Everyone has been very helpful."

"Good. If you ever need anything, just let me know. I know they tend to push deadlines harder the closer we get to

Christmas. Everyone trying to make sure they don't have to work over the holidays."

Sienna didn't want to still be in Sicily by Christmas. It was her mother's favorite holiday, and she didn't know if she'd be able to fight off the flurry of memories seeing Catania at Christmastime. Hopefully, her targets would be dead long before she heard her first carol.

The elevator opened behind them, and the other three people on her team stepped off. Ciro was tall and lean, and he had flirted with her heavily since day one, even though he had a wedding ring on his finger and pictures of his wife and children all over his desk. His infatuation might come in handy.

She wished she could say she wouldn't flirt with or manipulate or fuck a married man just to get what she needed to finish this, but it would be a small price to pay to get what she came to Sicily for. It's not like she'd ever see him again after this. His infidelity would be between him and God.

Behind Ciro was Jack, an Englishman who had been lured away from the competition with a sizable bonus package he didn't mind bragging about to anyone who would listen. Sienna would have loved to tell him her deal was much better and her pay likely higher too, just to watch his ego deflate, but she needed him to keep thinking she wasn't competition. He would be more likely to overlook her that way.

Finally there was Isa, the only other woman on the team. Sienna had been trying to feel her out over the last few days, but Isa didn't seem all that interested in forming a friendship or even a polite working relationship. Whenever Sienna approached her to ask a question, she kept her answers as short as possible.

She'd have to be careful around Isa. Jealousy could derail her plans as easily as anything else. And Isa certainly seemed to be jealous of something, whether it was the fact that Sienna was younger or she'd even been hired in the first place, Sienna wasn't sure, but she would not let this woman get in her way. Even if she had to constantly force herself not to slap the sour look off Isa's face.

They weren't the only four people on the floor. IT was a big department for a company this size, but her team specialized in app development, not the internal tech needs of the company. Every time she overheard a story in the break room about some stupid thing one of the on-call techs had to deal with, she sent up a silent prayer of thanks.

Their job was to maintain and develop applications for both internal and external use. She'd been hired to help build an app for a new package delivery service they were hoping to launch sometime next year, branching out from commercial shipping and freight to consumer package delivery.

She'd spent most of the first week in meetings, and in her spare time, she explored the systems the company used to maintain its operations. They were impressive, to say the least, and they gave her access to a wealth of company data.

But it was too early to dive into that yet. She had to pace herself before she went looking for the information she needed. Everything she did from her desk and the laptop they gave her was monitored—every keystroke filed, every word she typed cataloged. It appeared her uncle was very suspicious of his employees.

She didn't know yet if logging in when she wasn't supposed to or in an area she wasn't cleared to access would trigger an internal alarm, and until she knew that for sure, she couldn't risk logging in and getting caught. She'd have to be patient.

Ciro looked her up and down and gave her a wink as he crossed the lobby toward his desk. Blushing, she jogged to catch up with him, ignoring the way Isa rolled her eyes as she headed for her own cubicle.

"You look very dapper in that suit," Sienna said, storing her purse in the bottom drawer of her desk and smiling up at him when he leaned his shoulder against the wall of her cubicle. "Is it new?"

He ran a hand down the front of his jacket and over his suit pants, and she tracked its path with her eyes because she knew he wanted her to, letting her gaze linger on his crotch before snapping back up to his face. She bit her lip and ducked her head, and he chuckled.

"I've never seen a woman blush as pretty as you," he said, and she rolled her eyes with her back turned. "How many more times do I have to ask before you say yes to a drink with me after work?"

She dropped into her chair and swiveled toward the three large monitors arranged side-by-side on her desk. Glancing at his crotch again, she let her gaze linger long enough to make his cock stiffen and then lifted her eyes to meet his, biting her bottom lip.

"Are you sure your wife wouldn't mind us going out?"

He shifted, trying to casually adjust himself, and there was a twinkle in his eye as he watched her. "Of course not. We're just friends, right?"

She grinned and arched a brow. "Right. Friends."

"So, Anna," he said, "would you like to have a drink with me tonight?"

Sienna fixed a pretty pout onto her mouth and watched his eyes drop to her lips. "I can't tonight. Ask me again on Monday."

He grinned wide and straightened. "Monday, then."

Turning from her cubicle, Ciro crossed the narrow aisle between their desks and sent her one last flirtatious wink before dropping into his chair and disappearing from view.

Sienna shook her head. The man was easily twenty-five years older than she was.

Not that the age gap seemed to bother him much. And if he was too busy thinking with his dick, it would make stealing his credentials to get into parts of the building she didn't have access to that much easier.

Logging into her system, she checked her email. Not even the years she spent working in IT for the German engineering firm had prepared her for the flurry of emails she received here. Emails scheduling meetings, asking for her input, or just being copied on something someone thought the entire IT floor needed to know, even though it had nothing to do with her actual job.

Every morning it took her almost an hour to wade through the mess, archiving what wasn't important and replying to what was. Email in and of itself could be a full-time job.

Next she glanced at her calendar. No meetings until after lunch. Afternoon meetings weren't ideal on a Friday, but at least next week she would begin her three days in the office, two days at home schedule. Showing up to a pointless hours-long meeting was much easier when you didn't have to wear pants.

She was pulling up the specs for the preliminary project she'd been briefed on at yesterday's meeting to look at the details when a shadow fell over her desk. She looked up to see Isa staring down her nose, a hint of disdain in the subtle curl of her lip.

"Hey, Isa," Sienna said, forcing mock cheer into her voice. "Did you need something from me?"

"Just wondering if you know what you're doing."

Sienna cast a sidelong glance at her monitors. "With…the project?"

Isa made a big show of rolling her eyes. "Just remember

that relationships between employees are strictly forbidden. It's in the company handbook. Which I'm sure you haven't bothered to read."

"I don't think I'll have a problem with that one."

Isa snorted. "Sure. Just try not to get fired like the last one. The workload is hell when we lose a team member. It'll be doubly so with this in the pipeline."

Isa didn't bother to wait for a response, turning on her heel and marching toward the break room at the back of the office.

"Don't mind her," Jack said in English from the other side of the wall separating them, his accent smooth and posh. "She's just mad because Ciro won't fuck her."

Ciro poked his head out of his cubicle at the sound of his name. "I hate it when you two don't speak Italian," he said. "It isn't fair."

"I don't want to go out for drinks if it will make Isa upset." Sienna switched back to Italian, keeping her eyes trained on her computer and ignoring Ciro's grunted protest. "I'd prefer not to make an enemy my first week."

"Who's enemies?" Ciro replied. "Isa is just like that. Bitc— grumpy," he amended at the sight of Sienna's raised eyebrows. "You'll see. It wouldn't matter if you said yes to a drink or not."

"Well, he is at least right about that," Jack agreed.

"You see? So when I ask you on Monday to have a drink, you'll have to say yes."

Sienna sent him her own flirty wink, shaking her head when he grinned in triumph. Men were entirely too easy to manipulate with the hinted promise of a quick and dirty fuck. But if Ciro was going to make this whole thing easy for her, she'd hardly waste time being upset about it. Maybe it would keep her mind off Luca and all the memories of him she hadn't been able to bury since he kissed her.

Isa flounced back to her desk, staring daggers at Sienna before flopping into her chair. The sound of her angry typing filled the air, and Sienna rolled her eyes.

Trying to get on Isa's good side might not be the best use of her time. Especially if Isa had an unreciprocated crush on Ciro. Because Sienna wasn't going to back down from getting what she needed out of him.

She couldn't get closer to her targets until she got access to the information she needed. And Ciro was her first step in getting it.

Chapter Eight

Luca stood before the wide floor-to-ceiling windows in the second corner office and stared down over Sicily. Cars, bikes, and Vespas whizzed around like ants through the well-lit streets. In the distance, beyond the colorful stretch of buildings, the moon glinted off the Tyrrhenian.

From this vantage point, everything seemed so small, inconsequential, ripe for the taking. Maybe this was why his brother had claimed the top floor of the towering building for himself. So he could feel like the king he was desperately fighting to be.

Turning away from the window, he surveyed the already furnished office. He wondered if he should be irritated or impressed that his brother had been so confident Luca would maintain an office here he'd already moved in all the furniture he would need.

A large, antique desk similar to the one in their father's study faced the windows, exactly how Luca would have placed it. The chair behind it was new but covered in a dark brown leather aged to look as old as the desk.

Tall, wide bookcases lined the wall behind the desk, and two chairs faced the front. The office wasn't as big as Matteo's, but there was still room enough between the desk and the door for a small loveseat and two more chairs across from it, creating a more intimate meeting area.

It was impossible to imagine needing this much space to do casino or even strip club business, but Luca knew Matteo's plans spanned far beyond reviving the failing Romano strip clubs they'd assumed control of or ratcheting up the profits of their already well-performing casinos. Casinos Luca had spent a lot of time pulling out of the gutter.

But still Luca had no concrete idea what Matteo's plans were beyond occupying Sicily's throne. Matteo had come back with a singular focus. Force every other Sicilian Don to bend the knee to him and allow them all to operate at his mercy—and only his mercy—on the island.

They'd completed the first phase of Matteo's plan by taking out the new and struggling Romano Don, Elio, and installing his younger, more pliable cousin, Davide. It had been a good move, not just for Matteo's plan, but for Carina's thirst for revenge. She deserved every drop of blood she and Alexei squeezed from that family for the way they treated her.

The second phase was controlling Varda's army to the south. Aroldo Varda had been a threat to Bianchi interests for years, constantly pushing the boundaries of their territories to see what he could get away with. In the end, all he'd gotten for his trouble was shot and all his loyal men with him. Dom now held control of the Agrigento territory in his iron grip.

Now they had their sights set on ruining Nero Gallo. Luca suspected Matteo probably would have played nice if Gallo had somehow miraculously agreed to their deal, shifting his plans to get what he wanted. Recalculating without sharing the new information with anyone until he was good and ready. He wouldn't put anything past his brother at this point.

He turned at a knock on the door, but no one entered. Must be Maeve. His brother rarely, if ever, bothered to knock for anything. Luca moved behind the desk to keep a barrier between them.

"Come in."

Maeve poked her head around the door and smiled. "I didn't realize anyone else was here this late, but I saw your light on. Thinking about joining us in the office full time?"

He looked around the space. "I am. I figured it's probably best to get settled in, find a rhythm before we get to work absorbing Gallo Industries."

"Smart," she said, pushing the door open fully and stepping into the frame. She clasped her hands in front of her, eyes wandering the office and lingering on the sofa before snagging his gaze. "If there's anything I can do to make your transition smoother, please let me know."

A week ago, he'd have flung back some flirty remark about working long, hard nights and then pictured her riding him on that very couch she kept eyeing. Now all he could picture was Sienna. Nothing in the last three years had dulled his senses where she was concerned.

He could still hear the sounds of her throaty moans and breathy sighs, the way her voice trembled when she begged him to fuck her. He'd shoved the need down for her a long time ago, but that kiss he should not have claimed from her mouth the other day had brought it all rushing back to the surface again.

Now he could barely think of anything else. He had to stop himself from jumping in the car and driving across the island just to see her at least five times a day. He still had so many questions.

Fitting her back into the box he'd kept her in for so long

wasn't working. He'd tried. And with each passing second, it was getting harder and harder to forget she existed.

If she was here for revenge, as he suspected, Christ knew she'd earned every bit of it and more. But fuck it all if he didn't want to help for the simple satisfaction of making whoever had taken her from him pay. Violently.

And he'd long suspected he might know who'd done it. Which would be a problem for all of them. Sienna might not want his help taking down her family's killer. She hadn't come to him to ask for it. But he had the sneaking suspicion they had the same target.

If he was right, this whole thing would become a lot more complicated. But there was at least one thing he could get working in Matteo's office that he couldn't get back at the casino. Better tech and security. Better information.

"Actually, can I get my own login for the database search program you use?"

Her eyebrows lifted, and her cheeks flushed, clearly surprised when he didn't flirt back with her. He'd have to deal with that later. Right now, he needed to confirm his suspicions about Sienna.

"Sure. I can get you set up with the program in just a few minutes."

He moved away from the desk toward the window, giving her plenty of room to skirt around it, and looked out over the city while her fingers moved rapidly over the keyboard. It was a shame Maeve's grandfather, Dublin's reigning mob king, wanted to marry her off after her year abroad helping Matteo gain control of Sicily. She was, no doubt, a much better asset behind a computer.

She stopped typing and took a step back. "Was there something specific you were looking for?"

He glanced at her from his spot by the window. She was loyal to his brother, not him, and if he didn't trust Carina enough to tell her about Sienna, he sure as hell didn't trust the woman who reported only to Matteo.

He shook his head. "Just some general research. I want to make sure we didn't miss any angles we could have worked. Especially when we make that hit next week. Thank you," he added as she moved to the doorway.

"Sure thing. If you need anything else, let me know."

She paused in the doorway, and when he said nothing, she gave him a tight smile and stepped into the hall, closing the door softly behind her. Leading Maeve on for several months was something he was going to have to feel bad about later. Once he figured out what he was going to do about Sienna.

Dropping into his chair, he ran a cursory records search in Italy for Sienna Gallo. There was her boarding school education in Milan. She'd hated that school and the nuns that ran it. Then her university education in Rome. She'd leveraged her low-ranking position in the Gallo organization to get her parents to agree to an education. The perfect way for her to be an asset to the family.

There was the occasional society page mention of her being seen at clubs and on the arms of sons of prominent men at social functions. She'd seriously dated an ambassador's son at university. Not surprising considering how well-connected her uncle was.

But then it was nothing but newspaper stories about her family's murder, speculation on who could have done it and why. The police ultimately arrested and convicted members of a known small-time gang who liked to cover up their crimes with arson.

It had never sat well with him. The whole thing had always seemed like a hit. But it wasn't as if his father had given him leave to investigate. He regretted not digging into it more then. Maybe he would have been able to find her. Even though he wasn't sure how.

He didn't have access to resources like this one three years ago, and even if he had, she'd ceased to exist. There was no other mention of Sienna Gallo after the night of her twenty-second birthday. Not even when he ran a broader search in Europe. Wherever she'd gone, she'd become someone else when she got there.

Tapping his fingers on the edge of the desk, he brought up a new search window. She was renting an apartment. Apartments meant paperwork. He plugged in the approximate location of her building until he found the one he wanted and brought up leasing records.

An old building from the late 1800s renovated into apartments in the last five years. There weren't many units in the building, and he scanned until he found records for the four apartments on the fourth floor.

Two couples, a single man, and one Anna Marino. The name didn't suit her. Not even with her fake blond hair and blue eyes. She'd never be anyone but Sienna to him.

He ran another search using the alias, which proved to be a treasure trove of information. There were similar schooling records for similar time frames but different schools than the ones she actually went to. There was a childhood background, but it was shallow, enough to make her look like a real person but not enough to give you too deep a glimpse into who she was.

It had information for parents who were missionaries and said she moved around Europe a lot and spoke four languages. She did speak four languages, but only because she liked to learn them. As far as he knew, she'd never lived outside Italy before she decided to run.

He sifted through all the information, zeroing in on the last three years. Three weeks after Sienna's twenty-second birthday, Anna Marino showed up near Berlin, renting first a room in a boarding house-type place and then, a few months later, a little cottage.

She worked remotely in IT for a German engineering firm making good money. And then, true to her word, a little over a week ago, she left Germany and created a paper trail moving south to Sicily. Where now she was living in Catania and working at…Gallo Industries?

His eyes narrowed on the screen. Son of a fucking bitch. There was only one reason she'd get a job right under her uncle's nose, hiding in plain sight. She suspected Gallo of murdering her family.

Luca certainly wouldn't put it past the fucker. The man was ruthless in the pursuit of what he wanted. That's why waging this war against him required a precise strategy and operating ten steps ahead. Something they couldn't do if Sienna started picking Gallos off one by one. Or wiping them out all in one go the way her family had been eradicated.

Fuck. He couldn't leave her to her own devices now, couldn't wait for her to seek her revenge and leave Sicily. Because if he was right and she was here to kill her uncle and his family as payback, then her goals clashed directly with theirs.

Logging out of the program and clearing his keystrokes, he glanced at his watch. It would be late by the time he made it across the island to Catania, but he had to talk to her. He needed to know what her plans were to make sure they didn't interfere with what they had in store for Gallo.

He wouldn't ask her to abandon whatever plans she'd come to carry out. He couldn't. But he needed to make sure his family didn't get screwed in the process.

Chapter Nine

Pushing her muscles through one last punishing flight of stairs, she exited onto her floor and followed the narrow hallway to the other end and into her apartment. She'd left all the lights burning out of habit, a silly bit of comfort to chase away the shadows and the demons hiding in them.

Grabbing a bottle of water from the fridge, she pressed it against her forehead and carried it into the bathroom. She twisted the nozzle for the shower and tested the temperature with her fingers.

At some point, she was going to have to make use of that incredible tub. But she'd pushed herself extra hard at the gym tonight, and if she slipped in there now, she'd probably fall asleep and drown.

Carefully removing her contacts and depositing them into the case, she stripped out of her shorts and sports bra. She avoided looking at herself in the mirror before stepping under the spray, closing her eyes, and tilting her head back, running her fingers through her long hair to wet it.

She'd considered cutting it off instead of letting it swing

almost to her waist more than a few times. It would certainly make it easier to maintain, cheaper too. But every time she reached for a pair of scissors, something stopped her. More accurately, Luca and the memory of how he'd liked to play with it stopped her.

Gliding his fingers through it when they were wrapped around each other, fisting his hands in it when he kissed her, pulling her head back to expose her neck for his lips or arch her back with his cock inside her. Some days, when she looked in the mirror and hardly recognized herself, it was the only thing that felt like a tangible tether to who she used to be.

She was rinsing conditioner out of her hair when a dull thudding resonated through the apartment. Was someone really playing music that loud at this hour? The banging suddenly stopped, and she frowned, reaching for the bar of soap and lathering it in her palms. She was running the suds over her stomach when the thudding resumed, then stopped a second time.

Shutting off the water, she listened for the sound again. There it was. Definitely not music. Someone pounding on a door. Her door. She rolled her eyes. Probably some drunk asshole with the wrong apartment.

Squeezing the excess water out of her hair, she quickly wrapped herself in a towel, prepared to tell the guy to take a fucking hike before he woke up the entire building. Peering through the peephole, she jumped back when Luca raised his fist to pound on the door a fourth time.

Opening it, she gripped the lapel of his suit jacket and yanked him inside, slamming the door behind him.

"Jesus Christ, Luca. Do you know what time it is?" She checked the peephole again to make sure no one poked their head out at Luca's late-night wake-up call. "What the fuck are you doing here?"

She turned to face him, cheeks heating when his eyes dragged up over her bare legs, lingering on the bottom of the towel skimming very high on her thighs and over the swell of her breasts. She gripped the knot tighter against her chest, her nipples pebbling under his hungry gaze. He might hate her, but he still wanted her.

When he didn't speak or bother to explain, she cleared her throat, drawing his gaze to her face. "Did you come all this way to gawk at me showering after a workout?"

His eyes flicked to the clock over the stove. "You exercise at midnight?"

"It helps me sleep. What do you want, Luca?"

"Who killed your family?"

The tone of his voice when he asked the question made it clear he already knew the answer, but she knew she couldn't share her plans with him. He'd definitely try and stop her.

"You drove three hours at this time of night to ask me that?"

He took a step closer. "I think I have a right to know who stole you from me." The statement caught her off guard, and her eyebrows shot up. "You're surprised?"

"Am I surprised you were so disgusted by your impulse to kiss me you ran away from me at lightning speed only to show up here at midnight and demand to know who killed me? Yeah. You could say I'm a little taken aback."

"Disgusted," he repeated, taking another step forward.

"Look, I know you hate me for not trusting you, but I—"

His hand shot out to wrap around her waist and yank her against his chest. "I do not hate you, Sienna. You could gut a man in the fucking street, and I wouldn't hate you. I hate that I couldn't protect you. I hate that you didn't think you could come to me. I hate whoever took you from me. But I do not and could not ever hate you. Do you understand?"

She nodded, unable to speak, her eyes dropping to his lips

as his hand fisted in the fabric of the towel at her back, forcing it up over the rounded curve of her ass. He growled low in his throat when she wiggled against his hold.

"You still haven't answered my question. Who killed your family?"

"I'm not having this conversation with you naked."

He gripped the towel tighter in his fist, dangerously loosening the knot between her breasts. "You used to like being naked with me."

"I never stopped liking it," she assured him, watching his eyes darken. "But I'm still not discussing my family's murderer with you while I'm wearing a towel."

He seemed to debate with himself over getting her naked or getting the answers he came for. Reluctantly, he released her, and she scurried down the hall to her bedroom, slipping an oversized sweater over her head and tugging on a pair of leggings. Covered from shoulder to calf seemed a much safer way to have this conversation with him.

He was standing in the kitchen where she'd left him, and she might as well still be naked save for a towel with the hungry way his eyes traveled over her. It had been so long since she wanted any man but Luca. Time hadn't faded her need for him.

"We should sit."

She crossed to the living room and sank onto one end of the couch, tucking her legs underneath her while she waited for him to join. He sat at the opposite end facing her, the city lights at his back through the window. He looked at her expectantly while she debated how much to share with him.

"Well?"

"I think my uncle ordered a hit on my entire family."

He swore under his breath, rubbing his forehead with his fingertips. "I suppose you have proof?"

She tilted her head, eyes narrowing on his face. "I didn't realize I needed any. I don't answer to you, Luca."

He scowled. "I never said you did. I always wondered if it was him. If someone had killed one of my brothers, I would have razed the island to the ground. And I don't even like them that much."

Sienna chuckled softly in spite of herself. "That was my conclusion. There was a reason I didn't run to him after what happened."

"And now you're back to make him pay."

"That's right. I finally figured out a way to get close enough to do what I need to do."

"Is that why you're working at Gallo Industries? To get close to him?"

Sienna jerked. "How the hell do you know I'm working at Gallo Industries?"

"Because after you died, I became very good at finding the information I wanted to know so I was never helpless again."

Her heart beat painfully in her chest, and she was glad he was too far away to touch. If she did, she might not be able to stop. Shoving that thought away, she focused on his question.

"Yes," she confirmed. "That's why I got a job there. In the IT department. Although you probably already knew that." She blew out a breath when he nodded. "My uncle is paranoid. He's always heavily armed and flanked by bodyguards. Except at the office. It was the only way I could think of to get close enough to him."

She shifted, trying and failing to read his expression. "He maintains tight security on the executive floor. I need access to credentials with enough clearance to get up there. Once I have that, I can take him out."

"I can't let you do that."

"Excuse me?" Of all the things she thought he might say, that one didn't even make the list. "I'm not asking your permission, Luca. I've been planning this for over two years. It's happening."

"I need you to wait."

Shoving off the couch with an irritated huff, she paced between the coffee table and the TV. "I can't believe you're seriously saying this to me right now. I don't deserve justice for my family? My uncle shouldn't pay for what he did?"

"That's not what I'm saying at all. But we have something in the works here, and if you take him out, it'll fall apart."

Her steps faltered, and she turned to face him. "You're making a move on my uncle? For what? How?" He hesitated, and she scowled. If he was going to demand answers, he was sure as hell going to give her some in return. "Fair is fair, Luca. Tell me."

"We've set in motion a plan to claim Gallo Industries under the Bianchi banner."

"You want me to hold off on avenging my entire family for a corporate fucking takeover?" she shrieked. "I can't take down the man who took everything from me because you want to make some fucking money?"

"Sienna—"

"Get out." She pointed at the door, but his eyes never left her face. "Out of everyone who might have tried to stop me, I never thought it would be you."

"This thing is bigger than me and you," he said, not budging from his spot on the couch. "Matteo—"

"Matteo's back?"

"Yes. He showed up for my father's funeral. We're taking over Sicily. We've already taken out Romano and Varda. Your uncle is next. I just…I need you to trust me."

"No." She shook her head, crossing her arms over her chest. "You need me to get out of your way."

"That's bullshit," he snapped, surging off the couch and stalking toward her. "You think I don't want him to pay for what he did to you? For taking you from me? I can promise you, there's nothing I want more. But I'd prefer not to get fucked in the process. I'd prefer not to lose our growing control on the island. I'd like for us to both get what we want. We can help each other."

"I want their blood on my hands. I deserve it," she spat.

He advanced until her back brushed the wall, his arms coming up to cage her in again. "And you'll have it. My word on that. We don't plan on leaving him alive anyway."

"Alexei can't have him. Nero is mine."

Luca sighed, pressing forward until the length of his body pinned hers to the wall. "I'll do everything I can to ensure you're the one who gets to take him out when the time is right."

Her eyes dropped to his lips and lingered there before darting back up to meet his gaze. "That's not good enough. How do I know you won't screw me out of what's mine?"

He dropped his head and whispered against her ear, "Baby girl, I'll load the gun for you."

She chewed her bottom lip, thinking. There were a million different ways this could go wrong. Her plan had been solid from the beginning. Get in and shoot her uncle so her family could finally have some peace. She'd hoped to watch the life drain from her uncle's eyes within weeks, not months, or potentially more.

But if her uncle was going to end up dead either way, it might be fun to watch him lose everything first. It was no less than what the bastard deserved. Gallo Industries was her uncle's baby. He loved it more than he loved his own sons. Taking it from him would be the icing on the cake of what she had in store for him.

Chapter Ten

"Fine," Sienna conceded. "I'll wait. But you better not make me wait long because I'll have the access card I need next week."

A slow grin spread across Luca's face, and he leaned down to kiss her, sliding his tongue against hers when she parted her lips with a sigh and dropping his hand to her hip to pull her closer.

"Whose card are you using?" He slipped his fingers under the hem of her sweater and traced circles over her warm skin, making her shiver.

"There's a guy on my team who has the right security clearance. I should be able to get what I need from him."

His gaze on her face sharpened. "How?"

"The usual." She lifted a shoulder. "Go out for drinks, flirt, bring him back here for a quickie so I can get access to his security badge."

"You will absolutely not be doing that," he said, hand tightening on her waist.

"It's not like it'll mean anything. I need his creds to get—"

"Sienna." Luca's voice was a warning growl. "You will not be fucking anyone for information."

She met his hard stare with her own and shoved at his shoulder. "You're not the boss of me. I will do what I have to do to—"

Luca silenced her with another kiss, rough and demanding. His hands slid through her damp hair, gripping it tight in his fingers and holding her against him while he claimed her mouth with his own. He bit her bottom lip roughly, making her whimper, then soothed it with his tongue.

Using his hands to adjust the angle of her head, he peppered kisses along her jaw to her earlobe. Nipping the lobe with his teeth, he traced the shell of her ear until she trembled, his breath hot on her skin.

"If he touches you," he whispered against her ear, raising goosebumps along her neck, "I will cut off his fingers one by one until he has nothing left to touch you with. Tell me you understand, baby girl."

He pressed his lips to the sensitive spot behind her ear, and she nodded, gripping the front of his suit jacket in her fists.

"How am I supposed to get his credentials if I don't sleep with him?"

His mouth worked down the side of her throat, nudging back the collar of her sweater and dragging his teeth over the skin where her neck met her shoulder.

"You're a very intelligent woman, Sienna. I'm sure you'll figure something out." He dropped one hand from her hair, sliding it under the hem of her sweater and cupping her bare breast, his palm rubbing roughly against her pebbled nipple. "But the only cock you'll be taking is mine."

He stepped back long enough to whip her sweater off over her head, then he was lifting her into his arms, sucking her nipple into his mouth and groaning when she wrapped her legs around his waist. He feathered kisses from one nipple to the other, circling it with his tongue before grazing it with his teeth.

"Tell me where the bedroom is, or I'm fucking you on this floor," he demanded before drawing her nipple between his teeth again.

"Last door at the end of the hall," she said between hitching breaths.

He carried her easily down the short hallway, fumbling with the door handle before finally swinging it open. She'd left the lights on in here too, but at least her new curtains were drawn. Expecting him to set her down on the floor, she squeaked in surprise when he dropped her onto the edge of the bed, urging her onto her back and covering her half-naked body with his.

The expensive fabric of his suit jacket dragged against her nipples, overly sensitive from his teeth, and she arched against him with a groan. His lips curved into a grin as he kissed and licked and nibbled from her chin, down her neck, between the valley of her breasts,

His tongue dipped into her navel before continuing down to the waistband of her leggings. Nibbling the exposed skin, he hooked his fingers in the fabric and urged her to raise her hips with a lift of his brow. Complying, she nearly came undone when she felt his warm breath against her pussy.

After peeling her leggings off and tossing them behind him, Luca knelt between her thighs. He placed her knees over his shoulders, dragging his tongue from the bottom of her slit to the top, circling it over her clit. She slid her fingers into his hair, grinding against his mouth.

"You taste better than I remember. Do you still come as pretty for me, baby girl?" He slipped first one, then two fingers inside her, shoving them deep and forcing a gasp from her lips. "I can't wait to find out."

"Luca," she whimpered, rocking against the slow, deep thrust of his fingers.

His mouth returned to her clit, sucking it roughly before swirling his tongue around it, his fingers keeping a steady pace inside her. Luca had always known how to touch her, to drive her wild, to push her closer and closer to the brink until he and the pleasure only he could give her were all she could think about.

"That's it," he crooned when her pussy clenched around him, working his fingers faster to bring her closer to the edge. "That's what I want. Come on my fingers, Sienna."

"Yes," she groaned, shuddering when he grazed against her G-spot and forced her higher and higher until she exploded around him. "Oh God," she breathed as he pulled his fingers out of her and licked them clean.

"I missed that sound," he said, shedding his jacket as he toed off his shoes and socks.

She sat up to help him unbutton his shirt and slide it off his shoulders, leaning in to trail her lips over his abs, his stomach muscles contracting as he undid his belt buckle and dragged down the zipper. He took a step back to slide his pants and boxers down to his ankles, kicking them off and palming his cock, giving it a rough stroke.

Sienna wet her lips, and his voice was hoarse when he spoke again. "On your knees in the middle of the bed for me, baby girl."

Dragging her eyes up to his face, she wriggled back into the center of the bed and shifted onto her hands and knees with her ass facing him. Before she could search for him over her shoulder, she felt the mattress dip with his weight. He ran his hands from her hips to her shoulders, circling the puckered scar there and then leaning down to press a kiss to it.

"I thought it was enough to know you were alive," he murmured against her ear, rubbing his cock along her slit as his fingers pinched and teased her nipples. "That I could let you have your revenge and walk away."

He buried his cock inside her with one languid thrust, and she dropped her head between her shoulders with a groan. "But I can't. You're mine, Sienna. From the first moment I saw you in that club until your last breath, you'll be mine."

"Yes," she whispered.

"It's just my dumb luck I get a second chance. I won't be wasting it by letting you go again."

Dragging his teeth over the nape of her neck, he sat up, gripping her hips and pulling his cock almost all the way out before slamming into her again. She rocked her ass back against him, squeezing him until he groaned.

"Fuck, baby girl, your pussy has always been made for my cock. You want more?"

She rocked back against him in response, unable to speak, and he slammed into her again, his hips setting a faster, more urgent pace than his fingers had. Filling her over and over until she was gripping the sheets with white knuckles, meeting him thrust for brutal thrust.

"Luca," she gasped, her body on fire from the way he was using it, his hands tight on her waist, his cock stroking deep inside her.

His hand slid down to her clit, and he rubbed it in rough, fast circles while he pounded her. "Come on my cock, Sienna. I want to feel you shatter for me."

She met every deep, grinding thrust with a desperate moan, his name a prayer on her lips as he fucked her until she could barely breathe. He bracketed her clit with his fingers, squeezing roughly, and she screamed his name as she came apart around him.

He pulled out of her, and she whimpered at the loss, letting him roll her onto her back before her arms gave out. He traced his fingertips across her collarbone, over her breasts, circling then pinching each nipple, grinning when she moaned for him.

"You're trying to kill me," she croaked when he snaked his hand lower, grazing it over her sensitive clit and making her jolt.

"Do you want me to stop?" His fingers stilled on her clit, his hand moving lazily up and down his shaft the only sound in the room. "Sienna. Do you want me to stop touching you?"

"No," she said, reaching for him and sighing when he didn't hesitate to cover her body with his. "I never want you to stop again. I thought I could let you go. I thought if at least one of us got to be happy, that would be enough. But you're mine, Luca. From the first moment you touched me until your last breath, you'll be mine."

He slid inside her in one savage thrust, grinding his pelvis into her clit. Scoring her nails across his back, she planted her foot flat on the bed and met his thrusts with her own, his hips working like a piston against hers.

His fingers dug into the curve of her ass, holding her while he pounded into her hard and deep. Falling back into his arms, into his bed, into his life, might be a mistake. It might jeopardize everything she'd done to get to this moment, but no one had ever given her what Luca did. His heart, his body, his soul. She would die a thousand times over if it meant she got to be with him, even for just a few stolen moments. Nothing else mattered.

As if sensing her thoughts, he dropped his head to the crook of her neck, slamming into her with short, fast thrusts, and whispered, "I'm going to make sure you get everything you deserve, Sienna. Gallo's blood on your hands. If you want him to beg, plead, scream, you'll have it."

"I want it," she gasped. "I want all of them to pay."

"They will," he assured her, grinding against her clit until she shuddered with the contact. "I swear it."

"Fuck," she panted, her body pulsing everywhere his skin met hers. "Luca. I want you to come inside me."

He groaned against her neck, fucking her into the bed harder. "Come on my cock, baby girl. Come hard for me, and I'll fill your pussy up."

Sliding her hands into his hair, she arched against his chest, dragging her nipples against his skin, pussy pulsing around him. Every brutally deep thrust of his cock pushed her closer and closer to the brink until her body went taut, and she saw stars.

"Yes, baby girl, just like that," he growled against her skin, giving her one last vicious thrust and emptying himself inside her.

"Jesus fucking Christ," she said, and he chuckled. "That was more intense than I remember it."

Rolling onto his side, he reached out to wrap an arm around her waist and haul her back against his chest. He kissed her scar again. "Just reminding you who you belong to."

"It'll always be you, Luca." She turned in his arms to face him, cupping his jaw with her hand and running her thumb over his smooth cheek. "Did you mean what you said? About my uncle's blood on my hands."

He turned his head to press a kiss against her palm. "Every fucking word. You'll have him and anyone else. They'll all pay for what they did to you and your family, Sienna."

"What if Matteo doesn't approve?"

"I'm not asking his permission. And until the time is right, no one else in Sicily will know you're alive but me. I'm not going to lose you again. Besides, you have access to insider information that could very well come in handy for us."

She smiled. "I'm going to enjoy watching him lose everything before I kill him."

"I was hoping you'd say that." He leaned in to capture her lips, deepening the kiss by degrees until she couldn't help but sigh. "You know, it's pretty late."

"It is," she agreed. "It would be very unsafe to drive back to Palermo at this hour."

"Staying would be the smart thing to do."

"Absolutely," she replied, rolling him onto his back and kissing down his abs, dragging her teeth over his hip, smiling when his cock started to harden for her again.

"Sienna," he said, his voice a warning.

"Hmm?" She blew a warm breath against the tip of his cock and watched it thicken.

"It's been a long time since I fucked your mouth, but I still remember how much you like it."

Sealing her lips around the tip of his cock, she sucked it hard, hollowing out her cheeks and making his hips jerk. "Luca? Show me what you remember."

Chapter Eleven

Luca woke to the feel of Sienna cuddling against his side, her leg sliding over his thigh as she wrapped her arm around his waist and pulled herself closer. She was still asleep, her breathing deep and even, and he ran his fingers through her hair. He hadn't gotten the opportunity to wake up with her a lot in their first year together, but the feeling of her warm body pressed against his was a gift after the pain of losing her.

The room was still dark, light peeking from under the thick curtains. Sienna was anything but a morning person, and she'd finally found a way to banish the sun.

His phone buzzed on the nightstand, and he reached for it, silencing it to keep it from waking her. A text from Carina wondering why he hadn't called about dinner yet. She was being entirely too persistent not to be up to something. Another from Alexei asking about something for the casino. He fired off a quick response to that one.

Then a flurry of messages from Matteo wondering where the hell he was and why wasn't he home. His brother's short, sharp tone was evident even through words on a screen, and

Luca gritted his teeth against the implication he was somehow at Matteo's beck and call.

I went out to get laid. As instructed.

Matteo's response was instantaneous. *When I said take the weekend, I didn't mean the whole weekend.*

You'll have to be clearer next time. Don't worry, I'll be home before curfew. Boss.

He dropped the phone on the nightstand and refocused his attention on Sienna curled against his side. In this position, he could see the large horizontal scar near her belly button. Like the ones on her neck and shoulder, it was raised, bumpy, and uneven to the touch.

He drew his fingers over it, trying to imagine her all alone in an underground bunker, digging bullets out of her body and quickly, clumsily, sewing herself up again. Every time he pictured it, he wanted to march into Nero Gallo's office and beat him until he begged for mercy. He wouldn't get any, but it would be fun to hear him try.

Tracing his fingertips down Sienna's spine and over the curve of her ass, he teased her exposed slit. She squirmed against his fingers but didn't wake up, so he did it again. Pushing past her lips, he dipped the tip of his finger inside her, and she squirmed again, this time moaning softly.

"Been a long time since anybody woke me up like that," she murmured, voice thick with sleep.

His fingers retreated, and he shifted her position on his thigh to give him better access. "How long?" He dipped his finger inside her again, pushing it in as far as he could in this position.

"Not since you," she assured him, clenching around his finger. "There hasn't been anyone since you."

He flipped her onto her back, gripping her thighs and spreading her legs wide before rubbing the head of his cock up and down her slit. "Say that again."

Her breath caught, and she reached up to cup her breasts, rolling her nipples between her fingers. "I haven't been with anyone since you."

Sienna was already wet and ready for him; his cock slid easily inside her. "Play with your clit," he commanded, pulling her thighs over his and pounding into her with fast, rough strokes. "I'm not going to take it slow, and I want to feel your pussy strangle my cock before I come inside you."

She whimpered but trailed her fingertips down to her clit, rubbing it in slow circles. He let her set a lazy pace while he continued to pound her, her fingertips grazing his cock each time he pulled out and making him jerk.

"Faster, Sienna."

When she didn't pick up the pace, he released one of her thighs and pushed her hand away. Smacking her clit, he groaned when her pussy fluttered around his cock.

"That's it, baby girl. That's what I want." He smacked it again, and she twisted her nipple roughly in response, her hips jerking wildly against his. "Are you going to be a good girl and come for me?"

He slapped her clit three times in rapid succession when she didn't answer him. Then her back arched beautifully, her pussy spasming around his cock, gripping him like a vise as he forced the orgasm from her body.

"Fucking Christ, Luca. Where did you learn to do that?"

He grinned, leaning over her to change the angle, seating his cock deeper inside her and feeling her shudder when his pelvis ground against her sensitive clit. "Where did you learn to like it?"

She bit back a grin, gasping when he lowered his head to capture her nipple between his teeth, biting it before pulling his hips back and slamming into her again, resuming his rough, frenzied pace. It wouldn't take him long to come, but he wanted to feel her explode around him again.

"You got another one for me, baby girl?"

"No," she replied, but her breaths were ragged, her pussy clenching tight around him with every thrust.

He bit down on her nipple again, pulling it away from her body with his teeth and releasing it. "I don't believe you."

"Fuck," she rasped, fingernails digging into the skin of his biceps where she was holding on. "Luca."

"Yes, baby girl. Give it to me."

She came for him again on a strangled moan, writhing under him, begging and pleading until he couldn't hold back anymore, and he followed her over the edge.

He collapsed on top of her, barely supporting his weight on his forearms while he licked and sucked the skin of her neck. She wrapped her legs around his waist, and he groaned.

"Let's run away together," he murmured. "I'll keep you naked and full of my cock all day long."

"Okay," she replied, voice lazy and relaxed. "But there are a few people I have to kill first."

Luca chuckled, pressing one last kiss to her neck and rolling onto his back. "About that. I should probably tell you what Matteo has planned so we can coordinate something."

Trailing her fingertips down his arm, she laced their hands together. "You probably should. Breakfast?"

"It's technically lunch time now. And I don't want you to put clothes on yet."

She laughed, sitting up and leaning over to peck his lips. "I do know how to cook. Is cacio e pepe still your favorite? I think I have everything to make it."

He kept his grip tight on her hand when she moved to slide off the bed and pulled her in for another kiss. "I've missed you."

Smiling, she kissed him again, tracing his bottom lip with her tongue. "I thought about you every single day. Come. I'll feed you, and you can tell me about your brother's plans to take over the world."

He watched her slip out of bed and pull on a robe, belting it loosely. Not bothering with any other clothes besides his boxer briefs, he followed her into the kitchen and claimed a seat at the round table while she pulled ingredients out of the fridge and pantry.

"That day I saw you at the hotel, we were meeting with Nero and his sons." She glanced at him from the corner of her eye but didn't speak. "Matteo offered to invest in Gallo Industries for an equal share."

Sienna's eyebrows shot up. "I can't imagine my uncle took that offer."

"He did not. He basically told us to shove it up our asses."

"Sounds about right." She set a pot of water on the stove to boil. "You had to know he wouldn't go for it."

Luca nodded. "We anticipated that. My brother was hoping he'd slip up and say something stupid."

Cracking black pepper into a skillet to toast, she frowned. "My uncle doesn't make many mistakes. Especially not with enemies."

"We've noticed."

She shot him a look over her shoulder and added salt and then pasta to the boiling water. "I assume you have a plan B."

"We do. Gallo's systems are a vault, as I'm sure you know. But we know enough to peg down some of his shipments. We plan to attack them, raid them for weapons if we can, and cost him a lot of fucking money if we can't."

"Hmm," she murmured, grating cheese into a bowl and checking the pasta. "What's the endgame?"

"Cut off his weapons supply, weaken his political alliances, and run Gallo Industries into the ground until he gets desperate and kills himself in a tragic yet convenient suicide. Or, more accurately, we kill him and make it look like a suicide."

"Why suicide?"

"As much as I'd prefer to walk into his office and put a bullet between his eyes for what he did to you, he's too well-connected. A suspicious death would draw attention from both the press and the authorities, and we can only line so many pockets to keep them looking the other way."

Sienna wet her lips with a nod. "That's probably true if you don't want to get caught. And I assume you don't. So you weaken Gallo Industries to give him a reason, take him out and make it look like a suicide, and then what? Make sure you're the highest bidder when the company goes up for sale? What about Stefano and Dante?"

"Matteo wants to own Gallo Industries. Move operations to Palermo. Rebrand it as Bianchi International and turn it into our flagship corporation. If Stefano and Dante aren't on board with that outcome, we'll take care of them as well."

Fishing pasta out of the water, she transferred it to the pan, swirling it to finish cooking with the toasted pepper and ladling in more water as she needed it. He'd never watched her cook before. He wasn't even aware she knew how. She'd obviously made this dish a lot, knowing all the steps by heart. He wondered if she had made it and thought of him since it was his favorite.

"They won't be," she said, adding the cheese and stirring quickly to melt it and thicken the sauce. "Stefano would follow his father off the edge of a cliff, and Dante is just a mean son of a bitch. Not as smart as Stefano, but every bit as ruthless as my uncle is."

"Noted."

"Your plan could take a while, though. The minute you start hitting targets, my uncle will tighten security and start randomizing shipments. He's got a whole backend app built for that."

"He switches them up so much already. We know we're playing a game of chance, but without direct access to his systems, it was the best we could come up with."

She nodded, transferring the pasta to two plates and adding more cheese and pepper before bringing them to the table. He twirled the thick strands of spaghetti around his fork and took a bite, eyes snapping up to meet hers. She only grinned at him.

"Good?"

He leaned over to brush his lips over hers. "You're phenomenal, baby girl."

"You know he's got more than one supplier, right? Or he used to."

Luca raised his brows. That was news to him. He wondered if Matteo knew that little nugget of information or not.

"He never puts all his eggs in one basket," she added. "You need an inside source. Someone who can not only give you shipments to ambush and sabotage, but also make sure it's random enough not to blow cover. And I know just the girl to help you."

Propping her foot on the edge of the chair, she sampled her pasta and added a little more pepper. "Plus, he most definitely has incriminating evidence hidden away. Who he's bribing, blackmail files, shit like that. My father used to talk about how stupid it was to store that much information for anyone to find."

"It does seem like a bad move."

"My uncle thinks he's bulletproof. But he isn't. Someone just has to look in the right spot."

"And then what? Go to the authorities?"

"No. They won't listen anyway. The ones that aren't in his

pocket are controlled by the ones that are." A dark look flickered across her face, and then it was gone again. "This will go faster if I can slip you information on what shipments to target for maximum damage, both financially and politically. But you'll want to be careful about who you bribe."

"Why's that?"

"The politicians in his pocket are scared of him. Whatever he's got on most of them, it's not good. I overheard my father talking about it more than once. Based on what I was able to see from police databases—"

Luca's eyebrows shot up. "You've hacked police databases?"

"I have." She smiled at the surprise on his face. "I could have hacked them before I left. But no one ever asked me to. Now I'm better at it."

"What did you find when you hacked the databases?"

She sighed. "Nothing. That's when I knew for sure it had to be Nero." He reached over and laid his hand on hers, giving it a gentle squeeze. "But the best way to bring him to his knees is to remove his allies first. And if you can't bribe them away from him, then you have to make it very inconvenient to support him."

"By taking out his government contracts."

"Yes. Once he's floundering with no hope of recovering, we can both get what we want."

Leaning his elbow on the table, his thumb tracing circles over the back of her hand, he studied her. "How risky is it? To get into his systems?"

Sienna shrugged, taking another bite of pasta. "No riskier than hacking any other database. I'll use all the same protections, and I have the added bonus of working there and having a more intimate knowledge of their security protocols."

"A position you put yourself in on purpose," he said.

"Yes. But now I have to figure out how else to finesse my fall guy after flirting with him all week."

"Why?"

She lifted a brow. "Because you threatened to cut off his fingers."

Luca gave her a pointed look. "I'll do it too."

"I don't doubt that." She tried to bite back a smile, but it didn't work, the edges of her mouth quirking up. "I'll figure something out."

"I don't want you to get caught, Sienna." His grip on her hand tightened. "I need you to make sure you're careful. Fuck knows what Nero will do to you if he finds out you're alive."

"Don't worry about that." She waved a hand in the air. "I know what I'm doing and how to fly under the radar.

"Just be careful."

"Of course," she replied. "How are you going to explain to Matteo the sudden acquisition of an inside source?"

"That's a great question," Luca muttered.

"He can't blow my cover, Luca. I've waited too long for this moment."

He reached out and pulled her into his lap, smiling when she wrapped her hand around his neck and guided his mouth to hers. "He'll never know it's you. How soon can you get access?"

"Ciro is going to ask me out for drinks tomorrow, and I'm going to say yes." Luca scowled, and she stroked her fingers over the side of his neck. "Don't worry, *amore*. I'll get him very drunk, but I won't let him touch me. He needs all his fingers to do his job."

Luca huffed out a laugh. "I don't give a shit what he needs."

"Just trust me. If all goes well, I should have access by Friday at the latest."

"All right. I'll get your number before I go." He kissed the tip of her nose. "Sienna. When can I see you again?"

"Friday?"

He sighed, wrapping his arm tighter around her waist. "That's very far away."

"I think I have something that might hold you over until then."

"Pasta to go?" he asked with a grin.

She drilled a finger into his belly but laughed. "I was thinking more along the lines of my bathtub is big enough for two."

Pushing abruptly to his feet, he cradled her against his chest and carried her into the bathroom. Setting her on the edge of the counter, he ran water into the tub, testing the temperature with his fingers before returning to her and unbelting her robe.

"Let's see how many times I can make you come before the water gets cold."

Chapter Twelve

Sienna scanned through the lines of code she'd spent most of the day writing, checking them for errors. Management kept changing their mind about the app's features. With the stroke of a pen, they could wipe out an entire day's work. No wonder they'd brought her on so early if they were so indecisive about even letting them build a test to completion.

There was something about being in her element, though. Even here, surrounded by the enemy. She'd always had a natural affinity for technology, constantly getting in trouble as a child for taking something apart to see how it worked. Even though she always managed to put it back together again.

When she turned thirteen, her mother's brother had gotten her a computer. But he made her promise she wouldn't take it apart before he gave it to her. It was love at first sight. And she kept her word by only dismantling the mouse.

Once she was older, it had taken some convincing, but eventually her father agreed to let her go to university and get a degree. The irony was, she had the career she'd always envisioned having. Except now she was trying to tear Gallo

Industries apart instead of protecting it from their enemies. Her loyalty to Nero Gallo had died with her family.

It had taken her more time than she wanted to admit to accept the truth. That her uncle had slaughtered his own brother, his own nieces and nephews—innocent children. She'd spent countless hours trying to reason it out, trying to pin it on one of their enemies.

Shortly before the massacre, a man threatened her father after he refused to haggle over a weapons sale. Then they'd needed to punish a foreign contact when they caught him double dipping.

But with every new bit of information she was able to uncover, every system she successfully hacked, a new picture emerged. She should have suspected Nero from the moment she chose to flee the country instead of run to his protection. But she'd reasoned with herself that she ran to keep him safe. In case whoever hurt her family wanted to hurt him too. She was a fool.

He'd grieved in the papers. Nero was nothing if not meticulous about the public's perception of him. Still, none of the news articles she'd found online matched the records she'd hacked her way into. Bare police files proved the entire investigation was nothing but a show for the press.

When the realization finally penetrated her blind loyalty, it had nearly broken her. As evil as her uncle was, she'd never doubted he loved his family, that family always came first. She'd loved her uncle and was excited to finish her graduate program and work for him.

But he'd taken everything from her. And for what? What purpose did it serve to kill them? What reason did he have for murdering innocent children? His own flesh and blood.

Deciphering the why of it consumed her in the beginning. She filled pages and pages of her journals, trying to reason it all out, trying to make it fit, and nothing made sense. Her father and brothers, her nephews, sweet little Pietro with his whistling gapped teeth. How were they a threat?

Nero had an heir and a spare in Stefano and Dante. And Stefano had been newly married then, the promise of producing his own heir on the horizon.

She might have driven herself crazy trying to make it make sense. Nothing about it ever would. So she'd decided to set aside her search for why and plan her revenge. Nero had obviously ordered the hit, and he deserved to pay for it.

She couldn't come back to the island as Sienna Gallo. She likely wouldn't have made it onto the island at all, let alone close enough to kill her uncle, if he knew she was still alive. So she'd waited, and she'd watched for an opportunity to get close to him, for a job opening at Gallo Industries.

Catching him by surprise at the office was the only way her plan would work. It was the only place he let his guard down. And as long as no one recognized her, she could go relatively unnoticed when she accessed the executive floor with Ciro's credentials.

Something she'd have before her head hit the pillow tonight. A spark of annoyance flashed through her as she edited a piece of code and saved her work. Luca had effortlessly convinced her to change her plans, to give him what he wanted with a simple promise that she'd get what she deserved in time.

It had never taken much convincing for him to get his way. From the moment they met, she'd only ever wanted to say yes to him. But this was too important to give up on why she was here. She might care about Luca, but she didn't care about their little war. And she would not sacrifice avenging her family so they could win it.

Jack's head appeared over the top of the partition between their desks, dragging her back into the present, and she offered him a smile.

"Heading out then?" she asked.

"I am. We won't see you in the office tomorrow, right?"

"No," she confirmed. "Wednesday is one of my work from home days. But I'll be back on Thursday."

"And home again on Friday," Jack replied. "I should have thought to negotiate that one for myself."

Sienna smiled, saving her work and stretching out her sore back. "I got lucky they agreed. My last position was entirely remote, and it spoiled me." Isa snorted, and Sienna pretended not to notice. "You want to grab a drink?"

"That's my line," Ciro said, smiling as he blocked the only way in and out of her cubicle.

"Well, you haven't asked me, so I'm taking matters into my own hands."

"Mea culpa," Ciro said, pressing a hand to his heart and stepping back when she stood. "I forgot about a prior commitment I had yesterday."

"You forgot your wife's birthday?" Isa said with a grunt, and Sienna forced herself to bite back a grin at Ciro's narrowed glare.

"Why are you keeping track of other people's birthdays?" Ciro muttered, mashing the button for the elevator.

"We've been working together for almost four years. It's not a crime to remember things."

"When's my husband's birthday?" Jack wondered as the elevator doors opened and they all got on.

Isa sniffed and flipped her hair over her shoulder. "Sometime in March."

"May," Jack replied with a teasing grin. "But close."

Sienna's phone buzzed in her purse, and she dug it out, smiling at the message from Luca.

Matteo was as agreeable as you can imagine. I'll see you Friday.

"What's so funny?" Ciro wondered, trying to read her text from his position on Jack's other side.

"Nothing. But I definitely need that drink now. I have something to celebrate."

"Oh? And what's that?"

Ciro motioned for her to move off the elevator ahead of him, and she heard his low, appreciative whistle when she put a little extra wiggle into her hips as she stepped out. Waiting until he caught up to match her pace, she smiled.

"A man who was getting too close finally got the hint."

Interest lit Ciro's eyes, and he leaned closer, dropping his voice so only she could hear. "That is good news."

Sienna bumped his shoulder with hers and turned to Jack and Isa. "Everyone's invited." She pinned Isa with a hopeful look. "My treat."

Isa looked from Ciro to Sienna and back again. "Fine," she finally agreed, trudging along behind them through the lobby.

"There's a bar not far from here. Great for drinks after work."

Ciro swiped his badge to exit, and Sienna did the same, eyeing where in his messenger bag he tucked it. The outer front pocket. Perfect. It wouldn't take her long to copy the information from both the card and the fob he had attached to the lanyard, but she had to get it away from him first.

They walked back toward her apartment and then cut up a side street toward a little café and bar that was quickly filling up with people. Ciro shouldered his way to a table in the back corner and held out a chair for her. As soon as she sat down, she repositioned the chair so her back was to the wall. She felt too vulnerable otherwise, too exposed to what she couldn't see coming.

A waitress eventually made her way over, informing them there'd be live music if they hung around long enough, before wandering off to get their drinks. Isa watched the people around them, mouth pinched into what Sienna suspected was a deep-seated disdain for humanity in general.

It was a risk to invite Isa along. If Isa became even a little suspicious, it could blow up everything she'd worked for. But Sienna could use Isa's infatuation with Ciro to her advantage. Keep them both on their toes. Ciro might not be interested in Isa like that, but he liked the attention.

"How long have you worked at Gallo Industries?" Sienna asked Isa, drawing her gaze away from the couple flirting beside them.

"What do you care?"

"Isa," Ciro scolded. "Why did you agree to come if you weren't going to play nice?"

Isa huffed out a breath but relented. "About six years. I worked in the IT department before moving up to development."

"It's fifteen for me," Ciro said proudly. "Over half of that in development. And Jack's been with us, what? Two years now?"

"Three next month," Jack replied, sipping his wine. "I should ask for some days at home when I negotiate my raise."

Sienna grinned and sent him a wink. "Well, I hope it's catching. The long-term job."

"Didn't seem to be for the last one."

"Teresa got married and moved away," Ciro said quickly, giving Isa's shoulder a warning squeeze. "She wasn't suited for the office anyway. Made to be a wife, that one."

Isa rolled her eyes behind Ciro's back, and Sienna could have sworn she saw Isa's mouth lift slightly at one corner when they made eye contact, but it was pinched and frowning again so fast it was hard to say.

"You worked in IT before this, yes?"

"I did," Sienna confirmed, nodding at Ciro. "For an engineering firm based in Berlin. It was good work, good pay. But I missed Italy."

"You said you're from Milan?" Jack asked, signaling the waitress for a menu.

"I was born there," she lied easily. She'd spent months memorizing these details when she paid handsomely for her fake documents. "But we traveled so much when I was younger it was hard to call anywhere home, I guess. Still, Italy will always have my heart. The wine, the food, the men," Sienna added, sliding a sly look to Ciro, who gave her a big grin. "Berlin can hardly compare."

"Of course it can't!" Ciro agreed, clinking his glass against hers. "Everything is better in Italy."

Ciro scooted his chair around the table and closer to hers when someone tried to get past them. It brought him and his bag within easy reach, but Isa visibly tensed. Her obsession with Ciro, who couldn't be less interested, was almost painful to watch.

Sienna bought two more rounds, goading Ciro into doing a shot with her even though she only pretended to drink it, spitting it back into her bottle of water. By the time Jack called it a night, Ciro was so buzzed he was flirting with both women, trailing his fingers up and down Isa's arm whenever she leaned in close to hear what he was saying. Which was often.

The after-work crowd thinned a bit, and the live band started to set up. When they played their first song, Ciro jerked in his seat, recognizing the tune.

"I love this one!" He twisted to look at Sienna, then Isa. "We should dance."

"I'm a terrible dancer," Sienna said with a pout. "You two go."

Isa's eyebrows shot up when Ciro laid a hand on the back of her chair and stood. "Don't you have to get home?"

"One dance." He looked over his shoulder at the people already gathered on the floor. "You know you want to."

Isa bit her lip. Her permanent frown fell away for the first time all night. She actually smiled, nervously tucking her hair behind her ear. When she glanced at Sienna, Sienna motioned them both away with a flick of her fingers.

"Watch our things, Anna," Ciro said, pushing his chair toward her and leading Isa onto the floor.

Sienna waited for the other dancers who'd gathered in the tight space to swallow them up before she reached for Ciro's bag. Leaving it on the seat of his chair and under the shelter of the table in case they looked over, she dug her hand into the front pocket and fished out his keycard and fob.

She'd tested out the device she'd purchased on her way from Berlin to Sicily on her own key fob, and it worked perfectly. Gallo Industries used encrypted fobs, but if she could copy the data, she could unspool it on her own protected machines at home. Assuming Ciro's fob and card weren't copy-protected.

She held his fob up to the machine, grateful the noise of the music covered up the series of beeps. *Read successful,* the readout on the device said. Removing Ciro's fob, she put a blank one in its place and pressed another button. *Transfer complete.*

She repeated the process with his card, her heart pounding as the first song ended and another one began. She saw them appear at the edge of the crowd and quickly pushed the lanyard back into his bag the instant it copied onto the machine.

Her leg bounced a nervous rhythm as she transferred the information to a blank card and shoved everything into her purse seconds before they sat at the table. She smiled at them both, surprised when Isa returned it.

"How was it?" she asked. Her voice was a little breathy, but no one seemed to notice.

"It was loud. But good," Isa said, that half smile Sienna was unaccustomed to seeing still on her face.

"I'm going to make you dance with me," Ciro replied as the song changed again. "It's even a slow one. You don't need to be a good dancer for a slow song."

She began to protest. The man really didn't deserve to lose any fingers, but nothing would make Isa more jealous than being chosen and then discarded. Sienna protested a little more for show, but eventually gave in.

"All right. One dance, but then I have to go."

Ciro grinned triumphantly. "Isa, will you watch—"

"Your bag," Isa snapped, that pinched frown back on her face. "Sure."

Sienna kept her small purse slung across her body, shaking her head when Ciro took her hand in his and laid his other low on her waist. She sent him a coy grin and moved it higher, leaving space between them as the song crooned through the speakers.

"You're very beautiful," Ciro drawled, his voice slurred by the alcohol. "You have the bluest eyes I've ever seen."

"Don't you think Isa's beautiful too? She's really got it bad for you."

Ciro glanced over her shoulder at their table. Isa was no doubt watching them both like hawks. "She tries too hard. There's no fun in the chase with her. You, on the other hand…"

"Ciro." She giggled, bracing a hand on his chest. "What if I said I don't sleep with coworkers?"

"I'd ask you to make an exception."

"And what if I said I didn't sleep with married men?"

"My wife understands my needs." Sienna highly doubted

that. "Besides, doesn't everyone want to be naughty sometimes?"

"Maybe. But you're old enough to be my father."

He grimaced at the word, spinning her out and back in, then grabbing her low on the waist again, forcing her to move his hand higher. "Age is just a number, *cara mia.*"

"Mmm," she murmured. "Still. If you want a sure thing, you really should give Isa a ride."

Ciro leaned in close as the song ended and whispered against her ear. "I like the game."

Sienna stepped away from him when the music finished with a flourish and clapped with the rest of the bar. "I really do have to get home. Behave yourself, Ciro." She glanced at Isa over her shoulder and ran a hand down his arm. "But maybe not too much behaving. I'll see you Thursday."

Moving past their table for the door, she sent Isa a wave and settled their tab at the bar. The night air was cool on her skin, and she dug her phone out of her purse as she walked back to her apartment.

"Hi." Luca's voice was warm and rich in her ear.

"Hi yourself." She jogged across the street when the light changed. "You have to promise me something."

"What's that?"

"That you won't cut off Ciro's fingers."

"What did he do?" Luca demanded, voice rough, and she chuckled.

"I had to dance with him. Just once. But I didn't let him touch my ass."

"Good. He might have lost a whole hand that way. Did you get what you need?"

"I did. I should definitely have something for you by Friday."

"Okay. I think I'll be able to get there around ten."

Sienna shivered in anticipation. As much as she used to

crave living life with Luca in the open, the intrigue of their clandestine meetings had always been just as fun. And now she had an entire apartment to bring him back to instead of the hotel rooms they used to rent.

She let herself into her building and took the stairs to work off the last of her adrenaline rush from her mission at the bar.

"I'll be waiting."

Chapter Thirteen

Luca made notes in the margins of the report he was reading. A question for the managers of the southern casino on why staff turnover rate was so high, a reminder to bring an update about the high-stakes poker lounge nearing completion to Matteo's attention, a quick tally to check the numbers on their projected revenue for the fourth quarter.

Historically they always turned a higher profit during the holidays, and with them looming right around the corner, plus the strip clubs in the Romano territory now under their control, it was going to be a banner year for the Bianchis. And it would only get better from here.

Shuffling the paper to the bottom of the stack, he read through the next one. He only stopped by the casino to pick up the last of his things and take them to the new office building. Maeve had acquired a second monitor in record time, and everything was ready and waiting for him.

But as soon as he'd walked through the doors, someone had handed him a stack of paperwork, two other people had come to ask questions, and he'd gotten lost in the shuffle of it all. And maybe a part of him was trying to avoid both his brother and Maeve at the office.

It had taken hours and lots of yelling to convince Matteo that details on Luca's inside source were none of his fucking business. It wasn't necessary for Matteo to know who it was. All he had to do was trust Luca wouldn't do anything to jeopardize the family or their interests.

He wouldn't give Sienna away to anyone, not even his own brother. Her safety was paramount in all of this, and she was taking enough risks as it was already. She'd talked herself into the lion's den, after all.

He didn't like the thought of her working at Gallo Industries with nothing separating her from her uncle except an elevator. She might look different with her blond hair and her blue eyes and those sexy glasses she hid behind, but it was hardly a foolproof disguise if she ran into them in the hallway.

The fewer people who knew she was alive and that he was communicating with her, the better. Until this was over and Nero and his sons were dead, he was going to keep her all to himself.

He heard noises in the hallway seconds before someone knocked on the door to his office and then let themselves in. Alexei's mouth ticked up at the corner, and he leaned against the frame, arms crossed over his chest.

"I thought you were moving to the skyscraper and leaving the rest of us peasants behind. Did you get tired of Matteo already?"

Luca snorted. "It's a tomb over there. And I get enough of Matteo's scowling at home."

"He does scowl quite a lot. Reminds me of your father that way. Do you think he actually knows how to smile?"

"I might have seen one once," he said, and Alexei huffed out a laugh. "But now I'm wondering if I imagined it."

Dropping into a chair across from Luca's desk, Alexei crossed his long legs out in front of him. "Rumor is you found yourself a Gallo spy. Nothing like waiting to present your inside contact at the eleventh hour." Alexei raised a brow.

"I wasn't sure I'd be able to hook them with my offer." Luca shifted in his seat, meeting Alexei's curious stare head-on. "When I had something, I said something."

"Mmm," Alexei murmured. "And you're certain your contact won't stab us in the back?"

"Absolutely. I trust them."

Alexei nodded slowly, eyes traveling over the space that was only half packed, a nearly empty box perched on top of a filing cabinet. "Let's hope your contact is good for it. Carina will be very upset if this isn't handled by the wedding."

"She's finally set a date?"

"She has. In the spring. She's expecting all of this to be behind us by then."

"I didn't think you'd get her to come around to a wedding that fast," Luca admitted.

"Neither did I." Alexei grinned, dragging his thumb across his jaw. "But I'm not going to complain about it. So make sure your contact doesn't fuck this up for me."

Luca rolled his eyes. "Don't worry about my contact. They're good for it. I'm meeting with them for information tomorrow."

"Good."

"Did you need something?" Luca asked as Alexei pushed to his feet again.

"What?"

"Did you need something, or did you just come in here for gossip?"

"Oh. Right. Both, really. Your sister asks a lot of questions. I like to be prepared. But also to let you know there's a guy on the floor who appears to be counting cards. Since Dom isn't here, I thought you might like to accompany me to make sure."

Luca pushed back from his desk and followed Alexei out the door. The casino floor was loud, the beeps and warbles from the slot machines and the constant low hum of conversation overwhelming the senses as they walked past the roulette wheels and small-time poker tables and stopped at the Blackjack tables.

This casino had five tables in total. Alexei gestured with a slight nod to a man dressed casually in slacks and a button-down sitting at table three. He was white, pale, probably in his early to mid-twenties, and he had a large collection of chips in front of him.

Luca watched as the dealer dealt the next hand. A pair of eights, which the guy split into two. Each time a card was dealt, he paused, his mouth twitching as if he was counting in his head and couldn't keep his lips still.

His next hit earned him a ten and a jack. Eighteen. The guy paused again, eyes darting from his two hands to the dealer's hand to the number of cards still left in the shoe. Then he made a mistake. He lifted his head and made eye contact with someone standing at the edge of his table.

The woman had long black hair and dark skin. She wore a tight red dress, a matching purse slung over her shoulder. She glanced down at the cards, then back up at his face, and tapped the table twice. A signal.

Luca shook his head. They were cheating and not even bothering to be subtle about it. The guy took a chance on one hand and hit. A two. Twenty out of twenty-one. The next one was a four, taking him over. But he'd already won the pot. The dealer only had nineteen.

Alexei moved forward to grab the guy before he could play another hand, but Luca stopped him. "He's not counting alone. Watch the woman in red."

Once the guy at table three won his hand, she stepped away with a small smile on her lips and turned toward table five. Two women and one man were already playing there. A blond in a conservative blue sweater slightly too big for her frame shifted in her seat, then stretched her arms out behind her. As soon as she did, the woman in red sat down.

"Well, fuck me," Alexei muttered. "Been a long time since we had anyone get this fancy. They've got to be Americans."

"Pity," Luca replied as he watched the dealer at table five deal the next hand, including the new player at the table. "You won't get to kill anyone."

"I hate that Americans are off-limits," Alexei said, almost pouting.

The table was hot, the cards coming out of the shoe favoring the players and not the dealer. A sure sign they were counting. The woman who'd joined them continued to make risky bets until her chips were stacked three rows deep in front of her.

Just before the decks reset, she threw her last hand and lost about ten grand, if he had to guess. But she still had fifty thousand in chips stacked in front of her.

When the dealer paused the game to shuffle the decks, Luca set off for the table, Alexei trailing behind him. As soon as people saw Alexei, with his bright green eyes and the imposing scar that ran the length of his face, they quickly moved out of the way.

The dealer noticed them crossing the floor and gave a signal for counters. Luca nodded and dropped into a seat next to the woman in red while Alexei claimed the spot beside the blond, leaning in to get a whiff of her strong perfume. Luca looked her up and down, and she sent him a flirtatious smile.

"Having fun?" he asked. She wrinkled her nose and

pulled an Italian language book out of her purse. "Having fun?" he asked again in English.

She raised a brow, replacing the book and scooting closer. "I am. Italy is beautiful. And I'm making the most of beginner's luck." She gestured at her chips.

His gaze dropped to the stacks and then darted back to her face. "Really? It looks to me like you're trying to cheat my casino out of money."

Her spine straightened, and the blond behind him gasped. Luca peeked over his shoulder long enough to make sure Alexei was behaving himself. He looked annoyed, knowing he wouldn't get to use any of the tools in his kit tonight.

Luca turned back to the woman in red. "I know you have a friend over there." He gestured to table three. "Anyone else?"

She shook her head, but her eyes flicked to table four. "No. Just the three of us."

Sighing, Luca rose from his chair and gripped her arm, hauling her out of her seat. "Leave those," he commanded when she reached for the stacks of chips. "I was going to let you have a few hundred euros as a kindness for spending time on my island. But since you lied to me, now you get nothing."

He pulled her away from the table. "Make sure all your friends leave with you, or you won't like what happens next."

Her eyes went wide, and she gestured at the tables. The blond in the blue sweater got up, giving Alexei a wide berth, and the guy at table three did the same. Then two more men at table four got up and followed them to the front door.

"That all of you?" Luca demanded, pinning each one with an angry stare.

"It is," the woman in red replied, breathless. "Please, we're just here on a little vacation. We don't want any trouble."

Luca shoved them through the big glass doors into the chilly night and released them. "If I see you back here, or in any of my other casinos again, I'll let him do what we do to cheats." Luca gestured at Alexei, who crossed his arms over his chest and glared down his nose at them.

"You can't threaten us," the tallest guy said, sweeping long brown hair out of his eyes. "We'll go to the cops."

Luca took a step forward until they were nose to nose. "You'll go to the cops and tell them what? You were trying to steal tens of thousands of euros from an Italian national?" He fished his phone out of his jacket pocket. "Why don't we call them right now? You can tell your story, and I can show them my video surveillance."

The kid blanched and took a step back, hands held out in front of him. "Don't worry about it, man. We won't come back."

"Yeah," the girl in red agreed. "We swear you won't see us again."

They held each other's gazes for a few more moments until Alexei stepped forward and broke the spell. All five of them took hurried steps back and then turned and jogged across the parking lot to a rented SUV. Luca chuckled as they peeled out.

"I wanted to rough someone up."

"I know." Luca slapped Alexei on the shoulder and turned to head back inside. "But we can't let you kill the tourists. Especially not the Americans. Dealing with the embassy is a pain in the ass."

Alexei grumbled as they walked back inside. "I liked Dom's war better than this slow assault on Gallo."

"Don't worry. You'll get plenty of blood on your hands before this is said and done."

"Will I?" Alexei raised a brow. "I thought Matteo was only going to take out Nero. Do you have other plans?"

"I do. Carina's not the only one who wants revenge."

"I'm intrigued. But I have questions."

"I'll answer them for you eventually. But sharpen your blades. Because once Gallo Industries is ours, I plan on dropping bodies. And I don't give a single shit if Matteo likes it or not."

A slow grin spread over Alexei's lips. "Music to my fucking ears."

Chapter Fourteen

Staring at the clock in the corner of the screen, Sienna tapped a pencil against the desk and waited. After successfully cloning Ciro's badge and key fob, she tested it on her devices. He had a higher security clearance than she anticipated. So high she'd immediately run a background check on him.

She didn't recognize him, and his paperwork checked out. But paperwork could be faked. Hers had. All you needed was enough money and the right contacts.

But his user logs were clean and didn't show signs of tampering. He never seemed to stray too far into a server or database he shouldn't be in, never worked after hours or on the weekends, and regularly took holidays where he'd have no activity on his log at all.

It was just as likely he'd worked on a proprietary project and been granted additional security clearance to access user and research data he needed. But she'd made a mental note to keep an eye on him anyway. He did at least have the access she needed to get onto the executive floor. When the time was right.

She'd spent countless hours imagining what it would be like to get off the elevator on the top floor, walk down the long hallway to her uncle's sprawling office, and shoot him between the eyes. Sometimes in her fantasy, she confessed who she was and made him tell her why he'd killed her family. But in reality, she probably wouldn't have time for that.

Knowing why had stopped being important to her a long time ago. Now she only cared that he paid for what he'd done. And she'd make sure he did.

Ciro's badge had proven useful in more ways than one, giving her easier access to the parts of the system she needed in order to find the internal tracking of shipments. With that out of the way, she'd had plenty of time to dive deeper into looking for the stuff Luca wanted. The information on which shipments contained weapons and which were normal freight.

She'd used spare time throughout the day on Wednesday and today to seek out the server she most likely needed, finding and abandoning them until she found the right one. It was trial and error since no one had handily labeled it Damning Criminal Info. But eventually she found it, three layers deep and in a different direction from where she'd started looking.

The protections around it were impressive, another hint that it was the right spot. It had taken her most of the previous night to crack through. And now that she had, she was itching to get in there again. To comb through the stacks and stacks of information until she found what she was looking for. Whatever info Luca could use to move this along faster.

But first she had to wait for Isa to get home. Something she was apparently taking her own sweet time in doing. For a woman who didn't like people much, she sure as hell was stopping often enough on her way back to her apartment.

Sienna's eyes followed the dot from the tracker she'd slipped into the ripped lining of Isa's bag the day before as it inched slowly along the sidewalk. One last turn, ten, maybe fifteen more paces, and Isa would finally be home.

Sienna imagined the woman pouring herself a glass of wine and sinking down on the couch with her cat. The ugly orange tabby she kept in a picture frame on her desk.

After discovering it was faster and cleaner to alter the user logs than clear them, she'd chosen Isa to take the fall. If someone found Sienna snooping where she shouldn't be, she'd get fired—or worse. And she couldn't risk Ciro getting in trouble and losing his security clearance.

That left Isa or Jack. And since she liked Jack too much to tangle him up in this, she'd easily selected the woman who hadn't stopped making snide remarks since they went out for drinks.

And if Sienna was going to make this look like Isa's handiwork, she needed to be sure no one could alibi her as being out at a club or having fun with friends. Although Sienna doubted Isa had many friends. The woman was impossible. Still, she waited another agonizing hour to be sure Isa wouldn't go back out again.

When the tracker didn't budge, she pulled up a window in a program she'd designed and used it as a filter for her login to the company servers. The black box glowed as it filled with neon green script, her fingers flying over the keyboard and carrying her closer and closer to where she needed to be.

After hitting enter, a series of screens popped up, one right after the other. She brought up the tracking software and ran a search for all the shipments scheduled to move in the next two weeks. The number totaled in the dozens. Too many.

Opening a new window, she cross-referenced those searches with her uncle's detailed notes on weapons deliveries buried deep in the classified server. It took a minute, the cursor blinking as the computer processed her coded command, but then the information flooded the screen. Three shipments of varying sizes, all scheduled to leave from different points around Italy and be distributed across Europe.

She grinned. That was exactly the kind of information Luca was looking for. And her uncle included more details than she'd been expecting. Including how many men were in the escort, how much product, the buyer, and the total amount due.

No wonder her father argued with his brother about this so often. Nero was leaving himself and his empire very vulnerable if anyone ever got their hands on this information.

Copying down what she knew Luca needed, she cleared the windows and glanced at the clock. He'd be here soon, but she still had a little time to do some more digging.

Pulling up a fresh search, she punched in the string of code to take her deeper into the archives, beneath an additional layer of security.

As she uncovered it all, Sienna imagined this is what her uncle would have had her doing if he'd let her live, if he hadn't forced her to become Anna Marino and fight for survival. If he hadn't turned her into a person consumed by thoughts of revenge and violence.

A new set of windows popped up, and she pushed those thoughts out of her head. They were for later. She couldn't let emotion distract her. Emotion would cloud her judgment, trick her into making a mistake.

In these windows, she hit pay dirt. Her uncle had more

than a few Sicilian politicians in his pocket. And each man had a folder attached to his name.

Inside were extensive, detailed blackmail files he kept as insurance in case they ever stepped out of line. Images of them meeting to accept bribes, a list of bribes and the amount and dates paid, images of them with mistresses and a few escorts. Of both genders.

According to these records, her uncle was paying off the mayor of Catania, the Regional President of Sicily's government, the chief of police, and not one but two prefects appointed by the national government in Rome to keep the provinces in line. No fucking wonder he'd been able to fly so far under the radar.

Her uncle kept a treasure trove of information these men would certainly not want leaked to the public. And now she and the Bianchis were going to benefit from it. She grinned as she saved the files to a secure folder on her desktop.

What she really wanted to know was who likely had a hand in helping to cover up her family's murder. She searched the records her uncle kept for payments for the window of time around the killings and zeroed in on two names. Fausto Restivo, the Regional President for the last two terms, and Gianfranco Carollo, Sicily's police chief.

They'd both been on her uncle's payroll dating back well before her family's murder, but two weeks before and two weeks after the attack, they'd each been paid large sums of money—more than triple their usual payment.

It didn't surprise her. Mafia influence still ran deep in this part of the country. Occasionally the government sent a politician to jail for dealing with the Mafia, but it hadn't happened in years. Maybe it was high time for another resignation and prison sentence.

The prefects seemed fairly new to the payroll, only being added in the last two years, and she didn't see anything connecting the mayor to anything except business dealings. Nero sent a lot of money his way, and it was likely a fee to keep him very well connected to the national government.

Nero had contacts in Rome, but none were on the payroll as far as she could tell. Just files on them. For now, he seemed content to play the game without money exchanging hands. If that ever changed, though, he was prepared.

Someone knocked on her door, and her eyes flicked to the clock. Two minutes after ten. Luca was nothing if not punctual. Something she'd always liked about him.

After confirming it was him through the peephole, she swung the door open and smiled. But the greeting didn't have time to make it past her lips before he had her back against the door, his mouth fused to hers.

She wrapped her arms around his neck and drank him in, skimming her tongue along his lower lip, tangling it with his until he groaned. His hands roamed under her shirt, squeezing her breasts through her bra and pinching her nipples with his fingers.

When he eased her shirt up over her stomach, she pushed his hand back down and pulled away. "Wait."

"I've waited five days. The wait is over."

She grinned, tilting her head for his lips, sighing when they skimmed over the scar on her neck without flinching. "Luca. I have information for you."

"Later," he murmured against her skin, nipping it with his teeth.

"I can't. I left my program open to answer the door. I have to go close it before I let you haul me off to bed for a few hours."

He went still against her, and she felt a puff of air against her neck when he huffed out an irritated breath. Sliding his hand down her stomach and over her hip, he took her hand and laced his fingers with hers.

"Fine. Hurry up and show me, and then I'm taking you to bed."

"I thought you came here for information," she said, leading him down the hallway into her office.

Before she could cross the space to her desk, he tugged her back against his chest, wrapping an arm around her shoulders and leaning down to whisper in her ear. "I came here for you. The information is merely a bonus that means I won't have to hide you for much longer."

She turned her head to look up at him. "Is that what you want? To not have to hide me?"

"That's the only thing I ever wanted." He pressed a quick kiss to her jaw. "Now. Show me what you found so I can get you naked."

He nudged her forward, leaning over her shoulder when she dropped into the desk chair. She handed him the list of shipments she'd written on a scrap piece of paper.

"This is perfect, baby girl. He already moved the shipment we were going to hit next week. We would have wasted time and resources. Any chance he'll move it again?"

"Probably not, but if you tell me which one, I can monitor it. There's something else I wanted to show you, though."

She opened the files she'd saved, and he frowned.

"I thought you said bribing the politicians would be a waste of time."

"Not a waste of time. I said you had to be careful. Besides, even if you choose not to use any of this, it doesn't mean we can't ruin a few careers before we're done."

She queued up the information in a slideshow, rapidly scrolling through each photo, each piece of damning evidence that could bring anyone down. Even on an island known for its corruption.

"Shit," Luca breathed. "I figured the mayor and the chief

of police. But Restivo is news to me. Did any of them help cover up your family?"

She nodded, tapping the keys and bringing up two photos side-by-side. "Restivo and Carollo."

"The president just got reelected too."

"I know. My uncle contributed quite a bit of money to his reelection campaign. The fucker."

Luca kissed the side of her neck, eyes flicking to the screen to watch as she carefully backed out of the system, double-checked that the logs reflected Isa's information, and closed her program. That had been a resounding success in almost every way.

Chapter Fifteen

When she turned to look at Luca, he was standing a few paces away, staring at her intently. She was suddenly self-conscious, pulling her hair forward to cover her neck out of habit. He frowned before his eyes drifted back to her face, and his expression softened.

"I knew you could do that before. That you were good at it. But knowing it and watching it are two different things. You're a wonder, Sienna. Can I get you naked now?"

She laughed, pushing away from her desk and crossing to him. She stopped close enough that there was space between them, but her body brushed his each time she moved. Reaching down to the hem of her shirt, she tugged it up and off, dropping it on the floor.

His eyes traced the lacy outline of her bra, lingering on the delicate bow between her breasts, entranced as she released the catch and let the material slide down her arms. Circling her fingers over her nipples, she pinched them lightly and knew the moment his control snapped in the way his eyes darkened and his body jerked.

Dropping his head, he kissed the top of her breast and

then further south until he wrapped his lips around her hard nipple, eliciting a soft groan from her.

"I don't have to be back in Palermo until dinner tomorrow." He lifted her in his arms and carried her to the bedroom. "I hope you don't expect to get much sleep tonight."

"Wouldn't dream of it," she assured him, hands moving to work open the catch of his pants as soon as he set her on the floor. "We have a lot of lost time to make up for."

He undressed her as quickly as she undressed him, their clothes landing in a discarded pile on the floor. He gathered her in his arms, his lips trailing a line of kisses from the outside of her shoulder to her neck. His fingers flexed on her hip while he tasted her, tracing the line of her scar with his lips.

When he turned and sank onto the edge of the bed, pulling her between his thighs, she frowned. He trailed kisses along her stomach, making her muscles contract and raising goosebumps over her skin. When his fingertips brushed over the scar next to her belly button, she jerked, but he held her fast.

"Don't," she said when he bent down to brush his lips against it.

He looked up at her, concern etched on his face. "Does it hurt?"

"No. I just..." She ran her fingers through his hair and tried to find the words. "It reminds me that I'm broken. Before, when I was with you, I felt perfect. You made me feel that way."

He tightened his fingers on her waist, drawing her closer and kissing the valley between her breasts. "You have never been anything but perfect to me."

She smiled, but it was sad. "Maybe. But now I just feel like damaged goods."

Luca's head snapped up, and there was fire in his eyes. "You are not damaged, Sienna." He scooted further back on the bed and pulled her with him, positioning her until she was straddling his chest. "I want you to ride my face. I want to remind you how perfect you are."

"Luca, I—"

"Come on, baby girl." Luca sent her a teasing grin, gripping her ass and easing her further up his body. "I know how much you like to come with my mouth on that pretty pussy of yours."

Biting her lip, she wriggled up until she was positioned over his face, his breath on her skin making her tremble. She'd never done this with anyone before or after Luca. And she was woefully out of practice.

"What if I suffocate you?" she wondered, fingers wrapping around the top of the headboard as his hands massaged the backs of her thighs.

"Then I'll die a happy man. You know what I want, Sienna. Give it to me."

The muscles in her thighs were tense as she lowered herself against his lips, gasping when his tongue dragged up the length of her slit. He avoided her clit with each pass of his tongue until she was gritting her teeth against the absence of him.

"Luca," she ground out, gripping the headboard with white knuckles.

"Hmm?" he murmured against her, fingers tight on her thighs but not moving her in any way. As if he was content to give her lazy licks that drove her crazy for hours.

"You're not… You have to…"

He pressed a kiss to her lips and then blew a cool breath across them, making her jerk. "Have to what?"

"Go faster. Or…something."

"I will." He grazed her thighs with his nails. "When you ride my face."

"I am!" She was desperate to feel him touch her clit, to sink his tongue deep inside her until she was screaming his name. "Luca," she groaned when he still didn't move.

"You can have exactly what you want, baby girl. All you have to do is take it."

When he dropped another kiss against her pussy she jerked, rocking against his mouth and moaning at the sensation. His tongue darted out to taste her, faster than before, and she rocked again. In response, he swept his tongue up to flick against her clit. Over and over until she cried out and then backing off when she started to shake.

He teased her mercilessly, dipping his tongue inside her and then drawing it out again and swirling it up to and around her clit. Over and over, working her until she was quivering above him, her hips jerking wildly.

Some part of her mind wondered if she should worry about whether he could breathe, but if he was still moving, he was probably fine. Right? And she was close. So fucking close.

"Fuck, Luca."

He didn't pause to speak or to tease her. He picked up speed, using his teeth to nibble her clit and her sensitive lips, dipping his tongue inside her again and spearing it in and out before dragging it roughly over her clit.

Every nerve ending was on fire, snapping like electricity across her skin. The more urgently her hips rocked, the faster he worked her with his mouth, and when he sealed his lips around her clit and sucked hard, she shattered into a million pieces. Pieces only Luca had ever known how to pick up again.

"Sweet mother of God," she panted, sliding bonelessly onto the bed.

He chuckled, turning onto his side and swirling his finger around her nipple. "For a minute there, I was worried you didn't remember what I taught you."

"I was trying not to smother you."

There was a hunger in his eyes that made her shiver, and she didn't stop him when he rolled her onto her stomach and covered her body with his. "Next time," he whispered in her ear as he slid inside her, "smother me."

She nodded, pushing back against him as much as his weight on top of her would allow. His thrusts were hard and deep inside her. Each time he drew back, the loss of him left her feeling hopelessly empty until he filled her again and the world recalibrated.

Never in a million years did she think she'd get to see Luca again, let alone have him like this, moving inside her, his body weighting hers to the bed, his lips hot on her skin while he whispered a single word in her ear. *Mine.*

That's the first thing he said to her when he walked up behind her in that club on her twenty-first birthday. After he'd scared off the guy she'd been grinding on with a look. He'd moved in behind her, placed his hands on her hips, and leaned down to whisper in her ear. *Mine.*

She had been from that day forward. She was now. She likely would be forever. Whatever happened, she was his.

"Luca," she gasped when he pulled back and slammed his hips into hers. Rough and demanding. "I need you."

"I know, baby girl." He scored her shoulder with his teeth. "Come for me again, and you can have me."

He fucked her harder, driving her body against the bed with each punishing thrust of his hips. Her sensitive nipples dragged against the rough fabric of the duvet, and she whimpered, which only spurred him on, his cock pumping furiously inside her.

He drove deep, angling his cock so he brushed against her

G-spot, and she cried out, her body going taut beneath him as her orgasm barreled through her. Her name was a prayer on his lips as he followed her over.

"Fuck, baby girl. The things you do to me."

"It's mutual. Believe me," she replied, voice muffled against the bed.

He rolled onto his side and pulled her back against him, snuggling her against the pillows. She felt his nose press against her nape and breathe her in.

She didn't know how he managed it, but in his arms, she still felt perfect.

Chapter Sixteen

The traffic from Catania to Palermo was a nightmare. He'd cut it too close, stealing kiss after kiss from her lips until he couldn't delay any longer. She'd wrapped around him in one more lingering kiss in the doorway, her tongue sliding against his until all he wanted to do was get her naked again.

But she'd eventually broken away, shoved him into the hall, and slammed the door in his face. If he didn't have this stupid family thing today, they could have spent the whole weekend naked like they had the weekend before. Talking, eating, fucking. They had so much to catch up on, and he hated leaving her.

A handful of nights in her bed, in her arms, weren't enough. It would never be enough. He wanted every night with her. Forever.

And because of that, he would probably be late, which would put Matteo in a shitty mood. His brother was always in a shitty mood when things didn't go his way. It was one of many things Luca hadn't missed in Matteo's absence.

An ugly yellow Mini Cooper cut him off, and he laid on

the horn, gesturing out the window as he took the exit for home and navigated crowded streets toward the villa. The driveway was full when he pulled in, and he eased his car in behind Alexei's Aston Martin.

Voices drifted down the hall when he opened the front door, and he followed the sound to the parlor, crossing to the decanter on the sideboard to pour himself a glass of wine. When he turned, Carina was looking at him with a single eyebrow raised.

"Looks like the gang's all here," Matteo said, gaze sliding over Emilia, where she sat between Dom and Carina.

Emilia's cheeks flushed pink. "I think that's my cue. I'll go hang out with the twins," she said of her brother and sister she'd been raising since their mother died.

"No," Dom said, reaching for her hand when she stood.

"We have important matters to discuss, Domenico," Matteo said, a bite to his tone. "Family matters."

"I'm aware. I drove two hours to make this little get-together when I have things I could be doing in Agrigento. Emilia is family now. My family."

"Really, Dom. It's fine. I—"

"Did you get married and not tell me?" Matteo wondered. "Because if not, your…girlfriend can go while we talk business."

Emilia tried to extract her hand from Dom's grip, squeaking softly when he tugged her into his lap and met Matteo's steely glare with his own. "She stays."

"Great," Luca said to defuse the tension, stepping between his brothers. "Now that it's settled. The report from my contact."

He unsealed the envelope with the information Sienna had given him and spread the pages out over the low table between the two couches. Alexei and Matteo reached out to grab photos, Alexei handing some to Dom, who kept one arm wrapped tight around Emilia's waist to keep her from bolting.

"Gallo's got more politicians than we thought in his pocket."

"Jesus," Alexei mumbled. "The Regional President?"

Luca nodded. "And the chief of police, two prefects, and the mayor of Catania."

"Chief of police makes sense," Carina said, looking at the photos in Alexei's hands. "I always thought the investigation into his brother's murder was a little suspicious."

"What do you mean?" Matteo asked, glancing up from the photos he was studying.

"Something like three or four years after you left, Nero's brother was killed, along with his whole family. Wife, five kids and their spouses, nine or ten grandchildren. All of them wiped out and then the house set on fire."

"That's awful," Emilia breathed, tears gathering in her eyes. It wasn't all that far off from how her mother died. Even if Dom insisted the bitch deserved it.

"It was." Carina sighed, slipping her arm through Alexei's and resting her cheek against his shoulder. "They eventually pinned it on a small gang, unaffiliated. But it always smelled like a hit to me. The Romanos thought so too."

Luca swallowed and shoved his hands into his pockets. "I didn't realize you followed that story."

"All of Sicily followed it. Mafia or not, Gallo is still a big name on this island." Carina tilted her head to study him. "Surely you heard about it."

"Of course I did. I just didn't pay much attention," Luca lied. He'd eaten up every article he could find about it until they stopped printing them. "The casinos were starting to get bad then. I was working a lot."

Dom snorted, tossing the photos back onto the table and pressing a kiss to Emilia's shoulder. "An understatement."

"So then what's the plan with all of this?" Carina gestured to everything laid out before them. "You can't just kill Sicily's president or chief of police."

"At least not without raising some serious red flags," Alexei added.

"How much is Gallo paying them?" Matteo wondered.

"About two thousand a month. Sometimes it's more. I assume those bumps come when they do him an extra favor."

"We could afford to double it." Matteo tapped his fingers on the arm of his chair. "Get them to defect to us."

"I don't think that'll work." Every head turned to look at Emilia, her hand flying to her mouth as if she could shove the words back in. "I'm sorry. I shouldn't have—"

"Why won't it work?" Matteo asked, voice cold, stare measured.

"It's really not my place."

"You've made it your place now. So tell me," Matteo demanded, ignoring Dom's warning growl.

Emilia glanced down at Dom, who nodded for her to continue, his hand skimming up and down her back. "I just… when I was paying off my mother's loan to Varda, it was the threat of violence as much as the desire to be out from under the debt that kept me paying. Often putting down extra to be done with it. Done with him."

Carina glanced back at the photos on the table. "So the money is changing hands. But it's probably the blackmail files that are really keeping them in line."

"Yeah. At least. That would be my guess."

"Very clever," Alexei said, and a small smile ghosted Emilia's lips.

"She's right," Luca confirmed. "My contact said much the same. They're afraid of him. If you want to go ahead with a bribery plot, along with sabotaging these shipments, you'll have to be careful about who you choose."

"Is using this shit going to out your contact?" Dom glanced up at Luca.

"I wouldn't think so." Luca studied the candid shots of men with their mistresses or lovers or exchanging money with Gallo. "Anyone can run surveillance on them and get these kinds of photos."

Matteo twisted his watch around his wrist. "We'll start with the shipments next week, and I'll see if Bonacci will make an introduction."

"Who's that?" Emilia asked.

"The mayor of Palermo."

Emilia's eyes widened. "You know the mayor of Palermo?" She shared a look with Dom. "Oh. You pay the mayor of Palermo."

Matteo arched a brow. "We do. Do you have a problem with that?"

"No, I just…" Emilia squirmed under Matteo's cutting gaze. "No," she replied softly.

"Lay off, Matteo," Dom grumbled.

"Emilia," Carina said, pushing out of her seat before Matteo could speak again. "Why don't we go check on the kids, and I can show you that necklace I was telling you about for Bella."

"Sure," Emilia replied, relief evident on her face. "That sounds great."

"You four try to behave while we're gone. You," she said, turning to Alexei. "Don't stab anyone without me."

"Of course not, *lyubimaya moya*," he replied, giving her hip a squeeze. "You know I love to watch you work."

Luca watched them go, wondering what it would be like to see Sienna with them. The three of them with their heads bent together in conversation. He hadn't imagined what a future with Sienna might be like in so long. He'd forced thoughts of her and what they might've had out of his mind just so he could survive.

But it felt infinitely more possible now than it had three years ago. Every second he spent with her or talking to her or thinking about her made the future he'd written off a long time ago seem that much closer.

They could have more once this was all said and done. He wanted more with her. And once Gallo was gone, there would be no one to stand in their way.

Except maybe Matteo. And Luca didn't give a fuck what his brother thought about his love life. If Dom could stand against him about Emilia, Luca sure as hell could stand up for Sienna.

"I don't know what the hell your problem is with her. But you're going to have to get over it," Dom said, drawing Luca out of his thoughts.

Matteo rolled his eyes. "Last I checked, we didn't read side pieces in on family business. As much as you might like to ride her, she isn't family. She's a liability. Those brats of hers being in my house are a liability."

"She is not a side piece, you fuck. Unless you consider Carina Alexei's side piece. I'm sure our baby sister would love to hear that."

Alexei stiffened, gaze sharpening on Matteo. "Do tell us."

"Of course she isn't," Matteo snapped. "They're engaged. And Carina is one of us."

"And without Emilia, we'd probably still be engaging Varda on the southern border," Luca reminded them. "She's never been anything but an asset to this family and our interests. You're the only one determined to treat her like shit because she's not what...Sicilian? Mafia born?"

"I have to put the family above everything else. Our safety, our future. It's my job to protect the family's interests from anything that's a threat." Matteo sneered. "Even if the threats are pretty redheads."

Dom's laugh was deep and mocking. "You're so full of shit. You whip out the line about protecting the family's interests whenever you're trying to get your way. Emilia has more than earned our trust at this point. She's mine, and she's staying. And if you don't like it, you can get fucked."

Shoving out of his seat, Dom crossed to the sideboard to pour himself more wine. Luca watched Matteo debate with himself, eyes darting between Alexei and Dom, who'd both made it very clear that Matteo's influence over them ended at their love lives.

Seemingly giving up for now, Matteo reached for one of the photos on top of the pile. Restivo tucking a thick envelope into his breast pocket while having lunch with Nero and Stefano Gallo.

"We're going to start with Restivo, but once Gallo is dealt with, I want the rest on our payroll."

"All of them?" Luca wondered. "The prefects too?"

"As many of them as we can get. In case we run into any" —his gaze flicked up and landed on Dom before dropping back down to the photo again—"issues."

Dom snorted, tossing back the rest of his wine and pouring a third glass.

"It might be better if we can try and get Bonacci elected president instead. Put our own man in higher office." Luca glanced at Alexei, who raised a brow and nodded slightly. "Restivo should go down with Gallo."

"We'll see. I don't want to rule anything out."

A maid stepped into the archway to announce that dinner was ready, and Luca followed his brothers down the hall to the family dining room. It still felt heavy in here. They hadn't used this room at all after their mother died. Not until Matteo came back to town.

Carina and Emilia appeared, the twins on their heels, and they all gave Matteo a wide berth before taking their seats. When the first course was served and Matteo still didn't speak, Luca shook his head. One big happy fucking family. How in the hell were they going to rule Sicily as a unit if they could barely stand to be in the same room with each other?

Chapter Seventeen

S ienna absently tapped her pen against the notebook laid open in front of her. She was on her third week in this job, and already she'd spent more time in meetings than she did doing the actual work they were paying her to do. Such a mind-numbingly boring waste of time.

At least in her old job, they didn't require her to sit in meetings for hours when all they really needed her for was a five or ten-minute presentation. This one was stretching beyond two hours, and she really had to pee.

If this was how every department of Gallo Industries was run, the Bianchis were doing the employees a favor by taking out Nero and restructuring everything. She'd have to give Luca some tips on best practices for the IT department. Things that had become second nature to her in Germany but were brushed off here.

Her old company prioritized the work she was paid to do over meetings. If her presence was required, she was given a window of time to pop in, say her piece, and pop out. If someone wanted her opinion on something else that came up, she got a message about it later.

Today's marathon meeting was going to set her back at least half a day, if not more, on the project she was working on. And she still had to get up to speed on another project Ciro brought to her yesterday. She might be here for other reasons entirely, but she still needed to do good work to maintain her cover. And her sense of personal pride.

She enjoyed her work. Even when she was stuck doing it for the uncle who'd killed her family and the company generating the obscene profits that made it possible.

Maybe that was contributing to her irritation too. She'd been on the island for almost a month, and not a single person had paid for what was done to them.

Luca and Matteo were having lunch with the mayor of Palermo and his close friend, the Regional President, tomorrow. But according to Luca, Matteo was undecided on whether Restivo should be left in power. Too bad for him.

She'd tell Matteo the same thing she told Luca if she had to. Restivo's career was over. As soon as her uncle fell, she was leaking every scrap of information she had on him to the press. There was no way he'd survive the fallout.

"And that wraps up our timelines for next quarter's projects. Any questions?"

Furtive glances went around the room, and when no one spoke, everyone exhaled a collective sigh of relief. Nothing was worse than getting stuck longer because some eager newbie had a burning question.

She followed the crowd out of the glass-walled conference room and back to her desk. Jack caught her eye as she passed his cubicle and raised a brow.

"That was a long one."

"Immeasurably. I'm going to take a stretch break and grab something to eat. Need anything from the lounge?"

Jack shook his head and refocused on his computer. He'd had his head down working on something all week, and she'd been forced to give up one of her work from home days to attend a handful of useless meetings. Lucky bastard.

Stretching out a kink in her lower back, she grabbed her purse from the bottom drawer of her desk and made her way down the hall to the ladies' room. It was empty, and she was grateful for the peace and quiet. Using the bathroom and washing her hands, she studied her reflection in the mirror.

She was due for another color soon. The blond was growing out, her roots darkening a little too much. She studied the ashy shade and the contrast to her skin that had gone pale during her years in Germany. Every run of Luca's fingertips through her hair made her wish it was brown again.

Pulling a vial of eye drops from her purse, she added some to her eyes and blinked rapidly. She hated the contacts as much as her hair color, more so under the bright fluorescent lighting. But a little discomfort was a small price to pay to make sure no one recognized her.

And it was only temporary. Her mission would be complete once Nero, Stefano, and Dante were dead. Then it wouldn't matter if anyone recognized her or not.

The door to the bathroom opened, and she smiled at a woman she only vaguely recognized. Giving her hair a quick brush with her fingers, Sienna stepped back into the hallway and headed for the employee lounge.

She wondered if the lounges on every floor were as nice as this one, with its comfy, overstuffed chairs and sofas and full refrigerator. A narrow pantry next to the fridge was always stocked with snacks, and fresh fruit was piled in a bowl in the middle of a large round table.

Grabbing a bottle of iced coffee from the fridge, she twisted off the cap and took a drink while she browsed the snacks inside the cabinet. Had she eaten breakfast? She couldn't remember.

After waking up late because she was supposed to work from home today, she'd seen the email that she was expected in the office for a meeting. Since she'd skipped a shower, she'd probably skipped breakfast too.

She took her coffee and a package of chocolate hazelnut biscotti to the table and sat, stretching her legs out underneath. A few minutes to herself, and then she'd go back out into the fray of people who wanted to stop by and introduce themselves to the new girl or ask questions or just chitchat in her general vicinity. God, she missed working from home.

Biting into the biscotti, she chewed slowly, her eyes closed as she savored the peace and quiet. Whatever she ended up doing after this, she wanted to do it from the quiet of a home office. People were exhausting.

The sound of voices drifted in through the open door, and she sighed as they got louder. She was just popping the last of the cookie into her mouth when Ciro stepped into the doorway, smiling when he saw her, followed closely by a man who stole her breath.

Drago. Raffaele Drago. One of her uncle's top capos. But she was more likely to see him at her uncle's estate, dressed in jeans and a button-down shirt with a gun on his hip. What was he doing in a perfectly tailored suit at the office? And why the hell was he talking to Ciro?

They both stepped fully into the room, and she gripped the edge of her chair when Ciro paused by the table. Ciro extended his arm toward her, and her heart pounded painfully against her sternum.

"Raffaele, this is Anna Marino. She's our newest hire in development. A very skilled coder."

Drago gave her a polite smile, and when no recognition flickered in his eyes, she relaxed slightly, loosening her hold on her chair to shake his hand when he offered it.

"Nice to meet new talent," Drago replied smoothly. "Hopefully they're giving you enough to keep you busy."

"Of course we are," Ciro replied with a cheeky wink in her direction. "Right, Anna?"

She smiled. "Absolutely. Speaking of," she added, pushing back from the table. "I should probably get back to it."

"Of course," Ciro replied, stepping back so she could cross to the door.

She wondered if either of them could hear her heart trying to beat its way out of her chest. She was almost to the doorway when Ciro stopped her.

"Actually, Anna. You might be able to help us out with this. You specialize in writing defense programs, right?"

Sienna took a deep breath and forced a polite smile onto her face before turning. "I do. That's mostly what I did in Germany."

Ciro nodded, and Drago looked intrigued. "I thought so. There's a proprietary project we're working on for a subsidiary, and we need to reverse engineer their systems."

"To find the holes?"

Ciro and Drago shared a look. "Yes," Ciro replied. "Exactly. We want to know where the weaknesses are so we can fill in the gaps and prevent any data leaks."

"Oh." She smiled at them both. "I can definitely help with that."

"Wonderful," Drago said, clapping Ciro on the shoulder. "Ciro can bring you up to speed. Hopefully you can get started sooner rather than later."

"Ah, yeah. Maybe. They just dumped another project in my lap this morning, and then—"

Ciro waved a hand in the air, cutting her off. "Don't worry about that. I'll arrange it. I'm sure Isa can do it. I'll come find you later to chat details."

"Okay. It was nice to meet you," she said to Drago before turning on her heel and leaving the lounge.

Sienna resisted the urge to run back to her desk, pacing herself through the rows of cubicles, the sound of typing and low conversation and the hum of machines barely audible over the blood pounding in her ears.

She hadn't come face to face with anyone who'd killed her family. Not yet. Not until today. She'd been so focused on her uncle and cousins she hadn't even considered the possibility of what she'd do if it happened.

There was no doubt in her mind that her uncle had tapped Drago to lead the hit on her family. There was no one her uncle trusted more. And he must have done so well he'd gotten himself promoted from murderer to businessman.

"It's your lucky day," Jack said when she rounded the corner and stepped into her cubicle.

"Yeah? Why?"

"Boss just stopped by. Said to tell you to go home. And that you can work from home for the rest of the week since you came in today."

Drago and Ciro moved into her line of sight, walking the other route from the lounge, and her skin prickled. She needed to get out of there before she lunged toward Drago and buried her nail file into his eyeball. She wanted to twist it until he shrieked the way Pietro had.

"You're a lifesaver, Jack."

He smiled. "I'm just the messenger. But you'll definitely have to tell me how you negotiated that into your deal."

Slipping her arms into her jacket, she chuckled. "I promise. I'll see you Monday."

Sienna turned to the side while she freed her hair from the collar of her jacket and carefully arranged it around her neck again to hide her scar. Hooking her purse over her shoulder, she took the stairs down to the lobby and buzzed herself out of the building.

Pausing on the sidewalk, she breathed in deep lungfuls of air. In through the nose, out through the mouth until her heart stopped racing. Luca might have asked her to wait on Nero, but he hadn't said anything about anyone else.

At least a dozen men had been involved in murdering her family. The names of each and every one were probably hidden in her uncle's files. What better way to pass the time while she waited for Luca's green light to kill her uncle than to take out the men who'd pulled the triggers?

Isa was home sick today. And before she closed her eyes to sleep tonight, Sienna was going to have the names she needed. And then she was going to start executing people.

Chapter Eighteen

"Little risky inviting Bonacci today, don't you think?" Luca wondered, standing at the front of his SUV with Matteo watching Bonacci's town car pull in behind them.

"No."

Luca raised a brow. "They've been political allies for years. What if Restivo tells him about the blackmail?"

"Considering one of the women Restivo has been fucking is Bonacci's pretty new wife, I doubt he'll say anything other than what I tell him to say."

A slow smile spread across Luca's lips. Another gift from Sienna's digging. Bonacci joined them, flanked by two body-guards who looked them up and down.

"I apologize for dragging you to the other side of the island," Bonacci said, adjusting his suit jacket. "Fausto is particular about these kinds of meetings."

"We understand the need for discretion," Matteo replied. "I'm glad you were able to join us. You and your family have always been valuable friends to us."

"I'm glad we could restore our relationship. It pained me

when your father let it lapse. I was sorry to hear of his passing."

Luca and Matteo shared a look. No doubt Bonacci missed the extra zeros in his bank account more.

"We appreciated the gift you sent. Bruno Giacosa wine was my father's favorite."

Bonacci nodded slowly. "We drank it many times. Your father was a generous man. But"—a smile crept over his lips —"the heir is even more generous, I think. Come. Let's not keep Fausto waiting."

They trailed Bonacci up the front walk to Restivo's palatial family villa. Rather than meeting at his home in Palermo, they were instead directed to Restivo's family villa in Catania. Matteo had grumbled about it, but Luca considered it a bonus. He'd insisted on driving separately and planned on having Sienna underneath him and coming on his cock before dinner.

The stone walkway was lined with neatly trimmed shrubs and what Luca imagined would be brilliant blooms in the right weather. A wrought iron chandelier hung on a long chain under the covered stoop. At night it would illuminate a set of double doors inlaid with silver accents and a silver door knocker in the shape of a lion's head, its mouth open in a silent roar and polished to a gleaming shine.

One side of the door swung open on a uniformed maid, young, pretty, timid. She stared mostly at their shoulders or the floor as she took coats and scurried away with them. Another woman in a different uniform came to escort them, leading them down a long hallway lined with religious art and relics preserved behind tempered glass.

Luca shared a look with Matteo and swallowed a grin. Restivo seemed to make a hobby out of collecting Catholic artifacts. Maybe he was trying to balance out the sins he regularly committed to keep his soul out of hell.

They stopped in the doorway of a long, narrow formal dining room with a dark wood table that easily sat thirty people. Elaborate place settings were clustered to one end, and the woman encouraged them to sit.

"Signore Restivo will be right with you. He's just finishing up an important call."

Bonacci's bodyguards flanked the door while they sat. Luca glanced over at them as a maid came out of nowhere to pour him a glass of wine. They made imposing figures in their black suits with their big, beefy hands clasped in front of them.

Staring straight ahead, they didn't move a muscle when Restivo skated in, his dark hair peppered with gray and slicked back. The man smiled with practiced ease, stopping behind his chair and bracing his hands on the back of it.

"Welcome to my home. I appreciate you coming all this way."

"It's not a problem," Matteo assured him.

Restivo flicked a glance at Bonacci, who quickly straightened and made introductions. "Fausto, this is Matteo Bianchi, owner of the Bianchi casinos now that his father has passed, and his brother Luca."

Restivo's gaze flickered between them, and he nodded before extending his hand. "I read about your father's death in the paper. Very sad."

"Yes," Luca replied, though none of them had been particularly upset to bury the bastard.

Restivo sat and gestured for the staff to serve lunch. A group of them stepped forward and set down plates in unison before moving out of sight again. Luca heard Matteo's barely audible snort. This meeting was a show of wealth more than anything else. Luca was over it already.

"What can I do for you? My friend here wasn't very forthcoming when he asked to have lunch today," Restivo said.

Matteo offered a charming smile. "I'm afraid we didn't give him many details ourselves. The truth is, we enjoy a number of mutually beneficial relationships with men such as yourself. Men who understand what an important role people like us play on this island."

"People like you?" Restivo asked, glancing at Luca and then fixing Matteo with an even stare.

"Don't play coy, Fausto," Bonacci chided. "You know what they're talking about."

Restivo spooned up a bite of risotto and then dabbed at the corner of his mouth with a perfectly pressed napkin. "The Mafia is an institution older than the government in Sicily. I believe institutions should be respected. But I'm not sure why you would want to speak to me specifically. Surely there are influential men closer to home."

"There are." Matteo's gaze slid to Bonacci, who inclined his head. "We've done business with a great many men in Palermo. But we'd like to become more well-rounded. It never hurts to have more friends."

"And what do I receive in return for my friendship?"

"More than what you're getting now," Luca promised.

Restivo's brows inched higher. "How much more?"

"Four. Per month. More when the occasion calls for it."

Bonacci nodded when Restivo looked to him for confirmation. The Bianchis are good for it. Settling back in his chair, Restivo took a drink of wine, studying them over the rim of the glass.

"I already have deep ties to Catania. Nero Gallo and I go back a long way. Loyalty is a precious thing."

Matteo shrugged. "Loyalties change as often as parties. I'm offering a mutually beneficial relationship. And my terms surpass Gallo's."

"What terms are those?"

Luca produced the envelope he'd tucked beside him and

set it on the table next to Restivo's plate. The man took another sip of wine before carefully setting his glass on the table and reaching for the envelope.

Luca had to give the man credit. Not a single muscle twitched when he opened it and calmly flipped through each photo. Evidence of his meetings with Gallo where cash changed hands, images of him in various states of undress with multiple women, sometimes multiple women at once, several photos of him balls deep in Bonacci's wife in more than one location. And position.

He closed the envelope, sealing it at the top, and laid it gently on the table. "I'm interested in your proposal," he said.

His voice was calm, but his eyes snapped fire. Sicily's president didn't like being outsmarted. If Bonacci found out Restivo was fucking his wife, their friendship would end, and Bonacci would run for president. And with Bianchi backing and their growing control over the island, he was sure to win.

"But?" Luca prompted.

"But I've known Gallo for a long time. If I abruptly cut ties, he might be suspicious."

Matteo waved a hand in the air. "I'm not asking you to sever ties with Gallo. You can take his money as long as you let me know what he asks of you when he asks it."

Restivo's eyes dropped to the envelope again, and a muscle pulsed in his jaw. "Agreed."

Bonacci leaned forward and clapped his friend on the shoulder. "Welcome to the fold, Fausto. Here's to a long and fruitful partnership."

They toasted, Bonacci smiling affably, Matteo grinning in triumph, and Restivo with a tight grimace on his face that almost passed for a smile. They finished the meal in feigned camaraderie, and Restivo walked them to the door.

"That was a clever play," Restivo said once Bonacci had

climbed into his car and driven away. "How long have you been watching me?"

"Long enough to know we would rather be friends than enemies."

Restivo scoffed. "You blackmail all your friends?"

"Only the ones who require the proper motivation," Matteo replied.

"I could go to Gallo in an instant. Let him know what you're trying to do to me."

"You could," Luca agreed. "But would your career survive the fallout? The island might live in harmony with the Mafia, but every young politician is eager to make a name for themselves by getting rid of us."

"Not to mention, Bonacci would be very upset to find out how often his little Celeste rides your cock every week."

Restivo gritted his teeth and shoved his hands into his pockets. "I know you've got something planned for Gallo. He's worried about it."

Luca raised a brow. That was news. "What makes you say that?"

"He told me," Restivo said, giving him a dry stare. "I've worked hard to get where I am. I'd like to stay there."

"Then make sure the information between us and Gallo only flows in one direction."

They stood there in silence for several minutes before Restivo ultimately nodded and turned to go back inside, slamming the door behind him.

"That went better than I was expecting," Luca admitted, following Matteo to their waiting cars.

"It did. But I still want to keep an eye on Restivo. Make sure he doesn't go to Gallo. That something your contact can do for us?"

"They might be able to. I can ask when I meet with them later."

"You know we didn't have to drive separately," Matteo said, pausing at the door to his SUV. "Is your contact afraid of me?"

Luca rolled his eyes. "No. I'm protecting their identity."

"It almost sounds like you don't trust me, brother."

Matteo's tone was sharp, but Luca wasn't interested in placating his feelings today. "That's because I don't. Not with this. When the time is right for you to know who they are, I'll tell you. And not before."

"Everything I'm doing is to put the Bianchis on top."

"Everything you're doing is to put yourself on the throne," Luca said. "The rest of us rising with you is nothing but a bonus. To pretend otherwise is insulting. To expect honesty you aren't willing to reciprocate is equally so."

"I came back to fix things."

"What things?" Luca stood at the door to his car.

"The family." Matteo twisted his watch around on his wrist. "I wanted to put everything back together again."

"If that's true, you suck at it. You can't put things back together while you hide who you are and what you want from us."

Luca climbed behind the wheel and slammed the door, cutting off Matteo's reply. He had better things to do than coddle his brother. Like see if he could coax Sienna to wrap her day up early. He needed the taste of her on his tongue to clear his head.

Plugging his phone into the car, he punched in her number and listened to it ring through to voicemail.

"You've reached Anna Marino. I'm unavailable at this time. Please leave a—"

Luca hung up and dialed again. This time she picked up on the third ring.

"Luca," she said, a little breathless. "I can't talk right now. Is everything okay?"

"What's wrong?"

"What?" He heard her take a slow, deep breath before speaking again. "What do you mean? Nothing's wrong."

"Sienna Caterina Gallo," Luca growled. "I know you too well for you to lie to me. Tell me what's wrong."

"Nothing, really. I just... I'm headed out to go...shopping."

"Sienna..."

"I made a list of people who killed my family," she clarified. "And since you won't let me start with Nero, I'm going to go cross off a different name."

Luca sat up a little straighter, fingers gripping the steering wheel. "Wait for me. I'll go with you."

She hesitated, and he imagined her eyes darting to check the time. "I don't have the three hours to wait for you. I know where he'll be for the next ninety minutes. It has to be now."

"I'm ten minutes away."

"Really? I thought you were meeting with the president today."

"We did. He wanted to meet at his family home instead of in Palermo."

"Oh." He heard rustling over the line, the sound of a zipper. "I forgot he's from Catania. How did it go?"

"I'll tell you about it when I see you. Sienna. Wait for me."

She sighed. "Okay. But hurry, Luca. I need this today."

He frowned when she disconnected the call. He'd have to find out what else had happened since the last time he saw her. And then why she hadn't told him about it. For now, he was eager to get to her. He wanted to watch her heal a small part of herself with this kill.

Then he planned to fuck her all night long.

Chapter Nineteen

Sienna paced the length of her apartment from the window to the door and back again, eyes darting to the clock over the stove with each pass. Nerves mingled with anticipation and buzzed along her skin.

This wasn't what she envisioned happening when she came back to Sicily. This wasn't the revenge she'd planned for. But seeing Drago the other day cemented it in her mind. There were more men responsible for her pain and suffering than just her uncle and cousins. And she might as well make good use of her time on the island if she had some to spare.

She'd spent hours and hours digging names out of her uncle's files. He'd been a little smarter with these, spreading the names out across different folders and databases instead of keeping everything in one spot. The fact that her uncle had killed his only brother was a secret he guarded better than most of the others.

Her father had been a popular man in the Gallo organization. Loyal to a fault. A good soldier and second in command. Not that his loyalty had earned him much. Just a bullet to the brain and his family annihilated.

It was smart, really, for Nero to take them all out at once. The need for revenge festered in the body, taking root and growing stronger with each passing year. The longer she had to wait, the more she wanted him dead. The more she wanted to see his lifeless eyes staring at nothing the way Pietro's had.

She only wished she had more time to make him suffer, to pour all of her rage and grief and anguish into him so he hurt as much as she did. But her plan didn't allow that much time. The whole thing was a long shot already.

And the Bianchis wanted it to look like a suicide. Their enforcer Alexei had far more practice with that than she did, but she'd been brainstorming ways to change her plan. As long as it ended with him dead by her hand, she didn't care how it happened.

Turning at the window, she glanced at the clock again. If Luca wasn't here in two minutes, she was leaving without him. She had a narrow window of where her target was going to be and for how long. If she missed it, she might not get the chance again.

The sky was painted in pinks and purples when Luca finally knocked on her door. He swept in, steps faltering when he saw what she was wearing. His eyes raked up and down her body, lingering on her breasts before stopping on her face.

"Are you planning on killing him or seducing him?" he wondered.

"Both," she replied, grabbing her purse off the counter and slipping it over her shoulder.

"Sienna." He gripped her arm when she turned for the door and tugged her back against him. "What did I say about men touching you?"

"Luca. We don't have time for you to be possessive. Once every two weeks, this guy goes to a strip club that's little more than a brothel on the edge of the red-light district. He buys drinks and God knows what else for about three hours, and then he walks back to his car and goes home to his wife."

"And your plan is to what?" Luca asked through gritted teeth, eyes scanning her body again. "Give him a lap dance?"

"No." She flipped her blond hair over her shoulder and smoothed it. "I'm going to offer him a blow job in a dark alley."

"The fuck you are." His brown eyes darkened until they were almost black, and he moved forward, pressing her body back against the counter and caging her in with his hands on either side of her hips. "You really think I'm going to stand by and watch you swallow a dick that isn't mine?"

His eyes dropped to her lips when she wetted them with her tongue, and he ground the hard length of his cock against her stomach. "Jesus. I'm not actually going to blow him. I'm going to offer."

"And then what?"

"And then once he has his dick out, I'm going to shoot him." She reached into her purse and pulled out the 9mm she'd stashed inside.

"You can shoot him without his dick ever being part of the equation."

Sienna sighed. They were wasting time. "I'm not arguing with you about this. It has to look like a mugging while he's vulnerable. Unless you don't care about flying under the radar with my uncle anymore. And if that's the case, I'll just wander up to his office on Monday and shoot him instead."

A muscle worked in Luca's jaw as he appraised her low-cut dress that clung to every curve and stopped at the top of her thighs, barely covering her ass.

"I won't miss this opportunity. You can stay here if it bothers you that much. I shouldn't be gone long."

Luca shoved away from the counter and stalked to the

door, yanking it open. He slid a hand over her ass and squeezed when she walked past him into the hallway.

He was silent in the elevator, on the drive, and as they walked the handful of blocks from where she'd parked her sedan to the alley closest to the strip club. But his hands never left her. Touching her hip, her back, her hand, her thigh.

"You probably should have stayed in the car," she said, nerves fluttering in her belly. How the fuck was she supposed to go through with this with him looking at her that way?

He snorted. "Not a fucking chance, baby girl. Because if he touches you, I'll shoot him myself."

"Luca."

"Don't worry. I want to watch you kill him. I just don't want to watch him touch you."

"Just trust me, okay?"

He slid his arm around her waist, tugging her tight against him, fingers slipping under the dangerously short hem of her dress to trace down the crack of her ass. "I trust you. But don't forget who this pussy belongs to." He teased his fingertips over her pussy lips through the thin material of her thong, smiling when he found her already wet. "And who's going to use it later."

At the sound of footsteps, Luca loosened his hold, tugging her dress back down and giving her ass a stinging slap before melting into the darkness. She squeezed her thighs together and peeked over her shoulder, trying to find him with her eyes. But the alley's shadows had swallowed him up, and she forced herself to forget him and focus.

Bringing him along was definitely a bad idea. Because she was prepared to do or touch whatever she needed to in order to do this. The idea that Luca would take it out on her pussy later wasn't exactly the deterrent he might think it was.

The footsteps grew louder, and the man she was looking for took shape. It was barely dark, but the towering buildings on either side of the narrow street blocked out the light as much as they offered privacy. There weren't many lights in this area. It wasn't well maintained by the city, and people didn't want to know what happened in the dark anyway.

She stepped into a shaft of weak light and twisted so it caught the sequins on her dress. The man slowed the instant he noticed her and subtly changed directions. Sienna smiled when he traveled further up the block instead of jogging across the street.

"Hey, doll," he said, tucking his hand into his pocket to adjust himself as he raked a gaze down her body. "You look too pretty to be in this part of the city. Are you lost?"

"No. But I still found you." She sent him a coy smile. "Are you looking for some fun?"

He grinned and stepped closer. "I just finished having some fun, but you are definitely persuading me to have some more." He looked her up and down again, not bothering to hide his erection now. "How much?"

"Fifty for a blow job. And more for...more," she added with another teasing grin.

He slid his hand around and cupped her ass, squeezing. "What if I wanted in that tight little asshole?"

"Three hundred. And a condom."

He sighed, releasing her ass and moving his hands to his belt buckle. "Let's start with your mouth on my cock. If you're any good at that, maybe I'll take some more."

She let him work his pants down to his thighs as she slid her hands up his arms to his shoulders and rotated him so his back was pressed against the stone wall. He grinned, wrapping his fingers around his cock and stroking it with short, fast jerks.

"You're going to be a good little cocksucker," he said, reaching his free hand up to probe against her lips with his finger. "I can tell. Well, on your knees," he said when she still didn't make a move to suck him. "Can't get me in your mouth from way over there."

Sienna took a step back, eyes wandering from his pumping hand to his face as she reached into her purse. "You think your wife will be disappointed when they find your body in an alley with your pathetic dick hanging out of your pants?"

He jerked, fingers stilling on his cock and eyes narrowing on her face. "What the fuck did you say?"

"Although, if that's the thing I was stuck riding for the rest of my life, I'd find that even more disappointing. Maybe she'll be happy to be rid of you."

He took a lurching step forward, but she was faster, pulling the gun free and shooting him once in the chest. He stumbled, then fell to his knees, hands reaching up to cover the wound.

"Who the fuck are you?" he demanded, hands slick with blood and weakly fumbling under his jacket to draw his own weapon.

"The last face you'll see before you die," she replied, pressing her gun against his forehead. "But you can call me Sienna Gallo."

His eyes went wide and then rolled back in his head when she pulled the trigger. Blood and brain matter spattered the wall behind him, and he slumped onto his side on the ground. She stood staring down at him, finger still on the trigger, waiting to see if he stirred.

At movement behind her, she whirled, gun raised, only to see Luca emerging from the dark, hands raised in defense. She lowered the weapon, slipping it back into her purse, and knelt next to the body, patting his pockets.

"What are you doing? We need to get out of here."

"I'm making it look like a mugging."

She freed his wallet from his jacket pocket and pulled out

the impressive wad of cash inside. He must not have found anyone he liked much inside the strip club tonight. His Rolex looked like a knockoff, but she took it anyway, along with the gold rings on his hand and the chain with a dangling cross around his neck. He wouldn't need any of it in hell.

"Come on, baby girl. We need to go," Luca said, reaching for her arm and helping her to her feet.

She resisted the urge to ram her heel into the bastard's crotch and followed Luca out of the opposite end of the alley and up the cross street. They zig-zagged back to her car a different way than they'd come, walking hand in hand. The gun felt heavier in her purse now than it had before, and her heart was pounding.

She'd done it. She wasn't entirely sure she'd be able to pull the trigger until she'd seen him standing there leering at her. Knowing he'd had a hand in what happened to her family and was just going about his life, enjoying himself in dark alleys and strip clubs, going home to his own family every night.

It hardly seemed fair that he was breathing and they were not. Now he was dead too, and it was no less than what he deserved for the innocent blood he had on his hands.

She wouldn't waste time feeling bad about killing him. She'd be too busy planning the next one.

Chapter Twenty

Luca's eyes kept drifting to her ass and the way it swayed in that sexy fucking dress as they walked back to the car. He'd nearly given away the whole thing when that prick reached out and grabbed her, but she hadn't let him touch her for long, and Luca wanted to see what she'd do.

He was hard for her in an instant when she pressed the muzzle to his forehead and fired. His baby girl had been practicing, and she had a lot of pent-up rage ready to be unleashed. It was hot as fuck watching her get what she wanted.

They ducked into the last alley between them and the car, and on impulse, he grabbed her hand to stop her and backed her up against the rough stone of the building, claiming her mouth. She froze for a fraction of a second, and then her arms were around his neck and her tongue was teasing along his lower lip.

He reached down to tug up the hem of her dress, desperate to sink himself deep inside her and too impatient to wait until they got back to her apartment. She squirmed against him when he slipped his hand inside her panties and stroked his middle finger over her clit.

"Luca," she gasped, hand sliding into his hair and gripping it tightly.

"Yes, baby girl," he murmured against her lips, nipping her top lip gently.

"We have to get out of here before the cops come," she insisted, even as she rocked into his hand.

"I don't hear any sirens, do you? No one cares about gunshots in this neighborhood." He slipped a finger inside her, grinning when she groaned softly. "Besides, I'll just look like a man enjoying his hooker."

Sienna rewarded him with a throaty laugh, shoving his shoulder with one hand and giving his hair a tug with the other until he was looking into her eyes. "Then you should hurry up and fuck me, because I've been thinking about your cock all night."

He took her mouth again, adding a second finger and grinding them deep inside her until she shuddered against him. "I think I'll make you come on my fingers first. Then I'll fuck you. Nice and hard because you let him touch you."

She groaned. "I had to, or he would have gotten suspicious."

"I don't care," he whispered against her ear, swiping his thumb back and forth over her clit. "I'm the only one who gets to touch you, baby girl. I'm the only one who can make you feel like this."

"Yes," she whimpered, and he increased the pressure on her clit.

Fuck, he loved that sound.

"I want to feel you come for me, Sienna," he said, teeth scraping against her jaw as he slipped in a third finger and fucked them in and out, her hips rocking against his hand with each thrust. "Then I'll remind you who this pussy belongs to."

Her fingernails bit into his scalp, and he relished in the sensation of her pussy fluttering around his fingers, squeezing tighter and tighter while her breaths became more ragged. Dropping his head, Luca scored her shoulder with his teeth, soothing the bite with his tongue.

When he nipped her again, she barely muffled her desperate cry in the crook of his neck as her pussy clenched tight around his fingers and her body went taut with her orgasm.

"You look so pretty when you come for me," he said, sliding his fingers out and up over her sensitive clit, making her shudder.

She sagged against the wall when he released her to free his cock, but she reached out to wrap her fingers around it, giving it one lazy stroke from root to tip, a smile curving her lips when he groaned.

"What's that look for?" he asked, thrusting against her expert grip.

"It's nice knowing I can make you just as desperate for me as I am for you."

"I'll never get enough of you," he assured her, turning her slowly in his arms until her back was against his chest.

He guided her hands to the wall and pressed them flat against the surface. Her dress was pushed up over her ass, her panties hooked out of his way. He slid them over her hips and down her long legs, slipping them into his pocket before kissing his way back up to her pussy.

Gliding his tongue along the length of her slit, he smiled when she groaned and rocked back against his mouth for more.

"I could eat you all night," he said, standing and pressing his hand against the small of her back to tilt her ass up. "But I need to be inside you." Looking down between them, he watched as he teased the head of his cock up and down her slit, then slid inside her with a groan. "Fuck, that's so good."

"Yes," she agreed, fingers curling into the wall and her ass pushing back against his grinding thrusts. "I love the way you fuck me, Luca. Never stop."

"I don't intend to," he promised her, drawing his hips back and slamming deep. "Whose pussy is this, Sienna?"

"Yours," she panted, breath hitching when he gave her the entire length of his cock in another brutal thrust. "Always yours."

"Fuck yes," he said through gritted teeth, setting a punishing pace, knowing he wouldn't last long inside her, not with the way she was gripping him, her ass bouncing with every thrust. "Mine."

He listened as her moans and sighs drifted out of the dark and wrapped around him. She was perfection personified, the way she responded to him, the way she wanted him, the way she needed him inside her as much as he needed to fill her.

Her pussy clenched around him, and he groaned, picking up the pace as he slid his hand around her hip to her clit, strumming it with fast, rough strokes of his fingers. Her body jerked under him, trying and failing to meet his deep thrusts with her own.

"That's it. Take my cock," Luca ground out, sliding his hand into her hair and gripping it in his fist.

He pulled her up until her back was arched beautifully, her fingers barely touching the wall, and pounded her until she was gasping for air. She clamped down around him, her breaths ragged, her hands scrambling for purchase he refused to give her.

"Fucking Christ, Luca. I'm going to come."

"Yes, baby girl," he panted. "Come all over my cock. Let me feel you."

She reached down to where his fingers were still swiping over her clit, digging her nails into the back of his hand as her body bucked violently under him and her mouth opened in a silent scream.

Releasing her hair in favor of gripping her hips, he pumped into her roughly, grinding inside her before pulling back and doing it again and again until she was panting and whimpering and shuddering beneath him.

With one last savage thrust, he sheathed himself inside her and gave over to his own release, his body on fire from it. Keeping his cock buried deep, he pressed her body against the wall and teased her earlobe with his teeth.

"Mine," he whispered, and she hummed her agreement, wriggling back against him. "This wasn't exactly how I expected tonight to go."

She laughed, soft and warm, and he pressed a kiss to her shoulder before reluctantly stepping back and rearranging his clothes while she did the same.

"Do you have to go back to Palermo right away?" she asked, running her fingers through her hair to smooth the worst of the tangles from where he fisted it.

He probably should, even though he didn't want to. They were making a run on one of Gallo's shipments in two days, and they still had details to finalize. Checking the time on his phone, he reached for her hand and calculated.

"No. I have a few more hours yet."

He'd be pushing the boundaries of how much sleep he needed to function, but more time with Sienna was worth it. Sienna had always been worth every sleepless night and long drive in the wee hours of the morning so they didn't get caught.

"But when this is all over, I'm moving you to Palermo and coming home to you every night."

She leaned into his side as they walked back to the car but

didn't say anything, and he felt the first warning bells going off in the back of his mind. No. That wasn't what her silence meant. She wouldn't up and leave Sicily this time because he wouldn't let her.

She'd promised him that first night they were together that she was his until their last breaths. And whatever he had to say to convince her he meant it, he would say it. He refused to lose her a second time.

Chapter Twenty-One

Luca pocketed his phone as he strode into the study, eyebrows winging up when he saw the men they'd chosen for today's mission already gathered.

"Look who finally decided to grace us with his presence."

Luca's eyes narrowed on Matteo's face. "I'm five minutes early."

Matteo waved a dismissive hand toward one of the couches. "For once. Have a seat. We're still waiting on Dom to do the final rundown."

"No, we're not," Luca replied, sliding his hands into the pockets of his jeans. "I told him not to come."

"Out," Matteo snarled, and the men quickly rose and made their way to the door. "You too," he added when Alexei didn't move.

"Oh, absolutely not," Alexei replied, twirling his knife between his fingers. "I'm staying to watch the show."

Matteo glared at him for a few more moments, but when Alexei didn't relent, he turned his irritation on Luca, and it sparked into anger. "Why the fuck would you tell Dom not to come? He's the one running this op today."

"Because Dom is busy in Agrigento. Now's not a good time for him to be absent from the territory, and I'm perfectly capable of running this one."

Matteo snorted. "You. Since when do you run ops?"

"Since you fucked off to God knows where and gave me no choice but to step in." A deep scowl creased Matteo's brow, but Luca ignored it. "I've run plenty of ops, killed plenty of men, and settled plenty of scores. All while keeping this family's financial interests afloat. Which is more than I can say for you."

Matteo stalked to the middle of the room until he and Luca were nose to nose. "Watch what you fucking say to me. At some point, little brother," Matteo said, emphasizing the word little, "you'll have to forgive me for my past transgressions."

"Forgiveness comes with honesty. And we're in short supply of both." Luca made a show of checking the time on his watch. "We've got a tight window. You can continue to waste time on an argument you'll lose, or we can do the final rundown and get going. Your choice."

"Alexei can lead this one," Matteo countered.

"He could. He won't."

Matteo glanced at Alexei, who still sat on the couch twirling his knife, a lopsided grin on his face as he watched. "Fine," Matteo bit off. "Get in here!" he bellowed, turning back and reclaiming his place in front of the desk as the men filed back in.

Once everyone was seated again, Luca turned to the expectant group. He'd worked alongside these men numerous times. They were steady, reliable, efficient, lethal. That's why he'd chosen them.

"We're going to run this one the same way we did the job in Naples two years ago." Luca ignored the look of surprise on Matteo's face. "Cause an accident, confiscate the weapons, leave no survivors."

"We're sure the shipment timing or location hasn't changed?"

Luca glanced at Matteo but addressed the men. "My contact is keeping an eye on it. They said it's still slated to leave on time. Which should be right about"—he confirmed the time on his watch—"now. We're running a little behind, but if we make good time, we should still be able to be in place to intercept."

The men began to get up and then hesitated, glancing at Matteo, who waved them out of their seats. Luca followed them to the door, pausing when Matteo called his name.

"Don't do anything stupid and get yourself killed. It'll be tedious running Gallo Industries without you."

Rolling his eyes, Luca followed Alexei into the hall and outside to the waiting SUVs. Climbing into the backseat of the second car, he pulled out his phone and fired off a quick text to Sienna. She was working from home today and keeping an eye on this shipment for them.

Truck just left the warehouse. No changes.

Thanks, baby girl. I'll text you when it's done.

Luca slid his phone back into his pocket and looked up to see Alexei staring at him, one eyebrow raised. The cars pulled out of the driveway, and they rode in silence, winding their way across the island.

Dom was technically closer to their intercept point, but it was true he couldn't be spared in Agrigento. Not for something as simple as this. And they'd timed it perfectly. The only snag in the plan would be if the ferry from the mainland where the shipment was coming from got delayed, and all that meant was they'd be waiting a little longer to execute. Hardly the end of the world.

The truck was headed from a Gallo warehouse on mainland Italy to a tourist port located in Antonetti's Syracuse territory. The port was used for personal vessels. Sailboats and yachts and shit like that.

According to what Sienna was able to dig up, they were selling these weapons to up-and-comers in the Greek Mafia. Men who wouldn't be pleased to have their pricey supply disappear.

Luca imagined their normal routine would be to load the weapons onto a private yacht in crates that could pass for supplies for a long journey and then cruise the three hundred nautical miles from Sicily to Greece with their contraband in the cargo hold. Today would not be their normal routine.

The plan was to ambush the truck at the precise moment it drove over the line from Gallo territory to newly seized Romano territory before it crossed Antonetti's border. Gallo would know it was a hit because the weapons would be gone, but they'd leave the truck for anyone to find and be sure to give it a splashy front-page story in the press.

Luca's phone signaled an incoming text, and he dug it out of his pocket, angling the screen away from Alexei's prying eyes. Sienna.

First check-in complete. Ferry just docked in Messina.

"Right on schedule," Luca said, sending back a confirmation text. "We shouldn't have any problems unless they hit traffic. They should do another check-in just as we get into position."

The sun was high in the sky by the time they were pulling onto the shoulder of the road outside Enna. It was close to the same location Dom had run surveillance on a few months ago. When they'd learned Gallo had been gifting weapons to Varda in exchange for protection should the Bianchis ever set Gallo in their sights.

Too bad for Gallo he'd bet on the wrong man. The weapons he'd given to Varda had been useless against Bianchi firepower. Now he was out the investment and the protection. Gallo didn't have the ranks to match them. That's why he'd gone running to Varda, and as soon as they stripped him of his wealth and influence, he'd collapse like a house of cards.

Luca climbed out of the SUV and moved around to the trunk. Pulling on thick gloves, he carefully hefted out one of the spike strips and carried it to the side of the road. They had a spotter a few miles up warning people away from this stretch. They only had one target today. No need to draw attention to themselves by taking out multiple vehicles.

Positioning two strips across the road, he leaned back against the side of the SUV hidden in the brush and waited. Alexei's knife was twisting through his fingers at a dizzying speed when Luca's phone signaled again.

Enna check-in complete. Be safe.

"Any minute now," Luca warned, seconds before a warning text came through from their spotter that the truck was on its way.

He watched from his vantage point as the truck rounded the bend ahead of them and came into view. It picked up speed on the straight stretch, and his muscles tensed in anticipation as it neared the spike strips.

The tires popped like gunshots when they hit the strip, and the truck swerved violently onto the shoulder, kicking up dirt and gravel. Luca thought they'd stay upright, but the front tires protested as the car veered back onto the smooth surface of the road, splitting off and catching under the back tires.

The truck shuddered and swayed before ultimately tipping over and sliding along the pavement for a few feet, metal scraping against asphalt and sending up sparks. As soon as the truck jerked to a stop, his men poured from the tree line and advanced, weapons drawn.

Smoke from the mangled tires rose into the sky, the smell

of burned rubber filling his nose as men advanced on the cab to make sure the driver was dead. Luca rounded the back of the truck and crouched down to undo the latch on the tailgate, only to find it bolted shut.

Gesturing to the man closest to him for bolt cutters, his head jerked up when shouts and then shots rang out from the front of the truck. It didn't last long. Everything was silent by the time he sprinted around to where his man was dismounting from the open door on the driver's side.

"What the fuck was that?" Luca demanded.

"There was a passenger we didn't anticipate," Torelli said. "He started shooting."

Luca gave an irritated huff. "Well, dig him out and clean up as much as you can. We can't leave a body with bullet holes for the cops."

"On it," Torelli assured him.

Luca left them to their work and went to check on the other group. The door was now pried open, severed bolts on the ground at their feet. The contents of the back of the truck were tossed around, some of the crates open with their guts spilling out. Gallo was hiding his weapons among a shipment of electronics.

"Load up the weapons quickly," Luca said, picking up a game console and tossing it back into a box full of other smashed video game parts. "I want to be gone in fifteen."

"What was the shooting?" Alexei wondered as the men began loading crates into the SUVs.

"A passenger who didn't have the sense to die on impact."

Alexei chuckled softly, standing next to Luca and watching them transfer the cargo from the truck to their waiting cars.

"So," Alexei began, keeping his voice low to avoid being overheard. "Does Matteo know your contact is a woman?"

Luca forced his voice to remain neutral. "No. Does it matter?"

"Not necessarily. He'd probably be more interested in the fact that you're sleeping with her."

Alexei's stare was searching instead of mocking when Luca met his gaze. "What makes you think I'm sleeping with her?"

"Well, I've had a few informants in my day. I've never called them baby girl."

"It's rude to read other people's text messages," Luca sniffed.

"I've never been one for manners. Getting that close to an informant is a terrible idea."

"It's fine."

"It won't be fine if one of you gets bored and she decides to go to Gallo and out the whole damn thing."

"She won't," Luca assured him. "Going to Gallo is the last thing she'd do. I know what I'm doing, Alexei." He leveled Alexei with a hard stare. "And I'd appreciate it if my brother didn't find out about her."

Alexei held Luca's gaze for a long moment before finally nodding. "All right. But I'll blow the whole thing wide open if it puts Carina in danger in any way."

"You mean if it puts the Bianchis in danger."

"No."

Luca sighed. "You know I'd never do anything to put the family at risk, Carina included. Everything is under control."

"I do know that," Alexei conceded. "But I care about Carina more than the rest of you."

Luca shook his head as the men finished loading up the last crate and more emerged from the woods with shovels and covered in dirt. The passenger was an additional complication, but Luca would bet money on the fact that Gallo wouldn't want the cops on this part of the island looking too deep into this, no matter how well he lined the pockets of the chief of police.

The accident, the theft, and the loss of weapons were a minor blow, but a blow nonetheless. If Gallo really was as worried about them as Restivo said, they'd consider this their warning shot.

It would be interesting to see how Gallo responded.

Chapter Twenty-Two

Curled into a corner of the couch and tucked under a blanket, Sienna scanned the documents she'd unearthed from her uncle's files. She'd spent days digging through whatever she could find looking for mentions of Ciro.

He'd finally read her in on that super secret project, and it made her more suspicious of him than ever. He maintained the story that the goal was to fake attacks against their system in order to create better security protocols.

It wasn't an unusual strategy. Hacking a system to clearly see the holes so you could patch them was a common tactic. But what Ciro and, by proxy, Drago, were asking for was far more than that. They didn't just want a hacking report. They wanted her to actively skim data, though they wouldn't tell her what kind.

Plus, the system he was having her work was complex. Whoever had designed it was good. Very good. She imagined anyone who got past those defenses wouldn't have long before they triggered some kind of alarm and got kicked back out again.

Uninterested in putting herself in the crosshairs of whoever owned what appeared to be a series of shell corporations spread across Europe, she'd spent more time looking for dirt on Ciro than she did building the program he thought would be a magic bullet. She wanted to know why he was so cozy with Drago and how deep he might be in with her uncle.

So far, she'd turned up nothing on the criminal side. She considered her uncle might be referring to him using an alias, but that was a stretch, considering he hadn't done it for a single man so far. What good was blackmail if everyone was tagged by a fake name?

After abandoning that angle, she'd started combing through front-facing employee records. Gallo Industries kept a detailed list of projects each employee contributed to, and Ciro had fifteen years' worth of history.

On the surface, everything appeared on the up and up. The very project she was working on was listed as the most recent project for both Ciro and her. It was labeled as contract work for a company name she didn't recognize but was traced back to a consulting firm in Paris.

Ciro had worked on three different projects for the same company in the last six months. Each business targeted was different, but all of them were categorized the same. Contract work to improve security systems. If she had to bet money on it, she'd say her uncle was trying to access someone's company secrets. And he was persistent about it.

But Ciro was clearly in on the game. It was obvious from the way he'd asked her to join the project to the cagey way he'd avoided some of her more direct questions. Even if he didn't know the extent of Gallo's plans—and he likely didn't—he knew he was doing something wrong.

Which is why she'd spent the last half hour combing through his financials. Nothing stood out as overtly odd, and that was the puzzling part.

His pay had never changed on the Gallo side. He got his standard raises every two years, and a few times during his tenure, he'd negotiated a bigger pay bump. Every December, he received a hefty bonus, but nothing off the charts, nothing out of the ordinary for a man in his position with his experience. However he was getting paid for this corporate spying, he wasn't depositing it into his regular bank account.

A comb through her uncle's back door financials had yielded no results. Maybe she was losing her touch. Or it was just late, and she needed to finally give up and go to bed. The idea of sleep didn't appeal, not with the nightmares she'd been having this week.

Pushing off the couch, she crossed to the kitchen and pulled a mug down from the cabinet. She'd make some tea, give it another hour, and then try to sleep again. Weeks like this one were when she missed the drug-induced sleep she had when taking painkillers after the shooting.

But they'd run out, and she'd gone into enough of a withdrawal that she decided not to seek more. She needed her head clear and her memories feeding her revenge. Especially the ones that kept her up at night. Maybe what she needed was another kill.

The high from the guy in the alley had faded, and she had two other names on her list she could easily take out without raising her uncle's suspicions. One man had a lethal tree nut allergy and a very predictable habit of meeting a mistress about thirty minutes outside Cefalù.

It would be easy to follow him to lunch at his usual spot and slip hazelnut oil into his food. Maybe she'd be bold enough to ask Luca on a date. He seemed to enjoy watching her kill the last guy. And she enjoyed him after. She'd almost forgotten what it was to be claimed by Luca. The high was better than any drug.

The water in the kettle boiled, and she poured it over the

strainer, letting the tea steep before adding sugar and a squeeze of lemon. The door handle rattled, and she jerked toward the sound, the spoon she was stirring her tea with falling against the side of the mug with a clink.

When the handle rattled again, she slid a knife from the block and crouched below the counter so whoever it was couldn't see her reflection in the windows. The lock clicked, and the door swung in, jeans-clad legs stepping over the threshold.

Shoving to her feet, Sienna advanced, knife raised, stopping a hair's breadth from the pulse point in Luca's throat before recognizing him.

"Fucking Christ, Luca," she said in a whoosh of breath, lowering the knife and taking a step back.

"I don't know whether to be turned on or worried you'll gut me next time I come over," he said, closing and locking the door behind him. "Both, I think."

"What are you doing breaking into my apartment at this hour?" She settled the knife back in the block and set her spoon in the sink.

He came up behind her, wrapping his arms around her waist and pressing a kiss to the side of her neck. "Is it breaking in when you gave me a key? I think the better question is, what are you doing awake at two in the morning?"

"Oh, and you were going to just slip into bed and let me get my beauty rest?"

"Of course, baby girl," Luca replied in mock offense, fingertips grazing the underside of her breast.

Sienna rocked her ass back against his already hard cock, grinning when he groaned softly in her ear. "Something tells me otherwise."

"Fine," he replied, flicking his tongue against her earlobe. "You caught me. I can't get enough of you. So sue me."

"I can hardly say I mind, as often as you get me naked when you come over. Which is to say, every single time."

He chuckled low in her ear, scraping his teeth over her skin and making her shiver. "Why stop a winning streak, then?"

His hands pushed under the hem of her sweater, his cool fingers dancing over her hot skin as he eased it up.

"Let me shut down my computer program first."

Pausing the upward exploration of his hands, he glanced over her shoulder at where her laptop sat open on the coffee table. "You were working at this hour?"

"I couldn't sleep," she said by way of an explanation.

She hadn't woken up Luca with nightmares yet. He was too heavy a sleeper. If he knew about them, he'd likely only worry. And what good would that do?

"Plus, Ciro has—"

"If you say he touched you…"

Laughing softly, Sienna set her untouched tea in the sink and crossed to the living room. "No. It would seem he's embroiled in a little corporate espionage. Potentially on behalf of Gallo Industries, though I haven't confirmed how he's getting paid."

"Who else if not for Gallo?"

"That would be the ultimate question, I guess. But for the last six months or so, he's been doing side projects for a firm in Paris trying to hack various corporations."

"What corporations? Italian ones?"

"All over Europe," Sienna replied, pulling her laptop into her lap and backing out of all the systems and files she'd accessed. "They look like very well-protected shell companies. If I had to guess, I'd say they all link back to the same corporation."

"Have they been able to get in?"

She shook her head, altering the user logs to reflect Isa's

credentials and clearing her keystrokes. "It looks like they keep hitting different subsidiaries, hoping to find an in. But the level of security is truly impressive. Even if they could get in, I can't imagine they'd have much time to steal anything of value."

"Interesting."

"It is," she agreed. "Especially because I have no idea why my uncle would be interested in a real estate mogul based in what appears to be Bruges."

"Belgium?"

Sienna stopped short in her retreat from the couch and turned to look at Luca, raising a brow at the look on his face. "Yeah. Why?"

"Something Matteo said a few weeks ago."

"One of them was a leasing conglomerate. Clearly a subsidiary company for a larger corporation. Another was international real estate. The last one is localized to Bruges. Office buildings and commercial rental properties."

"That could prove to be a very interesting development."

Sienna frowned. "Why? Does that mean something to you?"

Luca's look of concentration melted into a smile, and he pushed off the couch, reaching down to pull her to her feet and planting a kiss on her lips.

"You might have just given me a clue to a riddle I've been trying to solve for six months."

"Okay," she replied, drawing out the word. "I have no idea what that means."

"That's okay. I do. And I think it puts me in a perfect position to wheedle some information out of my brother." He hauled her onto her toes and took her mouth again, angling her head to take the kiss deeper. "Baby girl, you're a wonder. And I'm going to take you to bed now."

She grinned as he lifted her into his arms and carried her

down the hallway. "I'll never say no to you taking me to bed."

Chapter Twenty-Three

The water smacked against the shower walls as he rinsed his hair under the spray. It wasn't quite big enough for two. At least not if your goal was a proper shower. But that hadn't been his goal the last time he'd had Sienna in here with him. She'd been pressed against the cool tile, and he'd been pressed against her.

He hadn't been able to talk her into it this morning, though. When a call sliced through his dreams, she'd jolted out of sleep, looking tired and a little frazzled. Matteo was calling an all-hands family meeting, and he needed to get back to Palermo by lunchtime.

Plenty of time to make Sienna scream his name, but she'd slipped out of bed, belted on a robe, and disappeared into the kitchen to make coffee. He shut off the water with a sigh and reached for the clean towel she'd left on the hook. Soon enough, there wouldn't be three hours of distance between them, and he could have her in his bed every night.

Toweling off, he ran a hand through his damp hair and pulled on the spare change of clothes he'd started keeping in the trunk of his car. At least now he could stop showing up at home in the same clothes as the day before and pointedly ignoring his brother's raised eyebrows.

Alexei knew, at least, that he was sleeping with his informant, and he was right that Matteo would absolutely lose his shit if he found out. Luca was probably fighting a losing battle on that front. Especially because he couldn't keep away from her. A few more weeks, a couple months at most, and this would all be over.

They were queuing up to take some big hits at Gallo, both financially and politically, before Christmas. They were the topic of today's meeting, apparently.

A plate of cornetti sat on the kitchen counter while the moka hissed and bubbled on the stove. Sienna glanced up and smiled when she saw him, the fatigue easing out of her face.

She nodded her head at the pastries. "I hope strawberry jam is still your favorite. But if not, I got hazelnut spread too."

"Which is your favorite."

Her smile widened as she took the pot off the stove and poured the fresh coffee into a mug, setting a carton of milk and a spoon next to it. Before she could step away, he grabbed the belt of her robe and pulled her forward, brushing his lips against hers gently, then taking the kiss deeper.

Holding the hot coffee pot out to her side, she pushed onto her tiptoes, snaking her free arm around his neck, and he wrapped his arms firmly around her waist to hold her against him. When he pulled back, her lips were wet and swollen, and he leaned down to nip her top lip, making her sigh.

"Are you okay?" he asked, keeping his arm tight around her waist when she moved to step away.

She stared into his eyes for a long beat, and he read hesitation in them, but she said, "Of course, *amore*. Just that someone kept me up until sunrise. You know how I hate the sunrise."

Deciding not to press the issue, he gave her a quick squeeze and released her, adding milk to his coffee and stirring it through. "What are you up to today?"

"I'm working from home, but I wanted to do more digging on that Belgian thing from last night."

"Looking for anything in particular?"

"Yeah, payment records. I can't find any from my uncle to Ciro."

Luca frowned, taking the first tentative sip of his coffee and finding it just as strong as he liked it. It warmed him through to know she seemed to remember just as much about him as he did about her.

"Maybe they're just buried deep."

"Maybe. But why would they be? It might be nothing."

"I'm sure it's not nothing." He plucked a cornetto from the plate and took a bite, savoring the bright burst of berries on his tongue. "I trust your instincts on this. Let me know if you find anything."

"You're always the first," she said, stealing a sip of his coffee and making a face. "You should just chew on the raw beans."

Luca chuckled around another bite of pastry. "I'm meeting with my brothers and Carina later today. I imagine I'll get a finalized list of our next targets. If I send them to you, can you get me more information?"

"Of course. That's what I'm here for."

A look passed over her face, and a crease formed between her brows before smoothing out again. Something was bothering her today, and she didn't want to say what.

"Sienna." He waited until her eyes lifted to meet his. "If it's too dangerous or too much, just say the word."

"No." She waved a hand in the air and stepped forward, wrapping her arms around his waist and laying her head against his chest. "It's not that. I'm just eager for all of this to be over. Nero's death has been a long time coming." She drew in a shaky breath and released it. "I guess I'm just getting impatient."

He wasn't sure that was all it was, but he didn't have time to dive into it with her right now. He'd have to make time later. He wanted to know why she kept getting that sad, distant look in her eye.

"I promise we're going to end this as soon as we can," he said, easing her back and cupping her face in his hands. "Then we'll have the rest of forever together. Until your last breath. You promised me."

Her eyes misted, and when she tilted her head up for a kiss, he obliged her, sliding his tongue against hers and slipping his hands into her hair. She fisted her hands in the fabric of his shirt at the small of his back, and her grip felt desperate.

Pulling away from her was one of the hardest things he'd done in recent memory, and he used his fingertips to trace the outline of her jaw and her cheeks and her nose. He trailed them over the rim of her lips, smiling when she kissed the pads of his fingers.

"I…"

The word love hovered on his tongue. They'd never said it to each other, not once in their short year together. He'd felt it, but something about saying it had always felt weighty. Like letting the word past his lips would propel them toward a future they might not get to have.

It should be easier now with the promise of what awaited them once Gallo was dead and Sienna was resurrected. But he couldn't force it out.

"I know," she said, turning and kissing his palm before stepping out of his embrace. "Send me those targets once you have them, and I'll let you know what else I find out about Belgium."

"I will."

She busied herself wiping up the kitchen while he pulled his jacket from the coat closet and slipped it on. With his hand on the knob, he cleared his throat, and she glanced up with a quick smile.

He forced himself to pull the door open and step into the hall, take the stairs down to the lobby and climb into his SUV, and drive the fuck away from her. He didn't remember leaving her being this hard before. Then again, he'd never fathomed losing her back then. Or the way it would split him in two.

He hadn't realized he'd still been in pieces until he saw her again and began to knit himself back together. They would get through this. He would not let Gallo take her from him this time.

The drive across the island was quick and painless at this hour of the day, and he navigated the open roads with ease, hating the distance between them with every mile. But the faster he got business done in Palermo, the sooner they could be together for real this time. And he needed that like he needed air in his fucking lungs.

Pulling into the driveway, he parked in his usual spot and grabbed his dirty clothes off the passenger seat. The air had a bite to it this close to December, and he turned up the collar of his jacket as he jogged through the courtyard gate and around to the rear entrance closest to the stairs.

He'd used this door to sneak in and out as a teen, and that year he drove all over the island to be with Sienna. It creaked with age now, but it was still better than coming in through the front door where anyone might see him.

Quickly climbing the stairs, he dumped his clothes into the dirty laundry basket and stripped off his jacket, draping it over the end of his bed. Someone would come collect it and hang it up in the right spot, but for now, he was content to let his brother think he'd been home all morning and wasn't sneaking in after being out all night.

Some days, Matteo was worse than their father with his need for control and absolute fealty. A younger, more sober version of Lorenzo Bianchi, but still with the same unforgiving, unbending rulebook. Rules only Matteo knew and only shared when he felt like it. The dance with his brother was trying on its best day.

Adjusting the hem of his sweater, Luca made his way downstairs to the study at the back of the house. There were some casino financials he could go over before he had to head to the office for this meeting. Get his head fully into work mode before he had to face Maeve and the awkwardness that had now settled between them because he kept avoiding her.

He stopped short in the doorway when he saw Matteo seated behind the enormous desk, head bent over paperwork, a finger trailing down the page as he read and copied notes on a legal pad. So much for his quiet morning.

"I thought you'd be at the office already," Luca said, strolling in and grabbing the file folder off the top of the stack he'd left on the side table.

Matteo glanced up, setting down his pen and rubbing a hand over the back of his neck. "There's another tenant moving in today, so I decided to skip the noise of it. Dom and Carina should be here in about thirty minutes."

Luca nodded, bracing himself for Matteo's inquisition about where he'd been all morning. When none came, he sank onto the leather couch and flipped open the folder.

Luca scanned the report in front of him and did a quick tally of numbers in his head. Business had leveled out at their two western casinos, and it should be picking up this time of year. He made a mental note to go out there and see if money had plateaued because there weren't as many customers or if there was another issue at play.

The northern casino where he and Alexei had tossed out the card counters was doing very well, almost enough to compensate for the downturn in the west, but he'd prefer all of the casinos to be operating at max capacity. More profits were always better, and if any of the casinos were sluggish, they needed to know why so they could fix it.

Dropping that first folder next to him on the couch, he reached for the next one, pausing when he realized Matteo was watching him. Matteo didn't acknowledge that Luca was looking at him, and Luca wondered if Matteo was really seeing him at all or staring at something else.

Luca snapped his fingers, and Matteo jumped. "You with me?"

"Yeah." Matteo rubbed his fingers over his eyes and pinched the bridge of his nose. "I'm with you. Just…never mind."

"Just what?" Luca asked.

"Nothing. It's not important."

"Since when do you consider something you have to say not important?" Luca raised a brow when Matteo didn't even rise to the bait. Was everyone in his life slowly falling apart around him? "Matteo."

"I've…just been wondering if I'm taking this in the right direction. If I'm—" He caught himself. "If we're up to the task."

Luca had no idea what to say, the silence stretching uncomfortably between them. He'd never heard Matteo doubt himself before. Not before he left, and certainly not since returning. His brother had always been a steady force, driving forward toward his goal no matter the cost.

"I think it—"

He was interrupted by voices murmuring in the hallway, and when he looked back at Matteo, the indifferent mask he usually wore was back in place, all trace of vulnerability gone like it had never existed at all.

"I hope you didn't start without us," Carina said from the doorway, seemingly reading whatever nameless thing had transpired between them and looking from Matteo to Luca with a raised brow.

Luca lifted a shoulder. He had no idea what the fuck that just was. "We'd never leave you out, *sorellina*," Luca assured her. "Not since we saw what you did to Baranello."

Carina shook her head with a smile. "Better to be afraid of me, I suppose. Alexei sends his regrets. He's getting his hands dirty today."

"Can we get this going?" Dom said. "I have a meeting with my capos later."

"My capos, you mean?" Matteo pushed to his feet and rounded the desk, leaning against it and crossing his arms over his chest.

"Until you liberate us from the Agrigento territory, they're my capos. You said you had a game plan you didn't want to share on the phone. What is it?"

"I want to twist the screws on Gallo. It doesn't do much for us to drag this out too long. The swifter his fall, the easier it'll be to build Gallo Industries back up again once we have control."

"Music to my fucking ears," Luca said, ignoring Carina's curious nudge. "Don't keep us in suspense."

"I want to target larger and larger shipments, one right after the other, over the course of the next couple weeks. Then I want to make one really big move right before Christmas."

"What kind of really big move?" Carina wondered.

"I want to derail a train."

"Come again?" Luca said.

"Gallo Industries uses trains to move things quickly across Europe."

"And you know of a large gun shipment coming in on one of them?"

Matteo shook his head at Dom. "No. But that close to the holiday, he'll be running multiple trains carrying lots of cargo. A single train is bound to be worth tens of millions of dollars. Not a bad blow for a single mission."

"Risky, though," Luca said.

"Yes," Matteo agreed. "But worth it if we can pull it off. And I think we can. We have plenty of time to plan it and an inside man to give us all the details."

"We have to be careful with that," Luca warned. "I don't want to risk blowing their cover because you're trigger-happy."

"If he ends up blown, we'll protect him."

"Assuming you can get them out in time."

"This is how we end it, Luca." Matteo braced his hands on the edge of the desk. "Unless that's not what you want anymore."

Luca balled his hands into fists on his knees. "Obviously that's what I want. It's what we all want. But my contact has been loyal. I'd prefer not to throw them to the wolves."

"Get him to coordinate which shipments we can hit in the next two weeks to do the most damage with the least amount of blowback. Can he do that?"

"Probably."

"Good." Matteo nodded as if it was settled. "Then there's the Christmas party."

"What Christmas party?" Carina asked.

"Restivo throws one every year." Matteo's grin was wolfish. "This year we've been invited. And I've got it on good authority that Gallo never misses."

"It'll be the perfect opportunity to rub elbows with his people," Luca said.

"In a place where he has to watch himself," Carina added, and Matteo nodded.

"Who's invited exactly?" Dom wanted to know.

"The four of us and our plus ones should we choose to bring any."

"Alexei in black tie," Carina said, clapping her hands with a grin. "Excellent."

"I'll send you all the details. Just make sure everyone knows to be on their best behavior," Matteo said, pinning first Dom and then Carina with a look.

Carina drew an X over her heart, and Dom rolled his eyes.

"Great. That's all I have, so—"

"Actually, I have something else," Luca said, watching Matteo closely. "Curious what you might know about several shell companies across Europe tied back to a corporation based in Bruges."

Chapter Twenty-Four

She tapped her fingers impatiently on the steering wheel, eyes flicking to the clock on the dash. The man she was here for had deviated from his normal routine. As a result, she'd spent the last hour watching three old women decorate a scraggly Christmas tree in front of a trinket shop while her target was balls deep in his mistress.

According to his credit card records, he drove from Catania to the small village of Trabia, halfway between Cefalù and Palermo, every two weeks. Once he arrived, he bought lunch at a little seafood place on the water and rented a hotel room across the street.

Today, however, he'd pulled even with the curb, climbed out, and jogged in the wrong direction. Sienna thought at first he might have made her tail, even though she was careful to keep her distance. It's not like she needed to follow him. She knew where he'd end up either way. But she didn't want to let him out of her sight.

She'd watched him stop in the middle of the sidewalk, eyes sweeping back and forth. His watchfulness made her nervous. But he wasn't watching for her, face splitting into a wide grin when a brunette easily ten years his junior rushed into his arms.

They kissed, his hands sliding down to squeeze her ass, and Sienna reached for the door handle, prepared to follow them into the restaurant. But they'd turned and disappeared into the hotel instead.

She checked the clock again. One hour and eleven minutes ago.

The vial of hazelnut oil was burning a hole in her pocket. If they skipped lunch and she missed her window, she might not get another chance. She knew from Luca they were stepping up their assault. Planning multiple attacks to dig deeper into her uncle's pockets.

This might all be over soon, and she wanted to take down as many of the bastards as she could before it was finished. It had to be today. Quick, clean, accidental.

The man she'd shot in the alley hadn't raised a single red flag. Getting mugged and murdered with your dick out wasn't all that uncommon in that area. As far as she could tell, there hadn't been any internal chatter about it either. She needed this death to be as equally unremarkable.

That's why she'd chosen hazelnut oil. It was relatively flavorless when added to the right food, and he was incredibly allergic. She remembered the way he'd panicked, thinking he'd eaten a tiny bite of toasted hazelnut in a salad on her uncle's yacht once.

Dying that way was one of his worst nightmares, he'd later confessed to her father. It seemed a fitting end for him, considering how he betrayed them all. It also made her wonder if anyone in her father's inner circle had been loyal or if they'd all been spies for her uncle.

Movement out of the corner of her eye drew her gaze, and she watched the woman reach up to rub what Sienna guessed was lipstick off the corner of the man's mouth. He reached for the woman's hand and brought her knuckles to his lips. The sight of the intimacy made her lip curl back over her teeth.

Her father and mother used to show affection like that. Carlo Gallo could not be in the same room with his wife without touching her in some way. A hand on her back, a brush of fingertips on her arm, a kiss on her temple. Their relationship was a stark contrast to Nero's strained and dutiful marriage to his own wife.

Her parents had been happy and still madly in love after nearly forty years together. This man in front of her had obliterated it with the twitch of a finger. He didn't deserve happiness. And now his mistress was going to get a taste of what it felt like to watch someone you love die and then be forced into the shadows.

The love birds watched for a break in the traffic and then darted across the street to their usual restaurant. Sienna waited for a count of five before following them.

It wasn't terribly busy. They'd caught a lull between the lunch and dinner rush, and most of the tables were empty. Maybe their choice to fuck before eating would work to her advantage.

When she noticed them being seated next to the rocks leading down to the water, she requested a similar table, weaving through the mostly empty dining room and onto the patio. There were heaters dispersed evenly throughout and lights strung through a pergola overhead, and she imagined they would give a pretty, ethereal feeling to the space in the dark.

She sat at the next table with her back to them and ordered a glass of wine she had no intention of finishing. Once the waiter moved away, she leaned back, letting the wind carry their conversation to her ears.

"—thought about it some more?"

The man sighed. "We've been over this. I told you I can't."

"No. You told me you'd think about it."

"*Tesoro*," he cooed, and Sienna rolled her eyes at the endearment. "I am stuck with my wife. You know this. I've never been anything but up-front about it."

"I know, Maximo. But it's been two years. We would be so much happier together than with them. I've already found a lawyer. I can file paperwork before the holiday."

"Don't ruin today talking about what we cannot have, *tesoro*. Let's just enjoy our lunch and meet again after Christmas."

He signaled for the waiter, silencing their conversation, and Sienna took a sip of her wine, pretending to study the menu in front of her. The scallop risotto actually sounded good. Too bad she didn't want to linger long enough to eat a full meal.

She signaled the waiter and ordered a slice of tiramisu. There was never a bad time of day for dessert, and she wanted to finish eating and leave before they did. When the patio was quiet again, conversation between them slowly resumed.

"I can't believe I'm not even going to see you again until next year. That's too long, Maximo."

"I have to travel for work, and then there's the holiday," Maximo replied, irritation edging his voice. "Maybe we need a break from each other if this is how you're going to act whenever you don't get your way, Francesca."

Sienna imagined Francesca scowling when she made a disgruntled noise low in her throat. The topic shifted to something less charged when the waiter arrived with their lunch and her tiramisu. They spoke of exchanging gifts and how her job was going and if his sister was still sick.

A large group spread out between three tables on the other end of the patio, and their chatter cut off the conversation at her back. Reaching into her purse, she pulled out the small vial of hazelnut oil and unstoppered it.

She was debating how exactly to dose the coffee they'd just ordered between the kitchen and the table when Francesca suddenly excused herself to take a phone call. Once she was gone, Sienna readjusted her hair and her glasses and turned to offer him a tentative smile.

As soon as Maximo caught her eye, he smiled in return. When it was clear he didn't recognize her, she leaned in close enough to feel his body heat and asked, "Do you have the time? My phone died."

He turned to reach into his own pocket, but it wasn't enough time to upend the vial into what was left of his wine. Her heartbeat quickened. Francesca wouldn't talk on the phone forever.

"It's almost four." He set his phone on the table and turned more fully to face her. "You have beautiful eyes. So big and blue."

Sienna made a show of blushing, averting her eyes before meeting his gaze again. "Thank you. And thank you for the time as well."

"It was my pleasure. To help a woman as beautiful as you when she's in distress."

Sienna gave him a coy smile. "Aren't you on a date?"

Maximo grinned, leaning closer to whisper, "We're just old friends. Perhaps you and I could be something else?"

"Could we?" She shifted, and he did the same, twisting away from the table and dropping his gaze to her mouth. "What would you like to be?"

"Well." He licked his lips. "I know what I'd like to taste."

His eyes darkened when she rounded her mouth into an O. When he leaned forward, she quickly dumped the entire contents of the vial into his glass, grateful his body hid her hand from the view of the other table.

She expected him to go for her lips—Luca would hate that, she'd have to remember not to tell him—but instead he brushed a soft kiss on her cheek and whispered in her ear, "Maybe I'll see you here again sometime soon."

Sienna pulled back and smiled, trailing her tongue over her lower lip, satisfied when his eyes dropped to her mouth again. "Maybe you will." When the waiter stepped up to the table with their dessert, she leaned back. "Thanks again for your help."

"My pleasure."

They both returned to their own tables seconds before Francesca stepped back onto the patio. She stalked across the space and flopped down into her chair with a huff. Sienna didn't care to listen to whatever Francesca was getting ready to complain about, so she dropped bills on the table and pushed to her feet.

She passed them, turning to shoot a flirty wink at Maximo behind Francesca's back. Maximo's eyes darted from Francesca to her, and he smiled over the rim of his wineglass before taking a sip.

Forcing herself not to hurry, Sienna circled back toward the front door and around the side, stopping behind the privacy fence climbing with greenery that shielded the patio from the view of the street.

"Maximo!" Francesca shrieked. "Oh my God!"

There was the scramble of chairs scraping over the stone and desperate shouts for someone to call an ambulance. Francesca was sobbing and pleading with Maximo to just breathe.

Shifting, trying to find a clear view through the climbing vines, Sienna glimpsed Francesca sitting on the ground with Maximo's head in her lap. Francesca was stroking his hair and talking to him. But when Maximo's hand fell limply to his side, she let out a long, pained wail.

Whatever twinge of guilt Sienna might have felt was overcome by the satisfaction of knowing another one of her family's murderers was dead. His final moments might have been brief, but she hoped he suffered through them.

Crossing the road, she climbed behind the wheel and fished her phone out of her purse. A few missed messages from Luca while she'd been in the restaurant filled the screen. Pulling away from the curb, she decided to call him, smiling when his voice filled her ear.

Chapter Twenty-Five

"Hey, baby girl."

"Hey yourself," Sienna replied, and Luca smiled. "What are you up to right now?"

"Working from home. Matteo is out, and the house is quiet. A nice change of pace. What are you doing?"

"Just finished lunch. Want to meet up?"

Luca checked his watch. He wanted nothing more. But there was no way he could squeeze in a six-hour drive and spending time with her today. And he had a late meeting with Matteo and Dom to plan their next series of hits that took staying over at her place off the table too.

"Unfortunately, I can't. I'm swamped and don't have the time."

"What if I came to you?"

The smile in her voice had him doing the same. "To Palermo?"

"Yeah. Actually, what if I'm already here?"

Luca pushed off the couch and moved to the window looking out over the back of the estate as if he might somehow be able to see her. "You're in the city?"

"I'm close. I'm in Trabia, and I want to celebrate. With you."

"You killed someone."

Her laugh was light and sweet and made him ache for her. "Don't say it like that."

"Like what?"

"Like you're proud of me or something."

He grinned. "But I am proud of you."

"You're terrible." She chuckled. "Do you have a few hours to spare for me? I can get us a room at that hotel close to the casino. The one with the good room service."

"Come to the villa."

There was a pause as his words sank in. It was risky, inviting her to the house. Even with Matteo off island for the day, there was still staff wandering around. But now that he'd said it out loud, he wanted nothing else.

"That's an unnecessary risk, Luca."

"It'll be fine. No one knows who you are or that we were seeing each other before. We'll use your alias."

"I don't want you to call me Anna while you fuck me," she snapped.

"That's not what I meant. I'm not required to explain you to the staff, Sienna."

"But they'll talk. And if your brother finds out?"

Luca shoved a hand into his pocket and stalked back to the couch. "If they talk, they'll tell him I had a hot blonde named Anna over while he was out. I'm not a child, and this is my home too." His heart beat wildly in the silence. "If you really don't want—"

"What's the address?"

A wide grin split his face. "I'll text it to you."

Disconnecting the call, he shot her a quick text with the address and directions for parking in the lower garage if she wanted her car out of sight. Work forgotten, he paced the foyer until the rumble of an engine caught his attention. Peeking out the front window, he smiled when he saw a flash of black pull around the side of the house to the lower garage instead of Matteo's bright red Alfa Romeo.

Circling away from the front of the house toward the side entrance he'd guided her to, he pulled open the heavy door just as she was making her way up the path. She looked nervous, but she smiled when she saw him.

He held his hand out for hers and laced their fingers together when she laid her hand into his palm. Drawing her in close, he brushed a soft kiss against her lips and breathed her in.

"You actually came."

"I'm not sure there's much of anything I wouldn't do for you," she murmured, pressing another kiss to his lips. "But we should probably go inside."

He drew her through the door and bolted it. There was something indescribably exhilarating about leading her through his home, past things that were familiar and important to him. Her hand was warm and solid in his as they climbed the stairs and turned down the long hallway to his bedroom.

Motioning for her to go ahead of him, he closed and locked the door, leaning back against it. She spun in a slow circle, studying the room and pausing when her eyes caught sight of something that had been sitting on top of his dresser for the last three years.

Moving forward, she reached out to touch it, pulling her hand back at the last second and curling it into a fist. He crossed the room, pressing against her from behind and wrapping his arms around her waist.

"I thought I lost this." She brushed her fingertips over the antique hair clip, making it wobble so the tiny gems caught the light.

"You were wearing it the last time I saw you." He brushed his lips against her jaw. "When I surprised you for your birthday."

Picking it up, she turned it over gently in her fingers. "I remember every moment I spent with you that day, but I don't remember wearing this."

"It flew off the blanket when I shook it out. I figured I'd give it back to you the next time we were together." His hands tightened on her waist, and she leaned back against him. "Then it was all I had left of you."

"It's been three years." She set it carefully back on the dresser. "You could have gotten rid of it. Moved on. Why didn't you?"

He turned her in his arms, pressing his fingers under her chin and tilting her head back until she met his gaze. "I won't pretend I was a saint these last three years, Sienna. But I didn't want anyone else. None of them were you."

"But you'll move on eventually. Get married, have kids."

He frowned at the tears swimming in her eyes. She said it like he'd have those things without her. Except he didn't want them with anyone else.

"I wanted all of that with you, Sienna. No one else. No one before and no one since. Only you. And once Nero's gone and you're free again, if you don't want that anymore, that's fine. I'll take you in whatever way I can have you. But I won't lose you again."

She opened her mouth to speak, but changed her mind and closed it again. Wrapping her arms around his neck, she drew him down for a kiss. He let her take her time, building it slowly with teasing nips of her teeth and the soft glide of her tongue and the scratch of her fingernails through the hair at the base of his skull.

He slid his hands under the hem of her sweater, and she sighed, leaning into him and taking more from his mouth. He would eagerly give her whatever she wanted whenever she wanted it.

Sliding his hands up until they met the underside of her bra strap, he quickly undid it with his fingers and moved his hand around her ribs, working his fingers inside the loosened cup and pinching her nipple lightly. She hummed against his lips, and he smiled, giving her nipple a subtle twist that made her breath hitch.

When she broke the kiss, he wasted no time dragging her sweater up her body and tugging it off over her head. She made quick work of her bra on her own, and then she was shoving his suit jacket off his shoulders.

Her fingers were warm where they brushed his skin as she worked down the buttons of his shirt, and he groaned when she tugged it out of his pants and splayed her fingers over his abs.

"I thought I knew what I wanted when I came back to Sicily," Sienna said, trailing her fingertips up to his shoulders and pushing his shirt down his arms. "Now I'm not so sure."

"I told you Nero's death would be yours," he assured her, working open the catch of her jeans and sliding down the zipper. "Your cousins too, if you need them."

"I know." She hissed when he slipped his hand inside her panties and stroked her clit with his middle finger. "But I don't want to think about him right now. I only want to think about you and the way you touch me. The way I dreamed about you touching me every day for three years."

Luca used his free hand to shove her jeans and panties over her hips, smiling when she stumbled in a desperate attempt to free herself from them. He nudged her back against the dresser and used his knee to spread her thighs apart so he could sink his finger inside her.

"So wet for me already," he murmured against her cheek,

trailing kisses to her earlobe and tracing the shell of her ear with the tip of his tongue.

He added a second finger and slid them deep, grinding his palm against her clit until she shuddered. She was perfect in every way, and it was a miracle he'd managed to live without her for so long. Without the sound of her voice or the feel of her skin or the way she made him think and reason and see beyond what was right in front of him.

Her fingernails dug into his biceps as he stroked his fingers in and out, and he leaned down to capture her nipple between his teeth, swirling his tongue over the tip as he slowly eased it away from her body.

"Luca," she gasped, nails digging deeper.

"Hmm?"

"I… That…"

Releasing her nipple, he grinned, pressing a kiss to it and making her jerk. "Use your words, baby girl."

Her laugh was throaty and deep, and he couldn't resist capturing her lips. No time for slow now. He wanted to spark that fire in her that he loved so much. The one that made her writhe under him and beg for more and scream his name.

Her legs wobbled, and he thrust his fingers deeper, faster, working his thumb over her clit. She rocked her hips each time he made contact until she was riding his hand on her tiptoes, chasing each urgent thrust of his fingers inside her.

"Come on my fingers, baby girl. I want to feel you soak my hand before I slide my cock inside you."

"Yes," she replied with a shuddering breath. "Yes, Luca. Please."

At her plea, he shifted the angle of his fingers, curling them up so each time he pulled out of her, the tips of his fingers dragged against her G-spot. She wrapped her arms around his neck and pressed her chest to his, her hips still grinding against his hand.

"That's it, Sienna. Come for me," he murmured against her ear, sliding an arm around her waist to hold her upright.

He thrust deep inside her, grinding against her clit, and when she came, she buried her face against the side of his neck and screamed his name.

"Am I dead?" she panted, and he chuckled. "I think I might be dead."

When he slid his fingers free of her, she groaned. "If you felt that, you're not dead."

"Sometimes I think you're trying to kill me."

"Wouldn't death by orgasm be the best way to go, though?"

He lifted her into his arms as she laughed and carried her to the bed. Setting her down on the edge, he smiled when she immediately scooted back against the pillows, her eyes trailing down his chest to where he worked open the button of his pants.

She wet her lips as she watched him, and if he wasn't hard for her already, he would have been in that instant, with the hungry look in her eyes. Climbing up after her, he settled himself between her spread thighs and leaned down to take her lips again.

"I used to spend all my free time dreaming of ways to get you into my bed. This bed."

"All of it?" she wondered, wrapping her legs around his waist and hissing when he slid the length of his cock up and down her slit.

"Most of it," he conceded. "I wanted you in my world, Sienna. You were already mine, but I wanted everyone to know it." Tracing the length of her pussy with the tip of his cock, he buried himself slowly inside her, dipping his head to nibble her bottom lip. "Soon enough, they will."

"They will what?" she gasped, rocking her hips up to meet his deep thrust.

"They'll know you belong to me."

"Luca," she whispered. "I—"

He slid out and back in with a brutal pump of his hips, and her words were lost on a strangled gasp. Later. They'd hash out exactly how they would resurrect her later. Right now, he wanted to concentrate on the feel of her body under his. The way her pussy gripped his cock, the way her nails scored down his back, the way her breath fanned warm against his shoulder.

He'd imagined having her in his bed so many times, and now she was here. He didn't want to waste a second being anywhere but in this moment with her.

Leaning up on his hand, he slid his cock in and out at a steady pace, each thrust inside her hard and deep, loving the way she tightened around him each time he bottomed out in her, her heels digging into his ass, urging him faster. He captured her nipple between his fingers and twisted it lightly, increasing the pressure until she arched off the bed and whimpered.

"You are the most beautiful woman I've ever seen."

Her eyes opened, cloudy with lust and that beautiful hazel hidden behind the unnatural shade of blue, but she was here, she was his. Forever. Something he wanted to make sure she didn't forget.

Slamming his hips against hers, he squeezed her breast, thumb and finger working her nipple until she was vibrating under him, the muscles in her neck straining against the pain and the contact of his pelvis against her clit.

"Come for me, Sienna," he commanded. "Show me what I do to you."

He slammed home, giving her nipple another rough twist and groaning when her pussy spasmed on his cock with her orgasm. Her back arched, her skin flushed, her chest rising and falling with each panting breath. He'd never seen anyone more perfect.

Covering her body with his and grinding his cock gently inside her, he peppered kisses across her collarbone. Dipping his tongue into the hollow of her throat, he tilted his head and nibbled up the side of her neck across her scar.

"Luca," she whispered, her body wrapped around him.

"Hmm?"

"You are everything I ever wanted. I'm sorry we didn't get more time together."

Rolling off her, he settled back against the headboard and tugged her into his lap, shifting her until she was straddling him. Pressing against the small of her back, he rocked her hips forward then pulled them down, filling her again.

"We have all the time in the world, Sienna."

He pressed a kiss between her breasts, rocking her hips against his until she took control of the movements. Bracing her hands on his shoulders, she leveraged herself up and back down again, riding him at her own pace, eyes staring into his.

"If we never get another moment like this, it won't matter," she said softly. "Because this one was perfect."

Something in her tone settled into his chest like a heavy weight. She sounded like she was saying goodbye. But he didn't ever intend to say goodbye to her again. They would continue their assault on Nero, weaken him and Gallo Industries. Sienna would have her revenge, and then they could build that life together they always talked about. There was no other way this was going to end. He wouldn't allow it.

Snaking his hand up her thigh, he circled a finger over her clit and she jerked, dropping her forehead against his and riding him faster, more urgently.

"Luca," she breathed.

"I know, baby girl," he whispered, fingers digging into the

skin of her hip while he worked her clit with rough strokes. "Come for me one more time."

He gritted his teeth against his own release. He'd wait to follow her over the edge, wait to make sure she had everything she needed before he took for himself. Bracketing her clit with his fingers, he rubbed it quickly before squeezing it, delighting in the way her hips jerked and she slammed down onto him.

"Fuck, Luca."

"That's the idea," he said, squeezing again, her thighs quivering against his. "Do it for me, Sienna. Come nice and hard on my cock, baby girl."

"Yes," she panted, fingernails digging into his neck.

When he squeezed her clit a third time, her whole body went taut, and her violent, shuddering orgasm ripped his own from him until his vision dimmed and he saw stars. She collapsed against him, burying her face in his neck, and he circled her waist with his arms, pulling her in close.

"This is all going to be over soon. You trust me on that, right?"

"I do," she assured him, her words muffled against his skin. "When are you making your next hit?"

"We're doing three at once in two days."

"He's going to hate that."

Luca smiled, running his fingers through her hair. "Yeah. But I'm eager to get this over with." His phone signaled from his pants pocket at the foot of the bed, but he tightened his hold when she moved to scoot off him. "Where do you think you're going?"

"You should probably get that, and I should head out."

When she moved away again, he released her, watching her collect her clothes from around the room and disappear into the bathroom. He heard water run into the sink before it was drowned out by the sound of his ringing phone.

Shifting to the end of the bed, he dug it out of his pocket and checked the display. Matteo. The phone went silent and then almost instantly began ringing a third time. Casting his eyes to the ceiling, Luca accepted the call and pressed the phone to his ear.

"Where have you been?" Matteo demanded before Luca could even speak.

"Your first call was less than two minutes ago," Luca replied smoothly, glancing up when the bathroom door opened. "What do you want?"

"The ferry just docked, so I should be home soon. Did you finish going over the document I sent you about the company in France I want to buy?"

"I did. I made some notes. We can talk about it when you get home. Bye, Matteo."

Disconnecting the call, he held his hand out to Sienna, smiling when she immediately pushed away from the door and crossed the room to stand in front of him. She cupped his face in her hands and leaned down to press a quick kiss to his lips.

"I really should go," she whispered, her voice catching and reviving that heavy feeling in his chest.

He nodded, dressing quickly and leading her back down the stairs to the side door. She stepped out into the chilly afternoon and jogged quickly down the path to the lower garage, peeking at him over her shoulder before disappearing around the bend.

One day very soon, they were going to have the freedom to stay, to not sneak off and wonder when they might see each other again. Gallo's end drew ever closer, but Luca didn't see any harm in speeding up the inevitable.

Chapter Twenty-Six

Sienna stared at the clock in the corner of her computer screen and tapped her fingernails impatiently on the top of her desk. Three minutes and twenty-seven seconds, and she'd be able to sneak out and avoid giving Ciro that update she kept promising him.

So far she'd done more work on helping Luca and looking into Ciro than working on Ciro's project. She didn't even know enough about the defense systems to lie, at least not convincingly, and she didn't want to admit to him she hadn't even bothered to touch it. There was too much on her plate right now to worry about how Ciro would feel if she told him she'd pushed this project to the back burner.

Luca and his family had successfully pilfered over ten million euros in illegal weapons from the shipments they'd hit over the last ten days and trashed hundreds of millions in freight in the process. And when she wasn't working, she was busy finding them new shipments to hit when her uncle changed routes, drivers, or locations. Shipments that wouldn't signal the presence of a mole inside Gallo Industries. At least not right away.

They were speeding toward the end of the year, and soon Nero would be weak enough that their final plan could be put into motion. Then it was her time to shine. She knew exactly how she was going to do it.

Her uncle worked well into the night most of the time, but she'd found a way to monitor the activity on his credentials and knew his pattern. He worked the latest on Mondays and Fridays.

All she had to do was make up an excuse to stay late on a Monday night. Then she'd use Ciro's cloned credentials to authorize the elevator to take her to the top floor, casually walk down the hallway with her purse over her shoulder and the gun inside it, step into her uncle's office, and shoot him in the face.

He wouldn't suspect her, he might not even recognize her, and she wouldn't give him time to reach for his own weapon. She figured she'd have just enough time to watch him bleed out.

The problem with that plan was how much she doubted it now. She'd been so sure of it before leaving Germany. It was the best conceivable way to make him pay for what he did. It might not give her answers, but it would give her the satisfaction of knowing that the man who ordered the annihilation of her family had paid with his life. A few months ago, that was all she needed.

But with Luca in the picture, things were different. He had his own wants and desires, and the closer they got to the end, the more they clashed with hers. Even if he didn't know it.

She didn't care if Nero's death looked like a suicide. She didn't care if Stefano and Dante were dead too so the Bianchis could easily assume control of the company. Or at least she didn't care before. Now what happened in the aftermath of her uncle's death was all she could think about.

The Bianchis were going to the president's Christmas

party in a few days. Her uncle never missed it, and since Luca planned to come over after the party, she knew he'd give her every detail of what happened. The walls were closing in on Nero Gallo.

The papers had not been kind to his recent string of accidents, blaming faulty equipment, careless safety checks, or inexperienced drivers, depending on which column you read. Just this morning, she'd seen an article giving credence to rumors that a few government contracts were in jeopardy of being revoked due to safety concerns.

Behind the scenes, Nero was scrambling. He was losing commercial business—people wanted reliable freight companies to ensure packages and merchandise were delivered without incident this time of year—and he faced the prospect of losing several hefty government contracts on top of it.

In a recent meeting, her manager had hinted that the project she'd been hired specifically to work on for a customer-facing shipping experience was in danger of being plugged. Apparently investors were concerned and thinking of backing out.

The tide was turning on Gallo Industries, and people were keeping their distance. Her uncle wouldn't breathe for much longer. She was sure of it, and so, it seemed, was Luca.

The clock rolled over to five, and she reached into her bottom drawer for her bag. Isa scrambled past her a few moments later, refusing to make eye contact as usual. Sienna shook her head. She would most definitely not miss Isa when this was all said and done.

Jack stretched on the other side of the partition and ran a hand through his hair. Luckily, Ciro wasn't back from his latest meeting yet. She could still make a clean break and avoid another conversation.

"Got anything fun going on tonight after work?"

Sienna slipped into her coat and adjusted the collar. "Laundry. The funnest."

Jack smiled, fastening the large buttons of his wool jacket and stooping to grab his briefcase. Slinging her purse over her shoulder, Sienna followed him to the elevator.

"Any plans for the holidays?"

Sienna stalled in her reach for the elevator button before quickly recovering and mashing it with her finger. "Not really a big Christmas person. You?"

"My better half wants to go to the Christmas markets in Vienna."

"And you don't?" Sienna guessed, getting on the elevator when the doors slid open with a whoosh.

"We did the markets in Rome last year. They were bad enough. Vienna is bigger, farther." He paused to rub a hand over the back of his neck. "I'm already certain I know who will win this argument."

Sienna laughed. "I guess you'd better buy the tickets and pack your bags, then."

"Before the week is out."

They swiped their badges at security and split off in different directions on the sidewalk. Sienna popped the collar on her coat against the wind before pulling her phone from her bag and scrolling through her messages from Luca.

They were hitting two more shipments before the party, and Luca wanted to know if anything had changed or if there was anything they needed to watch out for. She let him know she'd check when she got home and then stuffed her hands into her pockets.

She needed to go grocery shopping, but with night settling in, the wind was too biting to think about making a stop now. She'd order something and make a list for tomorrow. Turning toward her apartment, she stopped short when she saw Ciro huddled with Drago and half hidden by the potted bushes she'd jumped behind the day she ran into Luca.

Calculating the fastest way around them without being spotted, she stepped to her right, but it was too late. Ciro made eye contact and then gave her a tentative grin. Drago glanced in the direction of Ciro's gaze, the frown on his face melting into a strained, tight-lipped smile.

She waved, prepared to make a hasty retreat and use the excuse that they looked deep in conversation, but Drago motioned her over. Sienna took a deep breath and weaved through the people leaving the office. She hadn't wanted to come face to face with Ciro, let alone both of them.

"Heading out?" Drago asked, even though it was clear she was.

"I am. I have a bottle of Nero d'Avola at home waiting for me."

"A perfect choice," Ciro commended. "One of my favorites as well. Well, we won't keep y—"

"What progress is being made on our side project? I haven't heard many updates on it from Ciro."

"Right," she said when Ciro tensed. "That's because I haven't given him any. I was swamped last week with all the changes coming through for the customer app. But it seems that one might be put on hold soon, so I can prioritize this for you."

Drago shared a look with Ciro, who seemed to relax the tiniest bit, and pinned her with a hard stare again. "That would be fine. When can we expect to know more?"

Sienna shifted on her feet, tucking her face further into the safety of her hood, away from the wind and Drago's searching eyes. "Hopefully it won't be too long once I can get in there and have a deeper look. In my initial browse, their security looked very comprehensive. What you want might not be possible."

Drago's scowl deepened, and Sienna had to force herself not to shrink away. Ciro reached up and patted her shoulder with a gloved hand.

"You do your best to get us as close as possible to our end goal, and we can handle the rest."

"Is there anything specific you're looking for?"

Drago turned sharply to face her and took a step forward, invading her personal space. "We've already told you what we want. Access to their systems to test their security. There's nothing more you need to know."

She flicked a glance at Ciro, who looked genuinely worried. This was the Drago she knew and remembered. Quick to anger, quicker to lash out.

"Of course." Clenching her hands into fists in her pocket, she forced a smile into her voice. "I only meant if there was a specific part of their system you wanted me to focus on, I could build a more targeted program rather than take a general approach that may or may not give you what you're looking for."

Drago studied her, his eyes searching her face, and it sent a chill down her spine. She needed to get out of there. If he recognized her, she'd be dead before the morning, and Luca and his family might very well have to begin their assault again.

"Drago, no need to scare the poor girl," Ciro said, moving to stand next to her and wrapping his arm around her shoulders. "We asked for her help, and she'll give it. Won't you, Anna?"

"You asked for her help," Drago snarled. "I want an update by the end of next week. Or I'll take matters into my own hands."

He pinned her with another searching stare before turning and disappearing into the crowd of people. Sienna sagged into Ciro's side when her knees wobbled before righting herself again.

"Sorry. I thought it would be okay to shuffle things a bit. I didn't mean to make him angry."

"No, no. He's just upset about something else entirely. I'm sure he didn't mean to take it out on you. I'll speak with him." Ciro paused for a beat. "Are you all right?"

"I think so." Sienna took a step away and gave him a bolstering smile. "I do want to help in any way I can."

Ciro reached up to brush a strand of hair off her face, tucking it behind her ear and trailing his fingertips across her jaw to her chin. "Of course you do." He looked off in the direction Drago had disappeared and lowered his voice. "Truthfully, the part of the system we most want to concentrate on is the client records."

Sienna nodded her head knowingly. "That makes sense. You can never be too careful with your buyer data."

Ciro smiled. "Exactly. And once you help us crack this, I'm going to take you out to a nice dinner to celebrate. And I won't take no for an answer."

"Dinner sounds nice." She leaned into his hand when he rubbed it down the length of her arm from shoulder to elbow. "But you should probably know I never skip dessert."

She turned for home and left him grinning in the middle of the sidewalk. Ciro was much easier to distract than Drago. And she had a twisting feeling in the pit of her stomach that she might have said exactly the wrong thing to dial up the suspicion that was clearly already hovering around the edges where she was concerned.

She needed to be more careful. She was of no use to Luca and the Bianchis if she was outed as a mole and lost her access. And Drago would hardly stop at getting her fired.

Chapter Twenty-Seven

Adjusting his cuff links, Luca looked up at the sound of heels on the tile floor, smiling at the Bianchi women. Well, Emilia wasn't a Bianchi yet, but she finally had a ring on her finger. A pretty little diamond that seemed to suit her perfectly.

"Emilia, you're a vision," Luca assured her, grinning when she blushed.

"What about me?" Carina wondered, turning so the sequins on her dress caught the light.

"Perfect as always."

"You're not so bad yourself," Carina replied. "Too bad you can't bring your mystery woman with us to the party."

Luca's eyebrows shot up, and Carina shrugged.

"Alexei told me. And I told Emilia."

Emilia blanched and held her hands out in front of her. "I haven't told anyone. Not even your brother."

"Really? I would have told Alexei right away."

"Told me what?" Alexei asked, tugging at the bowtie of his tux and looking as uncomfortable and out of his element as Luca had ever seen him.

"About Luca's mystery woman," Carina said, reaching for Alexei's hand and pulling it away from his neck. "Leave that alone. I just finished tying it."

"I should sit this one out. I look ridiculous," Alexei grumbled.

"You look delicious," Carina assured him. "Just think, if you behave yourself and don't stab anyone, you get to undress me later."

"I bet I would get to undress you even if I did stab someone," Alexei challenged, wrapping an arm around Carina's waist and hauling her onto her toes.

Emilia chuckled, and Luca pretended to gag. "Please. You'll make me lose my dinner."

Dom and Matteo appeared at the end of the hall, and Emilia froze next to Luca.

"He hates me," she whispered when Matteo raked her with a disapproving frown.

"He hates everyone," Carina said with a wave of her hand. "Don't take it personally. Besides, you'll be family by the summer, and then he'll have to shut up about it. Christ knows we're all eager for that day."

Luca snorted in agreement and turned to his brothers as they joined them. Dom reached for Emilia's hand, running his thumb over the stone of her engagement ring before bringing it to his lips.

"Ready?" Matteo asked, twisting his watch on his wrist. "Maeve is going to meet us there."

"Maeve is coming? Why?"

Matteo glanced at Luca as he pulled on his cashmere coat and stepped out into the cold. "Because I need a beautiful woman on my arm. Who isn't my sister," he added at Carina's disgruntled squeak. "You should have found one yourself."

To their credit, no one who knew about Sienna so much as

twitched at the mention of Luca not having a date.

"Suddenly you care about everyone's love life?" Dom asked.

"No, I care about appearances."

Luca ignored his brothers' petty squabble and climbed behind the wheel of his SUV, raising a brow when Carina and Alexei scrambled into the backseat.

"What are you doing? I'm staying in Catania after the party."

"I figured," Carina said, reaching for Alexei's hand and scooting closer. "But if I have to ride both ways with them, I'll be the one who ends up stabbing people tonight."

Chuckling, Luca started the car and pulled out of the driveway. One day, Matteo was going to have to reckon with his utter distaste for relationships and find his own bride. Luca was very much looking forward to watching his brother crumble under that particular pressure.

The ride was silent save for the occasional snippet of conversation that drifted up from the backseat. It was dark by the time they arrived in Catania, and the party was in full swing, a line of cars snaking up the long driveway as drivers dropped off their passengers and left through what looked like a bricked rear drive.

"Jesus," Carina whistled as the house came into view. "Looks like Restivo is putting his campaign funds to good use."

The already imposing house was tastefully decorated with thousands of fairy lights. They hung from the eaves and crawled over bushes and wrapped around columns. Candles ringed by festive wreaths flickered in every window, and when Luca climbed out of the driver's seat and handed his keys to the valet, the soft sound of Christmas music drifted over the hum of conversation.

They met up with Matteo, Dom, and Emilia at the end of

the walk and followed the line inside. The music was louder in there, but so was the conversation, flowing around them and filling the space.

White-jacketed waiters carried canapés and cocktails from room to room on silver trays. The men were dressed in tuxes, and the women were wrapped in sequins and furs and expensive jewelry.

"I feel underdressed," Emilia said, running a hand over her hip when a woman walked past them in a pouffy ball gown with a fur stole hugging her shoulders.

"You look stunning," Dom assured her, wrapping an arm around her waist and turning to Matteo. "But I'd rather not linger too long."

"We need to see and be seen, Domenico," Matteo said, eyes scanning the guests. "Especially by Nero. Have a glass of champagne and relax."

Luca stopped a passing waiter and started handing out glasses, clinking his against Emilia's and giving her a wink. She smiled, taking a sip.

"Just try not to drink too much," Matteo added, eyeing Emilia. "We don't want loose lips ruining this for us, either."

With a roll of his eyes, Dom led Emilia away, and Carina and Alexei followed.

"You're such a prick, Matteo," Luca said before slipping into the crowd and smiling politely at anyone who made eye contact.

He did as instructed, making small talk, introducing himself. Within an hour, he'd met three bankers and their wives, a real estate investor, and the COO of Italy's largest privately owned company. Restivo certainly didn't lack friends in high places.

By the second hour, Luca had exchanged business cards with two men in finance and one whose business dealt almost exclusively in corporate takeovers. Something Matteo obviously had a thirst for.

Dom found him halfway through hour three, looking ready to crawl out of his skin. Scowling, he grabbed a glass off a passing tray and downed half of it with one swallow.

"Is Nero even showing up to this fucking thing?"

Emilia stepped closer when several heads turned and patted Dom's chest. "You're doing great, love."

"My patience is wearing thin," Dom replied, wrapping an arm around her shoulders and pulling her tight against his side. "Any sign of him?" he asked Luca.

"Not that I've seen. But I admit I've been busy schmoozing and haven't been paying much attention. Restivo has quite the crowd gathered tonight."

Dom snorted, taking another sip of champagne. "A bunch of rich suits."

"Rich suits we need to be connected to if we're going to make much headway in the coming year," Luca reminded him. "That's the whole point of this."

"I thought the whole point of this was to bring Gallo to his knees?"

"In the short term. You have to hold on to the power once you seize it. A concept you're not unfamiliar with. How are things in Agrigento?"

"They're fine. We've got some men who are less enthusiastic than others, but nothing I can't handle." Emilia's brow pinched into a frown, and Dom kissed her forehead. "Don't worry, kitten. I've got plans to motivate them."

"I know. That's what makes me worry."

Dom gave her waist a squeeze, opening his mouth to speak and closing it again when she stiffened.

"Isn't that him?" she asked, gesturing across the room with her chin.

Dom and Luca followed her gaze, and Dom's grip tightened on the glass in his hand. "That's him."

Luca scanned the room for Matteo, catching him standing with Maeve in the far corner. When Matteo finally met his gaze, Luca glanced at Nero, waiting for his brother to catch his meaning. When Matteo finally did, he straightened, leaning down to whisper in Maeve's ear. She nodded, pulling her phone out of her clutch while he made excuses to the people they were talking to.

Matteo signaled Carina and Alexei on his way across the room, and they converged in a corner a few moments later. Luca watched Nero over Matteo's shoulder. The man glided into the room like a king, nodding and smiling to everyone who called out a greeting to him.

His wife floated at his side. Her dress and jewelry were understated but elegant, and Luca could tell it was expensive, even at this distance. Nero never did anything small, and as one of Restivo's biggest donors, both above board and below, he was on top of the pile in this crowd.

The couple made their rounds, shaking hands and kissing cheeks. But when Nero spotted their group in the corner, his eyes narrowed and his shoulders squared. He instantly abandoned his wife and crossed the room, stopping close enough to crowd Matteo but not so close as to draw attention to them.

"Bianchi," Nero said, barely containing the disdain in his voice. "What are you doing here?"

Matteo raised a brow and took a slow sip of champagne. "My family and I were invited."

Nero swept them all with a look of disgust before zeroing in on Matteo again. "What kind of game do you think you're playing, boy?"

"I told you weeks ago, Nero. No games. You rejected my offer, and I put myself in a position to find someone who might be better suited to my...goals."

"These are my people. I own them."

Luca reached into his jacket pocket and pulled out the business cards he'd collected. With a smile, Matteo and even Dom did the same.

"Apparently, they're in the market for new business. You should do a better job of keeping your people if that's what you're after."

"Though that might be a little difficult," Luca added. "What with all the hardship you've had lately."

Nero pinned Luca with an unflinching stare. "Minor snags in productivity."

"That's not what the papers are calling it," Carina said with a sweet smile.

Nero took a halting step toward her, and both Alexei and Matteo stepped into his path.

"We really are sorry about the problems you've been having. Truly," Matteo assured him. "Maybe you should focus more on getting your company back on its feet and less on us making new friends."

"If I find out you're behind this, you little f—"

"Careful, Nero," Matteo warned. "It's hardly in your best interest to threaten me. Not in a room filled with all of *our* friends." Matteo gave Nero a friendly pat on the shoulder and smiled wide. "It was great to see you. We should be heading out. We've already been here for hours. Enjoy your evening."

Matteo strode away, and Dom and Emilia followed. Carina tightened her arm around Alexei's bicep when he moved to take a step toward Nero and dragged him toward the door. When they were alone, Luca set his glass down on a nearby table and shoved his hands into his pockets, clenching them into fists.

He wanted nothing more than to pound Nero Gallo into the marble beneath his feet, but he could be patient a little while longer. They had one more massive blow to deal to

Gallo Industries, and then they could implement the next and final phase of their plan.

Nero gripped Luca's arm when he turned for the door, and Luca looked down at where Nero's hand wrinkled the fabric of his tux and then up into the man's eyes.

"You better tell your brother to watch himself. He has no idea who he's dealing with."

Luca shook his arm free and flashed Nero a wide smile. "We know exactly who we're dealing with. Merry Christmas, Nero."

Both SUVs and Maeve's sedan were already waiting for them when Luca stepped outside, and he accepted his keys from Carina.

"Did he say anything else?" Matteo wanted to know.

"Just that we have no idea who we're dealing with."

Dom snorted. "We know perfectly well. But you baited him, and now he's going to look extra hard at us." Dom swept a look at Luca. "Make sure your contact is prepared for that."

Luca nodded. "I've got a meeting set up with them tonight." He checked his watch and rounded the hood of his SUV. "I should probably get going. Can you give Carina and Alexei a ride back?"

"I have space in my car," Maeve offered.

"I'll ride with you," Matteo said to Maeve. "Luca, we're meeting with the capos early Monday morning. Don't be late."

Luca inclined his head before climbing behind the wheel. He hadn't been late for any of Matteo's goddamn meetings yet. Why his brother needed to incessantly remind him to be on time, he had no fucking idea.

Looping away from Restivo's sprawling villa, Luca made his way across Catania and pulled into a public parking lot just down the street from Sienna's building. Buzzing himself in with the passcode she gave him, he took the elevator to her floor and let himself into the apartment.

She didn't try to stab him this time, and even though all the lights were on in the kitchen and the living room, they were both empty. Following the short hallway, he peeked into the office. Dark and vacant. Pushing into her bedroom, he found more lights on, but now he heard the faint sound of the shower through the closed door.

Pushing open the bathroom door, he leaned a shoulder against the frame and watched her. He expected her to jolt when she saw him, as she usually did when someone caught her by surprise, but when her eyes met his through the glass door, she only smiled.

"You clean up good, Bianchi," she said, her voice echoing off the tiles as she slicked back her hair.

"And you look great wet."

She laughed, and he crossed the bathroom, shedding the pieces of his tux as he went. When he stepped under the spray, she instantly wrapped her arms around his neck and pulled him in for a kiss.

"I take it tonight went well?" she asked, tilting her head for his lips.

"I'd say so. We made some good connections, rubbed elbows with the right people. And pissed off your uncle."

"All in a day's work. Any update from Matteo on your next move?"

"Later," he said, lifting her up against the shower wall and guiding her legs around his waist. "Right now I want to see how many times I can make you come for me before the hot water gives out."

Chapter Twenty-Eight

It was pitch black when Luca woke, and he instantly felt the absence of Sienna beside him. He reached for his phone to check the time. Not quite four in the morning. He waited a few minutes to see if she was in the bathroom, then a noise drew his attention to the hall.

Her office light was off, but a pale golden glow painted the other end of the hallway, and he followed it. Her back was to him, the light over the stove the only source of it in the room. An electric tea kettle boiled at her elbow, the bubbles dancing behind the clear glass. She turned it off before it whistled and poured water into a mug.

Turning, she jumped at the sight of him, slapping a hand over her heart and sagging back against the opposite counter. "Luca. You scared me. What are you doing up?" She frowned. "Did I wake you?"

"No." He took a step closer. She looked tired, more so than usual. A deep crease in her brow, dark circles under her eyes. "Did something happen?"

"I just...couldn't sleep." Sienna held up her mug and offered a thin smile. "Tea helps. You should go back to bed."

"You've been saying that a lot more lately."

She dropped her gaze to her mug, spooning in a bit of sugar and a splash of lemon juice and stirring it slowly. Something had been bothering her for weeks. Ever since she came over to the house. In the times he'd seen her since, she wouldn't talk about it.

He suspected she was having nightmares, but she wouldn't say. Always dancing around the subject, never saying anything beyond she couldn't sleep. It felt like she was pulling away, and the idea of it left a sour taste in his mouth.

"Sienna. Please talk to me."

She gave her tea one final stir and set the spoon soundlessly in the sink. Her voice was soft, and she wouldn't meet his gaze when she said, "It's nothing. Really. I'm sorry I woke you. Just go back to bed. I'll finish my tea and join you in a bit."

Luca sighed. "You didn't wake me. I woke up and you were gone. That's it."

Running her fingers through her hair, she pulled it forward over her shoulders, hiding her scar from view. A tell that something was definitely bothering her. She only did that when she was remembering and trying to forget.

"I can't help if you don't tell me what's wrong."

"I told you nothing's wrong. I just can't sleep sometimes. It's not a big deal."

When he took a step forward, she took one back, and the pain of the simple act knifed through him. Almost instantly, she realized what she'd done and moved closer. Setting her mug down on the counter, she ran her hands over his chest and across his shoulders before pressing her forehead against his collarbone.

"I'm sorry."

He brought his arms around her back and pulled her closer. "For what?"

"For everything. For all the years we didn't have together, for everything we missed out on, for this whole mess we're in now."

"What mess?"

She wrapped her arms tighter around him and squeezed, burying her face against his neck. "It wasn't supposed to be this hard."

He heard the tears in her voice, and it shredded him. What was she so afraid of? This was almost over. They had the rest of their lives to look forward to, and she was talking as if they were days, hours, minutes away from another tragedy.

"I need you to talk to me, Sienna. You have to tell me what's going on. Whatever it is, we can fix it. Together."

She laughed, and it was a watery sound, the skin of his neck damp with her tears. "That's just it. We can't fix it. It's an impossible scenario."

"I don't know what you mean." He pulled her back so he could look at her face, gathering the tears on her cheek with his thumb. "Please, baby girl."

"Do you think we made a mistake? Being together again?"

His hand fell from her cheek, and he frowned. "How can you ask me that? Do you think it was a mistake?"

She shook her head. "Just answer the question."

"No. Of course it wasn't a mistake. Being with you, holding you, hearing your voice, loving you." He gripped her chin and forced her to meet his gaze. "How could any of that be a mistake?"

Stepping out of his embrace, she wrapped her arms around herself and took a deep breath.

"I was fine with how everything was supposed to go. I knew what I needed to do to kill Nero, and I was fine with it. Get in, shoot him, and avenge my family. That's all I wanted for so long. I spent two and a half years building my life around that inevitable conclusion. And I was resigned to it."

She laughed, but the sound was heavy and wooden. "And then I walked out of that fucking bathroom in that stupid goddamn hotel, and there you were. And every second of that year we spent together came rushing back with crystal clarity. You were never supposed to be part of the equation."

"And now that I am?" His voice was little more than a strangled whisper.

He thought he knew where this was going, but he desperately wanted to be wrong.

"And now I don't know what to do. I have to choose between you and my family, and I don't know what choice to make."

"There's no choice, Sienna. You can have both."

"How?" she yelled. "How do I have both, Luca? My uncle goes everywhere with at least two bodyguards and Stefano. His house is a fortress, and his cars are made by the same company that makes the fucking thing they drive the president of the United States around in. The best place to get him is at his office. He thinks the building's security protects him, so he lets his guard down."

"Which is why you got a job there."

She nodded, squeezing her eyes shut. "Steal Ciro's credentials, take the elevator to the top floor, shoot Nero Gallo." Slowly her eyes opened, and she stared right into his, gaze intense and searching. "Did you really think I was going to just be able to waltz back out of there again?"

Panic clawed at his throat, and he rushed forward, gripping her arms and shoving her back against the opposite counter. "This was your plan the whole time? Whenever I asked and you said you had it covered, your plan was to fucking sacrifice yourself?"

"It's the only way, Luca. You said the kill was mine, and it's the only way I can do it."

"Like hell it is. Did you honestly think I was going to let

you do that? No," he said when she dropped her gaze to his shoulder. "Of course you knew that. That's why you didn't want to tell me."

"It was already hard enough," she murmured. "I didn't want to make it harder."

He pressed his forehead against hers. "Did you think we were going to send Alexei to the slaughter to get to Nero?"

"I don't know. But you said I could do it without interference an—"

"Without interference, Sienna. Not without protection. If you seriously think I'm going to let you sacrifice yourself for this, you're insane."

"So you're going to take it away from me?"

"No." He jerked her back. "I'm going to give you both. I'm going to give you Nero's head on a fucking platter. And I'm also going to give you a life with me after. Assuming that's something you want."

Sienna flung her arms around his neck, yanking his mouth down against hers and claiming his lips in a fierce, needy kiss. Undoing the sash on her robe, he slid his hands inside, gripping her waist and lifting her onto the edge of the counter.

Pushing the fabric off her shoulders, he dragged his lips across her collarbone and between the valley of her breasts. He urged her knees apart and nibbled down to her belly button, dipping his tongue inside and making her twitch.

Kneeling between her legs, he looked up at her before dragging his tongue up the length of her pussy and flicking it against her clit. He swirled his tongue across it over and over until her hand went to his hair, her fingernails digging into his scalp, and she rocked her pussy against his lips.

Grinning, he used one hand to spread her apart for his tongue, sucking her clit into his mouth and scraping it gently with his teeth to make her buck and groan. When she lifted her hips for his mouth again, he shoved two fingers deep inside her, tapping against her G-spot until her legs trembled.

"Just like that," he murmured, sucking her clit hard while he worked her at an unrelenting pace. "Let go for me, baby girl. Just let go."

With one last rough bite to her clit, she clenched and spasmed around him, his name a sob on her lips as she came undone.

He stood, rubbing his fingers roughly over her clit before guiding himself inside her and grinding against her until she shuddered. How the fuck she ever thought he'd give her up, he had no idea. But he'd do whatever it took to prove to her that what they had between them was forever.

"You're mine, Sienna," he growled while he pumped his cock deep inside her, making her groan and dig her nails into his shoulders with every thrust.

"Luca."

"Say it," he demanded, refusing to relent until she exploded around him again. "Tell me. Now, Sienna."

"I'm yours, Luca. Always."

Gripping the back of her neck, he forced her to meet his gaze while he fucked her, hips slapping against hers. "I will never let you go again. Do you understand me? Never. You are mine. In this life and every life after."

"Yes," she whimpered. "Until your last breath."

He leaned in until their lips barely brushed with each punishing thrust of his hips. "And I won't be taking my last for a very long time. Come on my cock, baby girl, and I'll fill your pussy up."

He slid his free hand up from her waist to her breast, tweaking her nipple between his fingers, looking into her eyes and giving it a rough twist. She arched as much as his hand on the back of her neck would allow, and when her pussy clamped down around him, he chased her over the edge with his own release.

"We're in this together, Sienna," he panted against her shoulder. "You and me. This isn't like last time. I will protect you. Always."

"I know," she said, her voice a breathy whisper. She leaned her cheek against the top of his head. "I should have said something sooner."

"Yes," he agreed. "You should have. I'll punish you for it later." He grinned when she shivered against him. "But I need you to promise me something."

"What?"

He stood up straight and cupped her face in his hands. "I need you to promise me you won't do anything stupid. I will make sure you have Nero's blood on your hands before this is over. My word on that. But you will not sacrifice yourself to have it."

Her hazel eyes searched his for a long moment before she finally nodded. "I promise."

Chapter Twenty-Nine

Pushing through the glass doors of the lobby, Sienna paused on the sidewalk and considered her options. Normally she'd walk home for lunch, but these days her apartment felt empty without Luca in it.

She used to relish the quiet of her little cottage outside Berlin. It was backed against a dense patch of trees, small and cozy and private, nearly hidden from view of the big manor house. The people who owned the property and lived in the main house on the other side of the expansive yard didn't bother her or ask questions as long as she paid rent on time.

She didn't go out much, and she never had visitors. She preferred it that way. People were hard to trust. But then she'd returned to Sicily and seen Luca in that dimly lit hotel hallway, and suddenly she didn't enjoy the quiet anymore.

Luca tapped things when he was thinking. His fingers on the table, his pen on top of a notebook, the toe of his shoe against the floor. He tapped things, and he stared into space. He'd filled her apartment with his noise and his scent and his extra toothbrush in the bathroom.

The more time they spent together, the more she expected

to crave the solitude she'd grown so accustomed to. But eventually she'd come to realize she'd never stopped loving Luca's noise; she'd just adjusted to the quiet. And now that it was filling her life again, she didn't want to let it go.

There was a sense of relief in finally confessing her plan to kill Nero. She should have known Luca was thinking ten steps ahead while she was only looking at the next one, already busy working out how to kill Nero and keep her too. Her singular focus had been killing her uncle for so long that it was difficult to see anything else.

Now that the truth existed between them, she felt a little ridiculous for not bringing it up sooner, for not allowing herself to see the possibility of what was right in front of her. Luca. They could actually have a life together without her having to sacrifice herself to kill Nero. She'd started to let herself dream about it. Everything felt possible now.

But there was still so much left to get through. She knew the Bianchis had one last big strike they wanted to make before Christmas, but Luca had been light on the details. He was supposed to come over after they had their next sit-down to explain.

Then there were the actual nuts and bolts of exactly how to kill Nero without making anyone a martyr. Something Luca was adamant they'd be able to do. But she could hear the skepticism in his tone when they tried to flesh out some ideas. It wasn't going to be easy, and it was clear the Bianchis didn't have a plan for this part. She didn't doubt their resources. She just hoped they were a match for her uncle's paranoia.

Stepping off the curb to cross the street, she decided a restaurant would do for lunch today. Better the noise than the tomb-like silence of her apartment. There was nothing else she could do until she heard from Luca anyway.

The last target, save for Drago himself, had been off island for over a month. Sienna was beginning to suspect he'd already been taken care of by someone for an entirely different transgression with the way he'd abruptly fallen off the face of the earth.

And if she could kill Drago without setting off alarm bells with her uncle, she would. He was becoming more and more persistent about this project with Ciro. Ciro was constantly hounding her about what gains she might have made. It seemed Drago wasn't pleased with what little she'd been able to do.

She'd been working on it in her free time just to keep her hands busy while Luca was back in Palermo, but the security they were trying to hack was too good. Something Drago seemed increasingly frustrated by if Ciro's general twitchiness at the office was any sort of gauge. Even Jack had noticed, and Isa had been a ball of nerves about it all week.

Luca hadn't been able to get much out of Matteo about the companies she was digging into. He'd seemed frustrated by his brother's secrets when he called to update her the other night.

She didn't relish the idea of telling Drago the company he wanted access to appeared to be unhackable any more than Luca liked being in the dark where his brother was concerned. Intending to give Ciro and Drago what she'd gathered so far and leaving the rest up to them, she'd pivoted to trying to find out exactly what they were doing with this information and who they were doing it for.

She was starting to doubt they were working on behalf of her uncle, even though they were logging it as a company project. She'd yet to find any sort of money trail from Gallo coffers for the work. And why the hell would you do something like this if you weren't getting paid?

It had to be coming from somewhere else. And if she

could figure out where, maybe it would give Luca a different angle to exploit to get Matteo to open up.

Pushing into the café and out of the cold, Sienna claimed a table by the window when the waitress waved her in to seat herself. It wasn't as busy as she expected at this time of day, but the place was clean and cozy and had a nice wine selection.

She fingered the worn corner of the menu while she decided between a glass of Pinot Grigio or Carricante with the house-made pesto. And maybe a caprese salad.

A couple in the corner caught her eye, and her mouth lifted in a small smile. When this was finished, Luca was taking her out on a real date. No more hiding or sneaking around or pretending the other didn't exist. Whatever she had to do, she wanted to be Sienna Gallo again, and she wanted to do it on Luca's arm.

After sending the waitress away with her order, she reached into her purse and pulled out her phone to check for messages from Luca. He was meeting with his family as soon as Dom could get away from Agrigento, sometime in the next day or two. Once they did, he'd have more for her, and they'd be one step closer to finishing this.

When a shadow fell over her table, she looked up expecting the waitress to have her glass of wine, but instead she saw Ciro and Drago towering over her. Ciro looked uncomfortable; Drago looked borderline murderous.

"Mind if we join you?" Drago asked, sliding into the chair across from hers without waiting for an answer.

"Not at all," she said, though he was already plucking a menu out of the holder at the edge of the table. "Do you eat here a lot?"

Drago slapped the menu on the table and folded his hands over it, the sleeves of his long-sleeved shirt riding up and revealing the bottom edges of a tattoo. She wondered if it was still just the dragon that curled from his elbow to his wrist or if he'd added to it over the years.

"I want an update," he snapped, his voice low but his tone harsh. "Now."

"Sure." She forced a smile and dug around in her bag for the notes she'd jotted down for Ciro and the thumb drive with the half-baked program she'd whipped up to hopefully satisfy them. "I was going to give this to Ciro after lunch, but since you're here…"

She slid the drive and the paper across the table toward Drago, who handed it to Ciro. "Their security is very tight. Impressive, really. I'm not sure they actually need much help from us."

"It's not up to you to decide what they need. Did you build a program or not?"

"I did." She nodded at the thumb drive. "I took the liberty of—"

"You took liberties?" Drago hissed. "Who the fuck asked you to do that?"

Sienna glanced at Ciro, who shook his head slightly. Whatever Ciro thought this might be in the beginning, he clearly didn't seem to know the extent of what he'd gotten himself into. Sienna cocked her head and played dumb.

"I told you, their security is airtight, and you'd have a better chance of getting what you want if you targeted a specific system. I didn't know which one you wanted, so I created a few variations for different areas of the business based on the security measures they have in place for each one."

Drago leaned back in his chair, and the crease in Ciro's brow eased a bit. Drago looked from the thumb drive to her, scratching his fingers over the stubble on his jaw and studying her as if he was trying to decide how best to word his next question.

"How's it work exactly?"

Sienna leaned back when the waitress set her wine and food on the table, waiting until Drago waved the woman away before speaking again. "It's kind of complicated. But the gist of it is, you use it as a back door into their system with code that mimics their setup, so it takes them longer to notice you and kick you out."

She cut into her caprese salad and took a bite, chewing slowly. "It might not work, but it's your best shot. Unless you want to give me more information."

Drago's eyes narrowed almost imperceptibly. "If their security is really that good, how would more information help you?"

Taking a sip of wine, Sienna forced herself not to fidget in her seat. She was balancing on the razor's edge here. And she needed to be very careful she didn't say the wrong thing.

"More information is always better than less," she assured him, forcing a note of calm reason into her voice. "Ciro knows better than anyone that the more we know about a system, the easier it is to get in. There might be something you don't even know is important that could help."

She glanced at Ciro, who was watching the whole conversation with wide eyes, turning the thumb drive over and over in his fingers. When Ciro added nothing to the conversation, she turned back to Drago, who was still studying her.

"But if I don't have the clearance for that, I understand. The drive should get you started, and someone closer to the project than me can fill in the gaps."

Drago plucked the drive from Ciro's trembling fingers and held it up to her face. "And there's nothing in this drive that would give us away? No hidden signal or anything that would tip people off that we're hacking them?"

Sienna's heart beat sluggishly in her chest, and she swallowed the bite of pasta that had gone to sawdust in her mouth. "No. Of course not. My own signature is all over that program."

"Your signature?"

"Hackers have their own unique identifiers if you know what you're looking for," Ciro said, speaking for the first time since they'd sat down. "A signature."

"Right," Sienna replied. "I'm not trying to get anyone in trouble."

Closing his fist around the thumb drive, Drago pushed back from the table, and Ciro leapt to his feet beside him. "For your sake," Drago said, shoving his hand into his pocket. "I hope that's true. We'll be in touch if we need more."

Sienna tracked them to the door and down the sidewalk until the late lunch crowd swallowed them up. Sagging in her chair, she shoved her plate away, the food already turning to lead in her stomach.

If she had any doubts that Drago was suspicious of her, he'd just obliterated them all. Even if Drago didn't recognize her, he could still out her as a mole, and her uncle would hardly send her on her way with a stern lecture if that happened.

Luca and his family needed to hurry up and figure out their next move. Because her time was running out.

Chapter Thirty

"Dom's here. Conference room in ten."

Luca looked up at Maeve standing in his office door and then down at the intercom on his desk. Normally if she wanted to relay a message, she called from her desk outside Matteo's office. Not that he'd spent much time working here, even after moving all his shit over. If he wasn't in Catania, he was at the house.

Partly because it was just as easy to work from there as it was here and because avoiding Maeve had become his own personal Olympic sport. He should consider himself lucky they hadn't actually slept together before Sienna came back. Christ knew that would have made it infinitely more awkward than it already was.

"Is everything okay with you?" Maeve asked, stepping inside and pushing the door in without closing it all the way.

"Uh, yeah. What do you mean?" He shuffled the papers in front of him in an effort to avoid eye contact. "I'm fine."

Maeve chuckled softly. "Yeah. You look fine. Luca?"

"Yep." When she said nothing else, he finally dragged his

eyes up to see her staring at him, one hand on her hip, a smile tugging at the corner of her mouth.

"Whoever she is, you don't have to avoid me because of her." She frowned. "Unless she asked you to."

"Unless who asked me to what?"

"The woman you're seeing." Maeve dismissed his raised eyebrow with a wave of her hand. "I didn't come to Italy to be a saint during my year of freedom. You flirted with me, and I flirted with you, and it was fun."

"I don't want you to think I was leading you on."

"I can't say I'm not a little disappointed. If you're built anything like your brother…" She whistled, then laughed at his stunned expression.

"So you did sleep with Matteo," Luca said, pushing back from his desk and crossing the room.

"What? No. He spent some time in Dublin with my family and our organization. They like to box. Boxing is better for everyone involved if there aren't any shirts. Don't look at me like that," she said, stepping out of the way and opening the door. "I'm allowed to appreciate the art right in front of me."

Luca shook his head. "So we're okay?"

"We're fine. Besides, I'm only here a few more months anyway. Then I have to go home and face the music of my own impending nuptials."

Her teasing smile turned sad, and Luca reached up to squeeze her shoulder before dropping his hand.

Dom rounded the corner, stopping in front of them though his eyes didn't break contact with his phone. After a few moments of furious typing, he looked up and glanced at them both.

"Are we doing this or what?"

"We're doing it," Matteo said from behind them. "Carina and Alexei are in the elevator as we speak."

They turned toward the glass-encased conference room

just as the soft ding of the elevator arriving drifted across the empty office. Alexei trailed Carina through the maze, his shirt on backward.

"If you're going to be late because you stopped for a quickie, you could at least put your clothes back on the right way," Matteo said, and Luca chuckled.

"Who said anything about stopping?" Carina replied, poking her tongue into her cheek as Alexei righted his shirt. "The driver's seen worse."

"You two are disgusting," Dom said, pushing into the conference room and dropping into one of the leather rolling chairs.

"Oh, please," Carina replied, waving a dismissive hand. "You're one to talk. Emilia told me about that time on the beach. And in your car. And at the res—"

"I never should have introduced you two," Dom grumbled, setting his phone on the table in front of him. "Let's get this over with. I'd like to be home before dinner."

"What a family man you're turning out to be, Domenico."

Dom glared at the teasing note in Matteo's tone, his hand curling into a fist on the table. "Get on with it, brother."

"I have it on good authority Gallo is about to lose not one but two government contracts in the new year. Turns out Rome is no longer confident in his ability to safely and securely handle their needs. The votes will happen just after they reconvene after the holidays."

"So you want to skip the train derailment?"

Matteo shook his head at Alexei. "No. I want to put the final nail into the coffin for Gallo. With whispers of losing these contracts and a blow like that, no one would be surprised if he committed suicide."

"And how do you plan on doing that exactly?" Luca asked.

"I'm still running through options. Maeve has been trying

to find a way into his home security system. It's the place that makes the most sense if we're going to go suicide."

"No luck?" Dom wondered.

"Not so far. His office might be an easier option."

"Not necessarily," Luca replied.

Matteo's brow shot up. "And how do you know that?"

"According to my contact, you need a special badge to get up to that floor. And security is tight." He thought of Sienna's plan to sacrifice herself. "If we send someone in there, there's a good chance they don't make it out alive."

Carina reached for Alexei's hand and laced their fingers together. "So what do you suggest?"

"We make hacking the house a priority."

"Good luck with that," Dom said. "He guards that thing like the Vatican. He makes Stefano and his wife live in the compound just to be safe."

Luca tapped his pen on his notebook. "Which makes it easier for us, really. No survivors. Acceptable collateral damage to sell the story."

"Taking out the entire family," Dom said.

"Or blowing up the office building," Carina suggested. "You could easily spin that in the papers to mean if he couldn't have the business, no one could."

"Especially if we feed them stories about his declining mental state," Matteo murmured. "Truthfully, I don't care how he dies as long as he's dead, Gallo Industries falls into my hands, and we don't have to deal with the cops sniffing around."

"So the house then," Carina said.

"Splashy wasn't the way I wanted to go, but let's explore all our options. Alexei, put something together with Luca based on whatever you can get from his contact and Maeve, and we'll set it in motion."

"Why don't you give this one to Dom?" Alexei asked. "He

likes the messy work of obliterating someone instead of carefully carving them into pieces."

"Because I'm busy," Dom replied. "Besides, it'll be good for you. Not all kills can be precise and methodical."

"Right," Alexei agreed. "And we have you when we need a boring, basic explosion or gunshot to the face."

Carina chuckled and gave Alexei's hand a pat. "Don't pout, *amore*. The sooner we finish this, the sooner we can get married. Unless you want to wait."

Alexei tugged Carina closer and nuzzled her neck. "Of course I don't want to wait. I tried to convince you to elope with me last weekend."

"Will the two of you please get a room?" Matteo asked, rolling his eyes. "There will be no eloping in this family. We have enough secrets as it is. Now, can we get back to the matter at hand?"

Luca wasn't entirely sold on the idea of derailing a train carrying millions in freight, if only because it put Sienna in danger. They'd need her in place until the last possible second to make sure nothing changed, and it wouldn't leave much of a window to get her out of there.

If Sienna didn't think she could do it without getting caught, Luca wasn't going to make her. And Matteo could shove his displeasure about that up his ass. They had done enough to justify taking out Gallo at this point.

Sabotaging the train might make their story stronger when it came to killing Gallo, but it certainly wasn't vital to finishing this. Sienna would come first here. Her safety was paramount, and if he couldn't guarantee it, they'd have to find another way.

"Once we know the train route isn't changing, we can get everything set up. We'll need your contact in place to make sure nothing deviates. Can he do that?"

"Yes. But I'm not leaving them to the slaughter. We have to get them clear before Gallo digs them out as the mole."

"Of course," Matteo replied, but Luca wasn't convinced. Matteo often did whatever the fuck he wanted, no matter what he promised. "We owe him a debt. We'll make sure he's good once the train job is done."

"Matteo," Luca said, waiting for his brother to make eye contact before continuing. "I will not sacrifice them for your end game. If I can't guarantee their safety, I'll pull the plug on this myself."

Matteo cocked his head, eyes narrowing. "If I'd known you were going to get so attached, Luca, I'd have insisted you hand your contact off for me to manage. Weren't we just talking about collateral damage?"

"Not with them, not for this. If you think I'm kidding, Matteo, then test me and find out."

"Don't threaten me, little brother. I'm not in the mood. You don't have the authority to stop this once I set it in motion."

"Fucking watch me."

Matteo cast a quick glance around the table and leaned forward, resting his elbows on the glass surface. "This is the last piece of the puzzle when it comes to taking out Gallo without drawing suspicion. I will not abandon it because you became friends with your contact. I will do what I can to get them out when the time is right. That's the best I can do."

"That isn't good enough."

Matteo stood in dismissal, buttoning his suit jacket as he looked down his nose at Luca. "That's all you get. Talk to your contact about those shipment details, and we'll finalize the rest."

The room was silent once Matteo breezed out, and Luca sat back in his chair with a huff. The ring of Dom's phone broke the silence, and he pushed back from the table without a word, leaving the room to answer it.

"You're not exactly being subtle, you know," Carina said.

"Subtle about what?"

"About the fact that you're in love with her. Your mysterious mole inside Gallo Industries."

Luca looked up to see Alexei and Carina both staring at him, and he scrubbed a hand over his face. "It's a long and complicated story. That I will tell you when this is all over," he added when Carina opened her mouth to speak.

"Maybe over the dinner at our house everyone keeps avoiding."

"What is it with you and hounding me about dinner at your place?" Luca said, pushing to his feet and waiting for Carina and Alexei to do the same.

"I was going to announce the wedding, but since someone already opened his big mouth"—Carina looked pointedly at Alexei, who managed to look both apologetic and unbothered at once—"I figured I'd just do something nice. It's been a long time since we did something as a family just because."

"Since when do you care about being a family?"

"I don't know." Carina shrugged, pausing outside Luca's office door and leaning back against Alexei's chest when he wrapped his arm around her shoulders. "The idea is growing on me. With Dom meeting Emilia and now the two of them raising her brother and sister, you with your mystery woman, me and Alexei."

She smiled when Alexei leaned down to drop a kiss on the top of her shoulder. "It makes me think about Mama for some reason. Makes me wonder what she might think of all of us. Now look." She huffed out a breath. "You've got me all sentimental. I hate when that happens. If it comes to your contact or Matteo's ambitions, I'll stand behind you every time."

"We both will," Alexei assured him. "You're right. Matteo

has plenty to cover his tracks if we took out Gallo tomorrow. Doing this much damage is just an ego stroke for him at this point."

"If it comes to it. I'm going to see her now." He checked his watch. "She should be getting off work by the time I get there. Once we talk, I'll know more."

"Keep us posted," Carina turned to go, pausing to look over her shoulder. "And when this is all over, you can bring her to dinner."

Luca shook his head and slipped into his office to grab the rest of his things. He wanted nothing more than to be with Sienna out in the open. It's all he'd ever wanted with her. And they were so close to having it. He didn't intend to fuck it up this time.

Everything had to go off without a hitch. Because he couldn't lose her again.

Chapter Thirty-One

Sienna trudged up the block toward home. Fuck this whole day. After her run-in with Ciro and Drago the day before, she'd been on edge. Every time she looked up, either Ciro or Isa was staring at her. By the time she collected her things from the bottom drawer of her desk and made her way to the elevator, she was beginning to feel like a bug under a microscope.

Her feet hurt in these stupid shoes she'd bought on impulse. Her stomach was growling because she'd skipped lunch to attend two meetings. And she hadn't heard from Luca all day.

She wanted to tell him about Drago and Ciro but not over the phone. He would worry. It was a conversation best had face to face. But she didn't know when she'd see him again. Hopefully soon, if only to calm her nerves.

Rounding the last corner to her apartment building, she stopped short when she saw him. He was jogging up the sidewalk on the opposite side of the street, looking down at the phone in his hand. He stuffed it into his pocket as he glanced up to gauge the traffic, and seconds later, her phone went off in her bag.

She flailed around for it in the recesses of her purse, refusing to tear her eyes away from his profile as he quickly cut through the cars crawling along the road, people eager to get home or do some last-minute Christmas shopping. Freeing her phone, she glanced down at the screen and smiled.

I'm at your place. I'll be waiting for you upstairs.

Cursing the damn shoes, she quickened her pace to catch up with him. "Can you hold the door?" she shouted as he put in the code she'd given him and the door unlocked with a click.

His head whipped around, and his smile warmed her down to her toes. He leaned against the open door, eyes trailing her body from head to toe, lingering on her legs before moving back up to her face. And there was the exact reason she'd bought the stupid shoes.

"I could get used to coming home to you every day," she said, tilting her head up for a quick kiss.

"You will," he promised her. "Very soon."

She stepped through the door and quickly checked her mail. Nothing but junk and some local mailers. She dumped it all into the recycling bin before swiping her key fob over the scanner and buzzing them into the elevator.

Once the doors slid closed, Luca reached for her, drawing her against his chest and wrapping his arms around her waist. "How was your day?"

"It was long," she confessed. "But it's better now."

He leaned down and brushed a kiss against her lips as the doors slid open with a ding, and he took her hand when they stepped off and turned down the hallway.

She set her bag down on the counter and turned on all the lights out of habit, squeaking when Luca wrapped his arms around her from behind and nuzzled his nose into her hair, inhaling deeply.

"I missed you."

"I missed you too. It's too quiet without you."

He pressed a kiss to the side of her neck and then nibbled her skin gently. "Business before or after?"

"Before or after dinner? Or something else?"

He chuckled low, and the sound sent goosebumps skidding along her skin. He slid one hand around to her hip, dragging down the hidden zipper on her skirt. Once he flipped open the hook at the top, her skirt fell to the floor in a whisper of fabric, and his hand immediately moved to her ass, giving it a light smack.

"We'll do dinner and business after I fuck you, then."

Her pulse quickened, and she rocked back against him, grateful now for the height her heels gave her, even if her feet were protesting. She rocked again, moaning low in her throat at the feel of Luca's cock against her ass.

In response, he slipped a hand down the front of her panties, dragging his finger up the length of her pussy and over her clit, teasing it in slow circles until she shivered with anticipation.

"Luca," she grumbled when he refused to touch her where she needed it most. "You're being mean."

"Is that not what you want?" He moved his finger away again, holding her body captive against his while he teased her with light brushes of his fingers against her pussy.

"You know it's not," she replied, rocking against his hand.

"Tell me what you want then, baby girl."

Up and down, over and over, until she felt like she'd go mad from it. "I want to feel you inside me."

He hummed against her neck, giving her skin another teasing bite before sliding one finger deep inside her. "Like that?"

She gripped his forearm, nails digging in while he moved his finger in and out, making her gasp. "More."

Swiping his thumb roughly over her clit, his arm cinched tighter around her waist when her knees wobbled, and he slid another finger inside her.

"I've got you, baby girl," he promised, grinding the palm of his hand against her clit while he curled his fingers forward to tap against her G-spot. "Push your panties down for me."

She worked the thong over her hips and down to her knees, wriggling so it slid down her calves to the floor. Carefully stepping out of it, she groaned at the way Luca's fingers moved inside her.

"That's my girl," he whispered against her ear, slowly pumping his fingers in and out. "You remember the first time I fucked you?"

"In the club. In the ladies' room."

She'd been sweaty and hot and more than a little drunk. But she didn't think it was the alcohol that made her go with Luca when he grabbed her by the hand and led her back to the bathrooms. He'd pushed her inside and locked the door behind them.

There had been no hesitation when he darted forward and claimed her mouth, backing her up against the bathroom counter and then turning her around to face the mirror. He'd shimmied her skirt up, smiling when he realized she wasn't wearing any panties.

"What did I say to you?" He slid his fingers out and back in, grinding them deep and curling them forward until she jerked.

"You said I was yours," she panted. "And that you were going to prove it to me."

He growled low in her ear, his cock grinding against her

ass while his fingers picked up speed, fucking in and out of her, his palm smacking against her clit.

"You are mine, Sienna. Your body and your heart and your soul. They're all mine."

"Yes," she whimpered, reaching out to brace her hands against the edge of the counter. "Fuck, Luca."

"That's right, baby girl," he said against her ear when she met the short, rough thrust of his fingers with her own. "Come on my fingers, just like the first night I claimed you."

He drove her closer and closer to the brink, unrelenting in his pace, murmuring into her ear until she couldn't hold back any longer. Her orgasm raced up her spine and sizzled through her nerve endings until her entire body trembled in his arms.

"You are so beautiful when you come for me," Luca said, pulling his fingers free and bringing them to his lips. "You want dinner and business now?"

"No," she groaned, grinding her ass against him and making him hiss. "I want your cock inside me."

"Do you?" She heard the metallic scrape of his zipper before he kicked her legs apart wider and slapped the length of his cock against her already swollen pussy. "Is this what you want?"

She leaned forward and adjusted herself and then pushed back against him, groaning when the tip of his cock brushed against her clit. "I want you, Luca. In every way imaginable."

He slammed into her so hard and fast, she was rocked onto her tiptoes, the breath stolen from her lungs as he pulled out and pounded into her again and again.

"You have me, baby girl. Forever. Now give me what I want and come on my cock."

His hand snaked down to her clit as he resumed his rough pace. Every part of her was on fire for him. From the rough but reverent way he used her to the feel of his breath hot on her neck to the relentless way he pushed her harder, faster, higher.

Being with Luca was all-consuming, and she'd never wanted to give over to it more than she did in this moment. To truly be his forever, whatever it took, whatever it meant, whatever she needed to do to make it a reality.

And when he closed his fingers around her clit and commanded her to come with a harsh whisper, she came undone for him a second time. Following Luca wherever he wanted to take her would never be a question.

"Fucking hell, baby girl," he groaned once he'd spent himself inside her and collapsed on her back, trapping her body between him and the counter. "I don't think I'll ever get enough of you."

"Good," she sighed, and he chuckled, slowly standing and spinning her around to face him.

He kissed her soft and sweet, his fingers playing with the hem of her blouse. "Let's talk business and eat."

"Done already?" she wondered as he adjusted himself back into his pants and bent to retrieve her skirt off the floor. The hungry look in his eyes made her shiver when he met her gaze.

"Not a fucking chance. But you won't have much energy for talking if we keep going and wait to catch up later. And you'll need the fuel." He traced the outline of her pebbled nipple through the silk of her top. "Go change, and I'll heat up something in the fridge."

She pressed a quick kiss to his lips before kicking off her shoes and disappearing down the hallway. There didn't seem to be much of a point to clothes since he'd only take them off her again anyway, so she stripped out of her shirt and bra and pulled on a robe.

He had dinner on the table and was pouring two glasses of wine by the time she'd taken her contacts out and used the bathroom. He'd scrounged up the leftovers she hadn't been able to finish after her confrontation with Drago and a few other things she'd been meaning to throw into a salad.

"There wasn't much."

"I need to go shopping." She took her usual seat facing the window, and he sat down opposite. "So? What's the update?"

He took a slow sip of wine and watched her fork up a bite of pasta before responding. "Matteo is determined to go ahead with the train derailment. Even if that means outing you."

Sienna set her fork back down and propped the flat of her foot on the edge of the chair. "Okay. When?"

"Before the end of next week. But I'm not doing it if it puts you in too much danger. If I can't get you out, I'll do whatever it takes to talk him out of it."

"It might not matter."

Luca frowned. "Of course it matters. There's no way Gallo won't know he has a spy on the inside once we hit a train. You said the shipments are too randomized, down to hours, for him to draw any other conclusions."

"I did say that. And it's true. But I'm skating on ice that's thinner than I thought. Drago is suspicious of me."

"Drago." Luca chewed thoughtfully. "The guy from the secret project?"

"Yeah. I've been dragging my feet on giving them much of anything, and Drago is getting impatient with the lack of progress. When he cornered me at lunch yesterday, I must have said the wrong thing."

"He still doesn't recognize you, right?"

"No. I don't think so."

"Then maybe he's just a paranoid guy."

"He's definitely a paranoid guy, but this was different." She shook her head. "I'm just saying, Nero will get word of the derailment almost instantly. When he does, I imagine I'm going to be suspect number one. I'm not sure how much time I might have to actually get away."

Luca reached for her hand across the table. "We don't have to do this. I'll talk Matteo into something else."

"If this is what you need, I can do it for you." She linked her fingers with his and gave his hand a squeeze.

"What I need is you," Luca said, drawing her into his lap and pressing a kiss to her forehead. "Only you. We don't need the train to make it believable."

"Maybe not, but it'll look better. If we choose one that travels on a day I work from home, that would buy me more time."

"Then we'll do that. Whatever you need." He pressed his cheek against her shoulder and then sat up straight again. "Can you monitor it from anywhere? The shipments?"

"I should be able to. Why?"

"Then I want you safe in Palermo. We'll set up a meeting with the family, explain everything, and you'll be safely with us when it goes down."

She smiled, cupping his face in her hands and kissing him softly. "I should stop underestimating how dedicated you are to keeping me alive."

He smiled, taking her mouth again and drawing her closer to his chest. "You really should. Now eat up." He lifted a bite of pasta to her mouth, waiting until she closed her lips around it. "You'll need all your strength for what I'm about to do to you."

Chapter Thirty-Two

Luca paced the upstairs hallway, waiting for Matteo to reappear from his bedroom. He'd wanted to broach the subject of Sienna coming to stay with them since he got home from Catania this morning, but Matteo had been on his way out and light on the details about where.

He'd finally gotten back nearly an hour ago, but he'd barely paid attention as Luca climbed the stairs at his side, and then he'd shut himself in his room. Luca would get his way on this. He wouldn't take no for an answer, but he wanted to at least talk to his brother about it first.

If push came to shove, Luca had no doubt he could take Sienna to stay with Carina and Alexei in Marsala and be just as safe there as they would be in Palermo. But he selfishly wanted her here, in his home, among his people and his things. He hated that he needed Matteo's blessing to do it.

Movement on the other side of the door caught his attention, and Luca took a step closer. It had taken Matteo a matter of hours when he returned six months ago to move from his childhood bedroom into the owner's suite. Luca had never felt compelled to snoop among his brother's private things, but now he wondered how much Matteo had changed to make their parents' room feel like his own.

The door opened and Matteo stepped out, eyebrows darting up when he noticed Luca standing in the hallway. Luca caught a glimpse of a large, imposing bed covered in dark linens before Matteo shut the door, sealing him out and moving around him down the hallway.

Luca trailed his brother to the stairs and followed him down and back to the study at the end of the long hallway. Matteo hadn't changed much in this room, save for replacing the ruined painting behind their father's desk. To Matteo's credit, not even da Vinci looked good covered in brain matter.

Matteo's hair was damp from a shower, and he was as dressed down as Luca had ever seen him in navy sweats and a plain white shirt. His feet were bare, and for a second, Luca was struck by a memory of the brother he'd known growing up.

Back then, Matteo had been wholly different. Untouched by the fallout with their father and his time away, he'd had more trust and fewer secrets. Matteo had always dreamed big where the family was concerned.

But now he was far less likely to share those dreams with anyone unless they could give him something he needed. A far cry from the man he'd been before, the man who'd been eager to heal the damage their father had done and forge a stronger generation.

"Why are you following me, Luca?" Matteo demanded, dropping into the chair behind his desk and pressing a button to call a maid.

"Did everything go well off island today?"

Matteo had been spending more and more time on the mainland, but he wouldn't say what for. Another secret between them.

"I had a very long but productive day. Is that all you wanted? To catch up?"

Luca opened his mouth to speak but was interrupted by the maid stepping into the doorway. Giulia bobbed a quick curtsy and waited for Matteo's instructions.

"I want a glass of red and some of that tortellini, if there's any left."

"Carlotta is asleep, *Il Signore*," Giulia said of the cook.

Matteo pinned Giulia with a hard stare. "Then wake her."

Giulia nodded her agreement and mumbled an apology, then looked to Luca to see if he wanted anything. When Luca shook his head, she disappeared from the doorway at lightning speed.

"You're in a chipper mood. Want to tell me what really happened today?"

Matteo rubbed two fingers over his eyebrow to his temple. "Not really. What do you need?"

"I want to talk about the derailment."

"Right." Matteo sat up straighter, shuffling papers around on his desk until he found the one he was looking for. "What's the update from your contact?"

"Because of how Gallo has been rerouting shipments within hours, they'll have to stay logged in longer than I'm comfortable with."

"What does that mean?"

"It means they're putting themselves at great personal risk to do this for us."

Matteo waved a hand in the air. "I told you. I'll get him out once it's done."

"I don't want to wait that long. I want to pull them before."

"We need him monitoring the shipments. We can't pull him out before it's even done. That doesn't make sense."

"They can monitor the shipments from anywhere now

that they have access through a company computer. They just need a strong internet connection." Luca paused. "And we have a strong internet connection right here. At the villa."

It took a second for his words to sink in, but when they did, Matteo's head snapped up. "You're not serious. You want to bring this person onto our turf? Into our home? How do I know I can trust him and he won't stab me in my sleep?"

"I'm pretty sure you'll be safe behind the door you bolt every night. Besides, I trust them with my life. You can trust them with yours."

"We can put him up in a hotel. He can stay there until Nero is dead."

"No," Luca said, fighting to keep his tone even. He would not get what he wanted if this devolved into a shouting match. "I want them completely under our protection."

"We can post men outside his hotel. Why are you fighting so hard for this guy? He's an informant. One you've no doubt been paying well. But he's nothing to us outside this little arrangement you have. You don't owe him anything. The deal was information in exchange for cash, not protection."

Luca's phone rang, but he ignored it, rolling responses around in his head and then discarding them. He could come clean with Matteo about Sienna, but something told him the news would be easier to digest with her by his side.

He'd rather pull it off like a Band-Aid all at once in front of the whole family than explain it in pieces. He had no idea how they would take it, and most of it was Sienna's story to tell anyway.

"I guess I have a bit more loyalty to the one person who's made this whole plan possible instead of leaving us chasing our tails and hoping we landed a hit."

Matteo leaned casually back in his chair when Giulia came in with a tray and set it on the desk in front of him, but his eyes remained glued to Luca's face. When they were alone again, he spoke.

"You can think I'm a cold, unfeeling bastard all you want, brother. It won't hurt my feelings, and it won't change my mind. I will not make this family, our home, a target by bringing your contact here as a refugee. They knew what they were signing up for when you recruited them."

"This—"

Luca was silenced when his phone rang a second time. Annoyed, he pulled it out of his pocket to check the display. Carina. She'd have to wait to hound him about dinner until later. Although it was looking more and more like he'd be bunking in Marsala for the foreseeable future anyway.

"This family has been a target since you set this whole plan in motion months ago. Don't act like I'm the one who randomly decided to put everyone in danger one day."

"This life is dangerous," Matteo replied, forking up a bite of tortellini. "Your contact knows that as well as you or I do."

"Be that as it may, this protection is a condition of their help for the derailment."

Matteo gripped his wineglass so hard Luca thought he might break it. "Their condition or yours?"

"Mine. I—"

Silencing his phone when Carina called a third time, Luca threw it into the couch cushions and rounded on his brother.

"You used to care about loyalty. About paying debts when we owed them. What the fuck happened to you, Matteo?"

"Nothing happened to me."

"Something did. This is not the man you were before you walked out on us, on your birthright. This"—he gestured up and down with his finger—"is just a younger, more sober version of our father. And we both know how people felt about him."

"I am not Father," Matteo bit off. "I'm trying to put everything back together. I'm sorry I'm not doing it in the way you expected it to be done. But it's happening, and that's all I really care about."

The sound of someone running down the hall in high heels drifted to his ears seconds before Carina burst into the room, chest heaving with the effort.

"Jesus fucking Christ," she panted, crossing the room to grab the remote for the TV off the corner of Matteo's desk. "Answer your fucking phone."

She pressed the button to turn the TV on and changed it to a local news station. A woman with perfect hair and a professional blue suit was talking about the weather while pointing at a map, but the ticker across the bottom announced some kind of explosion in Catania.

Alexei appeared in the doorway and moved to stand next to Carina. He reached for the remote and changed the channel. Images of a burning building filled the screen.

Luca rushed forward, stopping inches in front of the TV mounted to the wall. The building looked like Sienna's apartment. He searched the screen for any identifiers, but everything was in flames, and the shot was zoomed in too tight.

He willed the camera to pan out, but it stayed tight on the inferno. The reporter appeared on screen, a talking head in the bottom corner. He heard her report in fits and starts, his heart squeezing painfully in his chest.

A residential building in Catania. Near Catania's business district. A gas leak led to an explosion a few hours ago. Firefighters on scene were having a hard time controlling the blaze. Most residents had been evacuated, but some were still unaccounted for.

No. He took a step back from the screen, shaking his head. Then the shot switched to an aerial one, and he nearly fell to his knees. It was her building. He'd visited the area often enough in the last few weeks. He'd recognize it anywhere.

It couldn't be. She couldn't be gone. She had to be okay.

Whirling away from the TV, he closed the distance to the couch in quick strides, tossing cushions and pillows to the floor in search of his phone. Digging it out, he pulled up Sienna's number and pressed it to his ear.

She was fine. She had to be. Sienna would answer the phone and tell him everything was okay. Tell him she hadn't been at home at nearly midnight or that she'd gotten out.

The sound of her voicemail punched his heart into his throat. He hung up and dialed again. Two rings, three rings, four. "Hi, you've reached Anna—"

He hung up and dialed her number a third time. This time when her voicemail picked up, he heaved his phone at the wall and watched it splinter into pieces.

"Luca…"

Carina laid a hand on his arm, and he jerked away. He had to go. He would not abandon her like he did last time. He would do everything in his power to get to her. Until he laid his own fucking eyes on her body, she was alive.

"How long has it been?" Luca said, his voice thready and hoarse.

"We just saw the news as we were leaving the casino," Alexei said. "But the explosion was almost three hours ago, according to the first report I saw. I have no idea how accurate that is," Alexei said.

"I have to go there." Luca spun for the door. "I have to see for myself."

"What the fuck is going on?" Matteo demanded, following Luca into the hall behind Carina and Alexei. "It's just a gas leak and explosion. Three hours away."

Luca sprinted up the stairs to his bedroom, retrieving his gun from the top drawer of his dresser and fixing it into the waistband of his pants. Grabbing his keys off the top, he took the stairs down two at a time.

This was the possibility she'd warned him about yesterday. That Drago was suspicious of her, and her time was running short. He just never imagined it would run this short.

He should have insisted she come back with him the minute she told him she could run this surveillance on Nero from Palermo. Why did he let her stay? Why the fuck didn't he help her pack and insist she come with him so he could protect her?

If she was gone for real this time… No. He shook the thought from his head. He couldn't go there. Not until he knew for sure.

"Someone should go with you," Carina said, jogging to keep up with his long strides toward the front door. "I'll feel better if you take Alexei."

"I don't need a babysitter."

"Not a babysitter," Carina insisted gently. "Backup."

Luca struggled into his jacket, trying to fight off the rising panic. The drive was too long for him to lose his shit now. He needed to hold it together. Sienna would need him when he found her. He had to find her. He had to bring her home with him.

"Fine," Luca said, reaching for the door and yanking it open.

His heart stopped, and he heard Carina's sharp intake of breath from behind him.

Chapter Thirty-Three

Sienna faltered when the door swung wide. She wasn't sure she should come here. But she'd made the mistake of not running to him once. She didn't want to make it again.

Luca froze when he saw her. People were standing with him, but with the light at his back, it was hard to make out who. Two men and a woman, judging by their height. His brothers and sister?

She took a tentative step forward, and in an instant, whatever invisible force holding Luca in place dissolved. He rushed to her, crushing her body to his and burying his face against her neck.

"I thought you were…"

His voice broke, and she squeezed him tight, breathing him in. In Luca's arms was the only place she'd ever truly felt safe.

"I could have been."

He set her down so quickly she would have stumbled back a step if he didn't keep his grip tight on her arms. "What happened? The news said… Your building was…" He sucked in a shaky breath. "I tried to call and…"

He stumbled over his words as if he was trying to make sense of his thoughts, and she reached up to cup his face in her hands, pulling him in closer until their foreheads were touching. His breath fanned her lips, and she squeezed her eyes tight against the sting of tears.

Luca was here and she was here and everything was going to be okay. She repeated that to herself over and over, concentrating on the feel of his body against hers. As if sensing what she needed, he wrapped his arms tight around her, drawing her against his chest and running his hand down her hair.

Slowly, so slowly, her racing heart began to quiet. She relaxed against him, and he pressed his cheek to the top of her head.

"I was afraid I was never going to see you again," he breathed, and the terror in his voice hit a chord deep inside her chest.

"I'm right here. I'm okay."

"Does someone want to tell me what the fuck is going on here?" a voice behind them demanded.

"Jesus Christ, Matteo," a woman grumbled, the irritation clear in her voice. "Let them have a fucking moment."

"Who the hell is that?" Matteo snapped.

"It's Luca's contact," the woman replied. "It's freezing out," she said a little louder in a comment clearly meant for them.

Luca ran his hands up and down her back to warm her. She only had a thin exercise shirt and leggings on. All she owned in the world, save for her car at this point. She'd think about that later.

"You ready?"

She peeked around his shoulder at the people still

huddled in the doorway, their faces hidden in shadow. "No. But let's do it anyway."

He smiled, kissing her forehead before tucking her in against his side and leading her up the front walkway. "This is my sister Carina and her fiancé, Alexei. And my brother Matteo." Luca took a deep breath, and his arm tightened around her. "This is Sienna Gallo."

"Holy fucking shit," Alexei mumbled.

Carina looked from Sienna to Luca and back again, a small frown creasing her brow. "I think some explanations are in order."

She stepped back from the door so they could enter, and Alexei did the same. Only Matteo remained rooted in place, body half blocking the door, gaze intense.

"How do we know we can trust her?" he asked, not tearing his eyes away from her face. "How do we know she isn't working for Gallo?"

Luca took a halting step toward his brother, and Sienna laid a hand on his chest to keep him in place. "You've trusted me so far. Or at least you've trusted the information I provided you. Give me a few more minutes to tell you all of it."

Matteo studied her a moment longer but eventually moved aside to let them pass. Luca led her into a soaring foyer with an antique copper chandelier hanging from the ceiling by a long thin chain. The floors were a beautiful tiled mosaic that clicked under Carina's heels, and the crisp white walls were adorned with expensive art.

They turned into an expansive room with a fire burning in the massive marble fireplace on one wall, overstuffed couches and chairs circled around it. Luca guided her to a loveseat and sat, pulling her into his lap and wrapping his arms around her waist.

An older woman in a maid's gray and white uniform

stepped into the doorway, and Carina asked her for a pot of coffee and something to eat before crossing the room and claiming a seat next to Alexei, who immediately reached for her hand. Once all eyes were on them, Luca pressed a kiss to her shoulder in encouragement.

"About three and a half years ago," she began, "my uncle sent men to my house on my birthday and slaughtered my entire family."

She took them through the story she'd only ever told one other person before. Luca. They listened silently, Alexei's eyes darkening with anger and Carina leaning into his side as Sienna went on. Only Matteo seemed unmoved, his expression undecipherable.

When she was finished, they sat in silence, staring at her. The maid came in with coffee and a tray arranged with fruit, crackers, cheese, and chocolate-dipped biscotti before bustling away again.

Matteo got up to pour himself a cup, adding milk and a spoonful of sugar, stirring it slowly as he returned to his seat. "Seems like an awfully big coincidence that you'd show up on the island at the exact same time we were moving to take control of Gallo Industries."

Luca tensed underneath her, but she ran a hand over his arm, urging him to relax. "Since you weren't putting out a newsletter with your takeover plans, what's left except for coincidence?"

Carina barked out a laugh, leaning forward to fix her own cup of coffee and dunking a biscotti into it. "I like her," she said before taking a bite. "We understand revenge in this house. Don't we, Matteo?"

Matteo slid his gaze to his sister, taking a sip of coffee without speaking.

"So your uncle knows you're alive?" Alexei asked, fingers trailing up and down Carina's arm.

"I'm not sure, actually."

"Why else would he blow up your apartment building?"

"Luca told you about the project they asked me to work on?"

Matteo tilted his head, something flickering across his face. "He did."

"Drago, one of my uncle's top capos… I think he was getting suspicious of me because of it. The company they wanted me to hack has some of the best security I've ever seen. I wasn't making much headway, and I asked one too many questions."

"So he suspected you as a mole."

Sienna nodded at Carina. "That's my guess. If my uncle knew it was me and wanted to kill me, I don't think he'd go for something so big and splashy like he did last time. If they had eyes on me, they might have seen Luca coming over last night."

He went still beneath her and then sighed. "We met on the street for the first time." He dropped his forehead against her shoulder. "Fuck. I wasn't thinking."

"If he saw us, then I'm guessing the explosion was just as much a warning for you as it was a tool to kill me."

"Why weren't you home?"

Luca's voice was strained, and she slid off his lap to sit beside him, waiting until he pinned her with those big brown eyes before explaining. "I was at the gym. It—"

"Helps you sleep."

She smiled, reaching for his hand and lacing their fingers together. "My apartment's not that far from the gym. I heard the explosion. I knew exactly where it came from. I didn't bother to drive by and make sure. I just came straight here."

"I tried to call you."

"I ditched my phone in case they were tracking me somehow. Though, I guess they probably weren't if they didn't know I wasn't home. I didn't mean to make you worry."

"I'm just glad you're okay." He kissed her lips softly and pressed his forehead to hers. "I would have torn Catania to pieces looking for you."

She smiled. "I know."

"So what now?" Carina wondered, drawing their gazes. "We can't hit the train without your access. And this is a clear warning shot from Gallo to back off if there ever was one. What's his next move, and how do we intercept him?"

Sienna shifted in her seat when all eyes turned to her. "I don't know. I imagine he thinks killing your mole gave him the upper hand."

Matteo turned his watch around with his fingers. "I'll call Dom," Matteo said. "Have him meet us here with a dozen of his best men first thing in the morning."

"Tomorrow?" Sienna said, hand jerking in Luca's. "You want to wait?"

"It's after three," Matteo replied, annoyed. "By the time we plan something and drive to Catania, it'll be light out. I have bigger plans in motion than your revenge."

"We're all exhausted," Luca said, rising to his feet and pulling Sienna with him. "We need more time to create a plan of attack, and we'll think better after a few hours of sleep."

Sienna rubbed at the ache in her temple. She wanted her uncle to pay, but not at the expense of Luca's family or their men.

"Right. You're right. Tomorrow, then."

As everyone scattered, Luca led her into the hall and up the stairs. His room smelled like him, something she hadn't taken the time to notice when she was here before. They undressed each other in silence, slowly, carefully. Then Luca drew back the covers and helped her into bed before crawling in behind her and fitting himself against her back.

"We're going to get him, Sienna," Luca whispered against her ear, his arm cinched tight around her waist and his knee tucked between her thighs.

She settled back against him in the dark and listened to Luca slowly fall asleep, his breath warm on the back of her neck. They were going to end this once and for all. She'd use every trick and tool at her disposal to avenge her family.

By this time tomorrow, Nero Gallo would be dead, and she would be alive again.

Chapter Thirty-Four

Sienna was already up when someone pounded on the bedroom door the next morning, but Luca jolted awake behind her, and she had to stifle a chuckle.

"Get up! Dom is almost here," Matteo shouted through the door.

Luca snuggled closer, his arm tightening around her waist. "How long have you been awake?" he murmured into her hair.

"About two hours."

He lifted his head to look at the clock over her shoulder and frowned. "You didn't get much sleep, then."

"No." There was too much to think about. "But you kept me very warm."

He smiled, pressing a kiss to her shoulder and rolling onto his back. "I can hear you worrying from here."

"No, you can't."

Sitting up, he leaned over her, drawing his fingertip down her forehead and the bridge of her nose. "I can see it on your face and hear it in your voice. This ends today."

"I know." Luca wouldn't like the plan she'd been building since sunrise, but it was most likely their best shot.

"We took down Varda's entire army in a matter of months. We can kill a handful of people in a few hours. Do you trust me?"

She traced the shape of his jaw with her fingers. "Of course I trust you."

"Then trust me when I say before your head hits this pillow tonight, Nero Gallo will have drawn his last breath."

"Okay," she said, her heartbeat pounding in her ears. "Let's go set everything in motion, then."

The house was buzzing with activity when they came down the stairs. More staff than she would have expected darting back and forth from what looked like a formal dining room and what she assumed was the kitchen. At least a dozen men were stuffed around the big table, drinking coffee and talking.

They acknowledged Luca and sent her curious stares when they walked by on their way down the long hall. Instead of turning into the living room they'd met in last night, Luca led her to the very end of a dead-end hallway and into a study decorated in rich browns and soft leather.

Carina and Alexei were already seated on one of the couches, and Carina smiled at her when they entered. Matteo sat behind a wide desk, and a man she'd never met before pinned her with a calculating stare from a chair opposite the couch.

"Who the fuck is that?" the man demanded.

Luca closed the door behind them and drew Sienna to sit next to him on the last remaining couch facing the desk. He reached for her hand and intertwined their fingers.

"This is Sienna Gallo, Nero Gallo's niece. Sienna, my brother Dom."

"You're dead," Dom said bluntly.

"I'm supposed to be," Sienna agreed. "Twice."

Dom's eyes never left her, but unlike Matteo's hard stare, she felt more like Dom was sizing her up to decide if she was trustworthy, whereas Matteo seemed as if he'd already decided she wasn't.

"Please tell me you didn't drag me out of bed and across the island at this hour to talk to dead people."

"Sienna was our inside contact at Gallo Industries," Luca explained. "Last night, Gallo tried to kill her by blowing up her apartment building."

"The girl with nine lives," Dom murmured, still watching her. "So I assume you've lost access?"

"They would have rolled out new security protocols immediately. I could try to hack in, but there's no telling how long it might take."

"That takes the train derailment off the table." Dom turned toward Matteo. "What's the plan, then? Without an inside source, we're back to shooting in the dark. Blindfolded."

Matteo sighed. "I don't know."

"What about the office? You've been going in and out of there for a few months," Alexei said to Sienna, tilting his head in question and flipping the blade of a knife between his fingers.

"I have very good fake documents. Had. But you need a certain level of access to get onto the executive floor, and the clone I made was blown up last night."

"I told you," Dom said. "Collateral damage. We divert the explosives we were going to use to derail the train and take out the office building instead."

"You want to blow up Gallo Industries?" Sienna blinked in surprise. It was a hell of a lot bloodier and splashier than she thought they'd go for. "A little on the nose considering the *accident* at my apartment."

"She's right," Carina agreed. "Two explosions so close together will draw suspicions. Suspicions we can't afford."

"Do you have a better idea?" Matteo demanded. "Because this isn't exactly how I envisioned this ending."

"Yes, I do," Sienna said. "Use me as bait."

"What?" Luca demanded. "Absolutely not. I told you before, you're not sacrificing yourself for this."

Sienna shook her head and took a deep breath. She'd been rehearsing this part. She had to make Luca see it was the only way.

"Not a sacrifice. Bait. I'm still working under the assumption my uncle doesn't know I'm alive. And he doesn't want me to be alive. If I call him and ask to meet, he'll come."

"Yeah, because he wants to fucking kill you," Luca snapped. "No way in hell. We're not—"

A knock sounded on the door, interrupting Luca's refusal, and Dom pushed out of his chair to open it. A tall, thin redhead stood on the other side, laptop balanced on one hand, the other poised to knock again.

Her eyes swept the room, and when the woman's gaze landed on Sienna, she gave a knowing smile and gave Luca a thumbs up.

"What is it, Maeve?"

"Right," the woman said, stepping into the room and closing the door behind her. "I think I might have made some headway into getting into the security system at the Gallo compound."

Crossing the room, she set the laptop on the edge of Matteo's desk and pressed enter to bring up a single black-and-white image, a shot of the rear gate at Nero's villa. Instead of studying in the library, Sienna would often sneak through the gate to meet up with friends while her father and uncle did business. It seemed like lifetimes ago now.

"There's a gap in the systems."

"A gap?"

Maeve nodded at Matteo. "He uses two of them. One for the external cameras and a second one for the internal cameras and the alarm itself."

"That doesn't make sense," Sienna mumbled.

"I was able to get into the external cameras." She brought up a series of live feeds showing the stone wall and grounds around her uncle's villa and the handful of men on patrol.

"I don't understand how that helps us," Dom said, bracing his elbows on his knees. "Seems to me it makes it doubly secured."

"Actually," Sienna said, pushing away from Luca and crossing to the laptop, "it might give us exactly what we need. May I?"

Bending over the machine when Maeve nodded, Sienna brought up a window and typed in a long string of code, the neon numbers and letters filling the screen.

"Before it happened, my uncle asked me about upgrading security at the compound and the office. I gave him proposals for both. It looks like he implemented the one for the office but cheaped out when it came to the compound. Instead of redoing the entire system, he added a second one."

"And that helps us how?"

Sienna grinned, typing in a final command and hitting enter. A box popped up. The controls to her uncle's internal security system.

"They had to be linked, and that link is a weak point." She turned the laptop around to face Matteo. "Now we have access to the internal cameras and the alarm system."

"You can do that, and you wanted to use yourself as bait?" Alexei wondered, eyebrows raised.

"She's been dead set on sacrificing herself to kill him since she got back," Luca said.

Sienna crossed her arms over her chest. "When I saw my

recommendations implemented at Gallo Industries, I just assumed he'd done the same to the compound. I didn't even think to check," she added, reclaiming her seat next to Luca when he held out a hand for her.

The room fell silent, all eyes shifting to Matteo, his elbows resting on the desk, fingers steepled. His eyes were intent on the screen, a frown creasing his brow. She knew he was methodical, meticulous, a planner. But with revenge so close, her fingers itched to claim it. Whatever he decided, she would not be left out of it.

"I'd have liked to blow up the train first, tied it all with a pretty bow." Matteo swept Sienna with a look somewhere between irritation and disdain. "But since that's off the table now, we'll have to make the best of the seeds we've already planted."

"What seeds?" Luca wondered.

"When I was in Rome yesterday, I had lunch with an old friend. A journalist. I let it slip that I was worried about Gallo's mental health. It hasn't been a good quarter for him. Profits are slipping, and the government has lost faith in his ability to honor their contracts."

"Clever," Carina said.

"We commiserated about what a shame it would be to see a man such as Gallo tumble. I then, of course, asked them not to print anything that could damage him."

"Of course." Dom shook his head and chuckled.

"But for some reason, we've had two other reporters call to ask to speak to you about Gallo and your thoughts on how he might weather this particular storm." Maeve bit back a grin.

"So if he up and killed himself, the story with your worries would go to print and explain everything away?"

"My anonymous suspicions. Yes," Matteo confirmed. "Dom, can you put together an op? He thinks he's bested me by blowing up my inside man." Matteo slid a look to Sienna. "Woman. I'd rather not let him celebrate for long."

Dom nodded. "If I can get the layout of the compound and the placement of the cameras from Sienna and Maeve, I can have something for you in an hour, maybe two."

"I can get that for you."

"And I'll do whatever I can to help," Maeve said.

"That's all for now, then." Matteo motioned for them to go. "We'll meet—"

"Actually. There's something else. A condition."

Matteo raised a brow at Sienna. "I hardly think you're in the position to be giving me conditions."

"Really? Because without me, you wouldn't be anywhere close to getting your hands on Gallo Industries."

Luca squeezed her fingers while Matteo sucked his teeth.

"What do you want?"

"Take out whoever you need to however you need to at my uncle's compound. But Nero Gallo is mine. I get to put the bullet in his brain."

"It has to look like a suicide, or the whole thing is pointless."

"I'm aware of that." Sienna turned to Alexei. "You can show me how. But I get to pull the trigger. I want my face to be the last one he sees before I send him to hell."

Matteo considered her for a long moment, fingers drumming on the edge of the desk. "Fine," he finally agreed. "We'll sweep the house and take care of everyone else. And you can pull the trigger on your uncle."

"Lucky you," Carina mumbled. "He never agrees to anything that easily."

"Sienna," Matteo began as everyone rose from their seats and headed toward the door. "If you fuck this up for me, I'll make sure you're the one who pays for it."

"I've been planning this for too long to fuck it up now."

Chapter Thirty-Five

Armed with access to the security system and Sienna's knowledge of her uncle's habits, they built a solid plan in under an hour. With complete confidence in his security, Gallo sent his men home at nightfall, leaving the compound vulnerable. Bad news for him, good news for them.

One team would slip into the villa through the courtyard and take the winding staircase usually used by the staff up to the third floor. Dante first. His bedroom was closest to the stairs. Then Stefano and his wife down the hall.

They'd use silencers so they didn't tip off her uncle before they were ready to deal with him, but they'd be dead all the same, and the suicide note would explain the rest. Alexei's handwriting wasn't an exact match to her uncle's, but it was close enough that no one was likely to ask questions.

She'd watch through the security cameras from the car to make sure there were no surprises, and when her uncle was the only one left, she'd get what she came back to Sicily for. His blood on her hands.

There was no reason it shouldn't go off without a hitch,

but that didn't stop the butterflies from doing loops in her belly on the drive. Three years of loss and pain and heartache hinged on this raid. If they weren't successful, her uncle would never pay for his crimes, and she'd end up dead or in prison.

"You okay?" Luca whispered against her ear, wrapping his arms around her shoulders.

"I will be. When it's all said and done."

Turning her, he kissed her forehead, the tip of her nose, each cheek, and finally, her lips.

"I swear you'll get what you need, and you'll get to come home with me. I'm going to fuck you in Palermo before we sleep."

She smiled, wrapping her arms around his neck and pulling him in for a greedy kiss. He gave her what she asked for, hands sliding down her back to cup her ass and pull her against him. All she'd ever needed to get back on solid ground was Luca by her side.

"I want to be alive after this."

"You're alive right now," he reminded her, giving her ass a squeeze.

"I want to be Sienna Gallo again. Back from the dead. I want the world to know what my uncle did to my family."

"How?"

"I have proof he ordered the hit and paid men in power to keep it quiet."

"I thought all of that was back at your apartment."

"I've been carrying around a flash drive with the files on my keychain." She laced her fingers through his, squeezing. "We can send it to a reporter to break the story."

"They'll want to do interviews. Drag the whole thing out into the light of day and make you relive it over and over again."

"I already relive it in my nightmares. What's a few interviews?"

"All I've ever wanted to do was give you everything you've ever deserved. As long as you're sure this is what you want, I'll support you."

"Thank you." She gave his lips a quick peck. "Besides, when it all comes out, it only strengthens the suicide claim."

"I can see the headline now. Beleaguered businessman faced with a failing company and accusations of murder takes his own life." He huffed out a laugh.

"May he rot in hell."

"That's the idea."

By the time they arrived in Catania, the sun had fallen below the horizon, casting long shadows through the trees. Sienna's heart pounded in her ears as the SUV rolled to a stop across the street from the Gallo villa. Her family's old home wasn't far, and she felt the acuteness of the loss being so close.

She moved to position the laptop on the center console, but Luca stopped her with a hand on her shoulder, cupping her face in his hands when she turned to him.

"I've never said this out loud, Sienna, but I've felt it since the moment I first laid eyes on you. I love you. And I'm not leaving here today without you. So don't do anything stupid."

Sienna pressed a soft, lingering kiss to Luca's lips. "I'm not leaving here without you either. I love you, Luca. Until your last breath."

"We're in position," Dom said through the walkie, drawing Sienna's attention to the tinted window.

"Luca." She gripped his hand as he reached for the door. "Come back to me."

He climbed out, turning to face her as he adjusted the gun at his back. "Whatever happens, it's all for you."

The door closed, plunging the car into darkness, and

Sienna quickly brought up the live feeds from her uncle's security system. Maeve had been monitoring everything from Palermo while they made the drive, and it seemed like everyone was exactly where they needed them to be.

Cycling through the cameras to make sure while Dom's orders squawked through the walkie, Sienna blew out a nervous breath. Everything was going to be fine. She trusted Luca, and Luca trusted his men. That's all she could really ask for.

Pulling up the two camera feeds closest to the entrances where they would breach, she typed in the string of commands to disable the alarm system. No one would hear them coming.

"Alarm is down," she said into the walkie.

A scant minute later, six men appeared on the left side of her screen, Dom at the front. They quickly climbed to the third floor, breaking off into teams of two while Luca's group entered close to her uncle's study. The bastard was sipping a glass of what she assumed was his favorite chianti without a care in the world.

The faint ping of silenced shots filtered through the speakers as they moved from room to room, clearing each one as they advanced. Dante dead, Stefano and his wife dead, her aunt dead. A part of her wondered if she should feel a pang of sadness for her aunt and Stefano's wife.

But that feeling was quickly replaced by memories of Rina's lifeless body shielding the twins and Pietro's empty stare. In three years, they'd done nothing, said nothing. They'd made their beds, and now they were lying in them.

Just as the teams were preparing to clear the last room, movement out of the corner of her eye caught her attention, and she looked up to see headlights at the south gate.

"Fuck." Grabbing the walkie and scooting toward the door, she pushed out into the night without thinking. "Someone's escaping!" she yelled into the walkie, reaching back for the gun she'd stashed in her purse.

"Where?" came the quick reply.

"They're leaving through the south gate. Black SUV. I can't see inside. I'm going after them."

"Sienna don—"

Luca's command was cut off when she dropped the walkie and sprinted toward the fleeing vehicle. The car lurched forward as the gate continued its slow swing, and she had just reached the bottom of the drive when it finally pulled through.

Stepping directly into its path, she fired relentlessly in the direction of the tires, barely able to see beyond the glaring headlights and her own fury. No one was walking away from this. They all deserved to die.

The driver of the SUV floored it, forcing Sienna to dive out of the way. Grunting when she hit the ground, the air forced from her lungs, she rolled and scrambled to her feet in time to see the car's taillights disappear around the corner.

"Fuck!"

Turning to head back to find the walkie she'd dropped, she stopped short when someone grabbed her arm, fighting and clawing against their grip until she realized it was Luca.

"What the hell are you doing out here?" he demanded. "I told you not to do anything stupid."

"I was trying to clean up loose ends." She rounded on Dom when he joined them. "Who the fuck did your men miss?"

"I don't know," Dom replied through gritted teeth, irritated with his men or her, she wasn't sure. "They confirmed all the kills. Everyone who should be dead is."

"And whoever that is"—Luca gestured toward the end of the street—"is probably on his way to tell the authorities the Bianchis just murdered the entire Gallo family."

"I'll send men to scour the area," Dom assured them. "And make sure Matteo knows Maeve must have missed somebody on the security feeds."

Sienna snorted as the walkie strapped to Dom's belt crackled.

"Anyone planning on coming to join this little party?" Alexei wondered. "Or do I get to kill this asshole myself?"

"We're coming." Luca reached for Sienna's hand and brought her knuckles to his lips. "You ready?"

"As I'll ever be."

They made their way through the open south gate and up the driveway. Around the side of the house was the door Luca's team had breached, and they stepped inside.

Everything felt familiar and foreign all at once. This part of the house, her uncle's domain, smelled of wood polish and tobacco. She hadn't spent much time here; most of her exposure to the villa was through her aunt's north wing, padding across the mosaic tile in flip-flops and sheer coverups thrown on over bikinis.

She'd spent hours lying around her uncle's huge in-ground pool. Laughing, drinking, tanning. Almost daily in the summertime, they'd come over before the sun was too high in the sky and swim until the staff called them in for lunch.

Her favorite memory was watching her nieces and nephews take running jumps off the diving board into the water, bobbing to the surface in their life vests, giggling and paddling back to the ladder.

Her uncle was seated at his desk when she rounded the corner into his office. He didn't recognize her when she walked in, his brows drawing together in confusion, followed by a sardonic laugh.

"Seriously, Bianchi?" Gallo said to Dom. "You brought a

woman in to finish the job? Not man enough to do it yourself, I take it."

Sienna felt Luca's fingertips graze her back, and the gentle touch warmed her. Their mystery man's escape aside, everything she wanted was so close she could taste it. She was ready to be done with this. There was so much life left to live with Luca. It was time to put this behind her.

"Hello, Uncle."

Nero's eyes narrowed on her face. "Who are you?"

"Don't you recognize me? A real blast from the fucking past, I guess. Since I'm supposed to be six feet underground." She cocked her head. "Did it really have to be my birthday, *Zio*?"

"Sienna," Gallo spat. "You're the one who's been helping the Bianchis? How?"

"You really should take greater care about who you hire at Gallo Industries. You never know what people are capable of."

"I'd ask how you managed it, but I don't actually care all that much."

Sienna's smile was sharp. "Of course you do. Because it means you lost."

"I haven't lost anything. You won't get away with this. You think people will believe I killed myself over a little business hiccup?"

"Maybe not. But they might believe you killed your entire family and yourself when your only surviving niece confronts you with the evidence of how you murdered hers."

Nero's lip curled back in a sneer even as his face paled. "You have no proof."

"See? Wrong again. You really should have listened to my father when he told you not to store all that incriminating evidence on company servers. No one is unhackable, *Zio*. Especially not you."

Sienna held up the thumb drive from her keychain. "On this drive is everything I need to bury you. The payouts to politicians and the chief of police to cover up my family's massacre, the lists of names and dates.

"Every bit of information is scheduled to be emailed to Valentina Di Salvo in a few hours. You know how much she loves to break big stories. She was the face of my family's murders for months."

Lunging forward in his seat, Nero was shoved back by Alexei. "You never did know when to shut the fuck up. I regret I didn't personally pull the trigger on all of you myself."

"I bet you do," Sienna murmured. "But tonight we'll both get what we deserve. And the world will know the truth about you."

She stepped forward and took the gun Alexei held out to her, moving into the position he indicated. To his credit, Nero didn't resist when Alexei held him in place.

"Don't you want to know the truth?"

Her finger stilled on the trigger. "I already know the truth about you."

"Not about me. About your father. About why I had to kill him."

She wet her lips. He was offering her the answer she'd craved for so long.

"Tell me, then."

"Your father, your brothers. They commanded too much respect." Nero shrugged so casually it made her want to scream. "Your father was rallying men against me. In talks with the Bianchis about marriage after my talks about Dante marrying Carina fell through."

Sienna's eyes darted up to Luca's and back to her uncle.

"You're a lying son of a bitch. They were nothing but loyal

to you." Tears bubbled up, and she shoved them back down. "They never would have betrayed you like that."

"Everyone's loyalty has a price. I didn't want to wait around wondering what theirs might be. I did what I had to do to preserve my legacy."

"And look what good it did you." She pressed the gun into his temple, enjoying the quick flash of fear in his eyes. "You're a fucking coward. Murdering women and children and loyal men because you're afraid. Fear has a price too. And now you get to pay it."

"You don't have the fucking guts, Sienna."

She chuckled softly, but there was no humor in it. "I'd have agreed with you once. But I've killed two men already, and I didn't bat an eye. I'd kill a hundred men if you were waiting for me at the end of it."

"Your father would have made the exact same decision if he was in my place."

"He wouldn't have." Sienna shook her head. "He never would have betrayed you like that."

"If you say so, little girl." Nero snorted. "You have no idea what kind of violence your father was really capable of."

"Maybe not. But I guess that means I come by it honestly."

Nero opened his mouth to speak, but the words died on his tongue when she pulled the trigger. He slumped to the side, blood trickling from the corner of his mouth and down over his chin. More blood painted the bookcase behind him, sliding down the expensive polished wood.

And his eyes, so much like her father's, were left wide and staring.

"Baby girl," Luca whispered in her ear while Alexei reached for the gun, prying it from her fingers. "It's done. You're done. He's gone."

Luca pulled her away so Alexei could finish staging the

body and the scene, pressing Nero's fingerprints into the gun and then letting it drop to the floor.

"No sign of our mystery man," Dom said from the doorway. "But it looks like we're finished here."

Sienna let Luca lead her away, pausing for one last look at her uncle's lifeless body. She wished she could say she felt happy he was dead. But his death was just the last in a long line of tragedy.

All that was left now was to start over.

Chapter Thirty-Six

Sienna sat curled in the corner of the sofa in the great room, surrounded by the wreckage of brightly colored wrapping paper and pretty ribbons and bows. It had been a long time since she'd celebrated Christmas with anyone.

It was different from her childhood. Smaller, quieter, less frenzied. But it was good and solid. For the first time in a long time, she was looking forward to what the new year would bring.

Her uncle was dead, her vendetta finished. They'd figured out it was Drago who'd escaped from the compound that night. Slithering away like the snake he was. But Matteo was sure he was holed up in the Syracuse territory with Antonetti.

Matteo seemed to want Drago's blood on his hands as much as Sienna did. Luca found his brother's singular focus on her uncle's right hand curious, but as long as he ended up dead at the end of it, she'd let Matteo's obsession carry her to her end goal.

She'd sent the evidence she had against Nero to the press and then agreed to a single sit-down interview with Valentina to explain as much as she could. If Valentina sensed holes in Sienna's story, she didn't press for answers.

Maybe it was a good enough story without all the facts. Now the world knew Nero for who and what he was. A monster and a traitor. A man willing to murder his entire family in the name of greed and fear.

Restivo had been forced to resign, and Matteo was working hard to get his man Bonacci elected president in the next special election. And the chief of police had locked himself in his office and put a gun to his head when the state police came to arrest him.

She imagined more of her uncle's contacts would fall like dominoes under the scrutiny of corruption. The Bianchis were eager to put their own men in the vacant spaces.

With the entire Gallo family dead save for Sienna, Gallo Industries would legally pass to her as the only surviving family member. Sienna thought about pushing back against Matteo's plans to absorb the organization, to claim what was hers, but she liked the idea of taking what was and creating something new, something better. Plus, it gave her time to focus on other things.

It was a strange thing, coming back from the dead, all the legal machinations, to say nothing of the emotional toll. Luca had taken her to visit her family's graves for the first time, holding her while she sobbed.

There was a tear in her soul that would never heal with them gone, but being able to visit, knowing the man who'd killed them was dead, gave her at least a little bit of peace. And now she could start over.

She'd never expected to have a life after Nero was gone, hadn't anticipated living that long. But she was in no hurry to rush it. She and Luca would figure it out together eventually.

"I thought you were going to go up and take a shower," Luca said from the doorway, holding two mugs in his hands.

"I was. I will," she amended, smiling when he waded through the strips of paper and sat next to her.

She held the steaming mug up to her face and inhaled the rich scent of hot chocolate into her lungs. Exactly what her mother always served on Christmas morning after the presents were unwrapped and the kids scattered to play with their new toys while the adults sat around talking or dozing until lunch.

"I don't know if it's how your mama used to make it. But I asked Carlotta to make it how her mama did."

Sienna took a careful sip, tears gathering at the corner of her eyes at the taste. It wasn't exactly the same, but it was close enough.

"Your aunt called again."

Closing her eyes against the sound of her aunt's voice in the message Luca had played for her, she swallowed around the lump in her throat. Her mother's family had been trying to get in touch with her since her interview aired. But each time she reached for the phone, she couldn't pick it up and dial. The guilt and the grief were too heavy.

"I can't give them what they want."

"Why not?"

"They want my mother back. And she's dead."

"No, Sienna. They just want you. You're enough." He pressed his cheek against the top of her head. "We can go see them next week if you want."

"What if they can't stand the sight of me?" She'd always been told she looked so much like her mother. "What if it's too painful for them?"

"Then you never have to see them again if you don't want to. But it'll eat you alive if you don't at least try."

Pursing her lips, Sienna considered what it would be like to reconnect with her mother's family again. To weave that tether back into place. To have memories and people connecting her to a past that only existed in her head now.

The fire in her apartment building had taken the last of what she had left of her family, the recipes she'd carefully written down, the journals full of sketches and stories. It felt like losing them all over again.

Those were her mother's people, and deep down, she knew she owed it to her mother to at least make the attempt. Her mother would want her to.

"What are you thinking?" Luca wondered, wrapping his arm around her shoulders when she leaned into his side.

"I was thinking about the last Christmas I spent with my family. The living room looked about like this does now." She gestured at the floor, smiling as she remembered the bow one of the kids had flung onto the angel at the top of the tree.

"Mama and I were in the kitchen. She was making hot chocolate, the kids were running around screaming upstairs, and I was sitting at the kitchen table. We were talking about my little brother's girlfriend. I can't even remember her name now. But I remember how excited Mama sounded at the idea of a proposal coming any day."

She wrapped her fingers around the warmth of the mug and took another sip. "I wanted to tell her about you. I wanted to shout about you from the rooftops whenever my family asked me if I was seeing someone or when I would get serious and settle down."

"Me too," he admitted softly.

"I regret that I didn't. I regret that my family died without knowing how happy I was, without knowing I had you to love me." She took a deep, shuddering breath. "I regret that I didn't come to you after..."

"Don't." He set his mug down on the side table and turned to face her, leaning in to kiss away the tear winding its way down her cheek. "You were right not to come here. We were hurting for money then, even though I didn't know it at the time. There's not a doubt in my mind my father would have sold you back to your uncle, no matter how I tried to intervene."

"We lost so much time," she whispered.

"We have so much life ahead of us, Sienna."

Luca cupped her face in his hands and pressed a kiss to her lips. She sighed. She could have done so many things differently, but Luca was right. It was useless spending any time worrying over what had been when the future was spread out in front of them.

She wasn't going to waste a single second of her life on what she could or should have done instead. For the last three years, she'd been simply existing, in stasis, waiting for her moment to strike. But nothing was holding her back now.

She intended to enjoy every minute of the rest of her life with Luca by her side. She'd make her family proud of her. Until her last fucking breath.

A Note for the Reader

Dear Reader,

From the very bottom of my heart, thank you. Out of all the billions of books available to read you choose mine. I had so much fun diving into the dark side of Mafia life in this book and I'm so excited for the Bianchi family's final chapter. I hope you enjoyed Sienna and Luca's story and I'm deeply grateful that you took the time out of your life to come along on their journey.

If you enjoyed this book, I would really appreciate a little more of your time in the form of a review on Goodreads or Amazon or wherever you purchased it.

I couldn't do this writing thing I love so much without you. This is the third book in the Sicilian Mafia Wars Series and I hope you are just as excited as I am to finish out the series with Matteo and Tessa's story. Purchase the final book in the series, The Lies We Tell, an enemies to lovers age gap romance on Amazon now.

For exclusive sneak peeks, updates, release dates, and more, sign up for my newsletter at https://meaghanpierce. com/newsletter or follow me on TikTok.

All my love,

Meaghan

tiktok.com/@meaghanpierceauthor

Also by Meaghan Pierce

Callahan Syndicate Series

Sweet Revenge

Bitter Betrayal

Deadly Obsession

Dark Secrets

Sicilian Mafia Wars Series

The Vows We Break

The Games We Play